PRAISE FOR *TOWARD TI*
MERCY AND 1

"The story of a hilariously prickly writer who finds inspiration in her imagination (or is it?), *Toward the Corner of Mercy and Peace* is about finding the courage to carve your own path while you still have time. Tracey Buchanan is a welcome new voice in women's fiction."

—Camille Pagán, bestselling author of *Everything Must Go*

"My new favorite female curmudgeon! Prickly as a pinecone, Mrs. Minerva Place would rather chat with the residents of Oak Grove Cemetery than her own nosy neighbors. Prepare to have your funny bone tickled and your heart melted as Minerva wrestles with the inescapable vulnerability of being alive."

—Lynne Bryant, author of *Catfish Alley* and *Alligator Lake*

"Tracey Buchanan delivers an unforgettable and unlikely heroine in Mrs. Minerva Place. A crusty old church organist who feels more at home with the dead than the living, Minerva is perfectly content to keep herself safe behind her own walls. At least, she's content until the day a child walks into her life and, entirely against her will, teaches her the meaning of love, forgiveness, and second chances. With a vivid, unforgettable voice, Buchanan leads the reader on a journey that reminds us that no matter our past wounds or present mistakes, everyone is worthy of love."

—Kathleen M. Basi, award-winning author of *A Song for the Road*

"With the sure hand of a skilled writer, Buchanan transports us to a world where ghosts from the past stalk a historian and living in the present is fraught with hardships. This author hits the sweet spot of humor and tragedy where anything, even love, is possible."

—Jacqueline Sheehan, *New York Times* bestselling author

"Cranky and clumsy Minerva Place has a problem: The whole town thinks she's odd and maybe a bit crazy. And what with her habit of visiting the local cemetery and talking to dead people, she wonders if maybe they're right. Still, if they'd just leave her alone, she'd be content. Then a young widower and his six-year-old son move to Paducah and turn her life upside down. This touching and deeply affecting novel brims with humanity and will leave you contemplating: What does it mean to be connected to others and what do we owe the people whose paths we cross? This gentle-hearted and intimate glimpse into the soul of Minerva Place will stay with you long after you've read the last words. It's a gem."

–Maryka Biaggio, award-winning author of *Parlor Games, Eden Waits, The Point of Vanishing,* and *The Model Spy*

"What a delight! *Toward the Corner of Mercy and Peace* is a charming story about ghosts, grief, and guilt with an uninhibited six-year-old and a middle-aged, organ-playing misanthrope you can't help but love."

–Barbara Claypole White, bestselling author of *The Perfect Son* and *The Promise Between Us*

"With lush prose and a unique voice, *Toward the Corner of Mercy and Peace* introduces a memorable and delightfully cantankerous character in Minerva Place. This novel, filled with a colorful cast of multigenerational characters, explores themes of loss, friendship, and grace. Lovers of heartwarming and quirky small-town storylines will adore this book!"

–Linda Mackillop, author of *The Forgotten Life of Eva Gordon*

"Minerva Place is a relatable curmudgeon who prefers communing with the dead to dealing with the living—her secret preoccupation is writing the stories of those entombed in the local cemetery, giving voice to these otherwise lost souls. The arrival of the widower McAlpin and his son in small-town

Paducah threatens to disrupt her ordered life. With acerbic humor, heart, and pathos, Buchanan limns the past and brings out the rich inner life of this unforgettable character."

–Carol LaHines, author of *Someday Everything Will All Make Sense* and *The Vixen Amber Halloway*

"Quirky Minerva Place will capture the hearts of readers much like the other eccentric characters who have endeared themselves to uplit fans and earned their place on our keeper shelves—Ove, Olive, Eleanor, and Britt Marie."

–Karen Sargent, author of *Waiting for Butterflies*

"Every small town has an eccentric Minerva Place. In this intriguing plot, and through her excellent writing skills, Traccy Buchanan brings her alive with fascinating success."

–Bill Cunningham, former Kentucky Supreme Court Justice, author of bestseller *On Bended Knees* and *I Was Born When I Was Very Young*

"Refreshing. Charming. Clever. Shaped by dour, unloving parents, Minerva Place grows up to be judgmental and severe with herself and others. She believes she is unworthy of love so walls herself off from human interaction. Her surprising avocation, researching the residents of Oak Grove Cemetery then creating imaginary character sketches of them is truly original. With delicate empathy, revealing neither too much nor too little of their stories, the author fleshes out the 'friends' Minerva meets in the Oak Grove Cemetery. The pace of the book is lightly brisk. It does not bog down in the middle or go off on random tangents just to up the word-count. Her use of language is spare and beautiful. Anyone who is a sucker for a good turn of a phrase, as I am, will love this book."

–Cindy Burkart Maynard, author of *Anastasia's Book of Days, Soyala: Daughter of the Desert, Finding the Way*

TOWARD THE CORNER OF MERCY AND PEACE

Tracey Buchanan

Regal House Publishing

Published by
Regal House Publishing, LLC
Raleigh, NC 27605
All rights reserved

ISBN -13 (paperback): 9781646033379
ISBN -13 (epub): 9781646033386
Library of Congress Control Number: 2022942687

All efforts were made to determine the copyright holders and obtain their permissions in any circumstance where copyrighted material was used. The publisher apologizes if any errors were made during this process, or if any omissions occurred. If noted, please contact the publisher and all efforts will be made to incorporate permissions in future editions.

Cover images and design by © C. B. Royal

Regal House Publishing, LLC
https://regalhousepublishing.com

The following is a work of fiction created by the author. All names, individuals, characters, places, items, brands, events, etc. were either the product of the author or were used fictitiously. Any name, place, event, person, brand, or item, current or past, is entirely coincidental.

Printed in the United States of America

To Kent

You've supported and encouraged me every step of the way as I've traveled this road *Toward the Corner of Mercy and Peace*

1

Mrs. Minerva Place knew they thought her odd. That, she didn't mind. Kept them out of her hair. But crazy? Crazy was a whole other matter. Preoccupation with a cemetery should not qualify one as insane.

"Oh, Minerva, don't be so dramatic," she said as she marched down Charity Avenue (was talking aloud to yourself another sign?). "It's just your imagination."

And with that lapse of concentration on where she was placing each step, her heel—a modest, practical heel though it was—got crossways with the gravel and turned her ankle. Faster than a blink she lay splayed atop the resting place of—she twisted to see—Electra Eliza Barkley.

Forevermore. This was a fine fix. Just how in the world was she supposed to get her fallen middle-aged body upright now? She blinked at the sky above her, waiting for motivation.

"Mrs. Place?"

Minerva squinted. Tiny Johnson's face hovered above hers upside down. His eyebrows seemed to be speaking. No, that was his mustache where his forehead should be.

"Yes." Of course it was her. What kind of inane question was that?

"You all right? You're lucky you didn't fall over there." Tiny pointed to a freshly dug grave. He laughed and spit. Tobacco juice arced toward her. "Wouldn't that have been something?"

Minerva rolled to her side. Tiny Johnson was the cemetery keeper and church janitor. She, being the church organist and an avid fan of the cemetery, encountered the lumbering Mr. Johnson more often than she would have preferred. He, like most men, made her feel edgy, self-conscious.

"You need help?" He offered a hand caked in dirt. She gripped the headstone, then—what choice did she have?—she reached for Tiny's hand. It was moist, which repulsed her further. She grunted as she stood, a muffled "oomph."

Tiny laughed again. "You're a big gal, ain't ya?"

"Thank you, Mr. Johnson."

She reminded herself that Tiny Johnson wasn't right in the head. Still, her face burned. "I'm fine." She motioned him away with hand sweeps. Hopefully he would forget this soon. If anyone else had seen her, the news would spread like poison ivy. Just yesterday the whole beauty shop lit up like a Christmas tree with news about Bess Truman. As if what the First Lady wore was their business. Honestly, people would meddle in anything these days.

"Why do I see you over here all the time? If you're—"

"Forevermore. Mr. Johnson, just go on and leave me be." Oh, my stars. He looked like he might cry.

Minerva clapped her moss-bruised hands. Tiny picked up his shovel.

"Well," he offered. She concentrated on the leaves and bits clinging to her tweed coat. The last thing she wanted was to make eye contact and reengage him.

Finally, Tiny Johnson ambled toward the grave he had been digging. Minerva gathered what she'd dropped—paper, pen, crayons, toothbrush. The jar of water had rolled out of her bag and rested by the headstone.

"Mrs. Barkley, I'll be on my way." She addressed the headstone with a nod as she bent to retrieve the jar. Her back tweaked just enough to let her know she would feel the results of this fall tomorrow.

"You say something?" Tiny called. The man had such keen hearing. He was already a few gravesites down the way when he stopped to check with her. Hope filled his question.

"No." Minerva didn't bother to turn around. She continued toward the corner of Mercy Lane and Peace Avenue, pebbles maneuvering under her careful steps.

The weather-worn marker engraved with a weeping willow and German inscription sat crooked, leaning as if it wanted to forfeit its job. She laid out her tools, dipped the toothbrush in the Ball jar, and scrubbed the words. As the water ran over the ridges like tears, her throat tightened and her nose tingled. This feeling startled her. Why so emotional? Something about the process made her feel as if she were a doctor listening to a patient's heart with a stethoscope. It was an intimate activity, grave washing. Or maybe this wave of upset was simply due to her fall. She swallowed the emotion and focused on the stone.

Once she cleaned the stone, she wrapped butcher paper around the front of the marker, then secured the paper with duct tape. She chose a dark crayon—purple for this Frau—tore the paper jacket off, held it flat against the stone, and rubbed. As the words appeared Minerva imagined this was how war spies felt when a message in invisible ink materialized. A snuffle of a laugh escaped through her nose. War spies. Minerva, really.

The words emerged like ghosts on the butcher paper:

Margaretha
Stuck
Denkmal
Für die Liebe und Freundschaft
Seiner früh verstorbenen Frau,
Margaretha Retter, Geburtsname,
Stecken, wird dieses Denkmal gewidmet
von ihren trauernden Ehemann und Kinder.
Sie wurde in Siebeldingen, Deutschland am 6. Juli 1819 geboren
Und verstarb nach kurzer Krankheit im Januar 1845.
Weich und Peaceful im Herrn
Ruhe ihre Asche.

On this October afternoon, the air awash with crimson, orange, and yellow leaves dancing their way to earth, she inhaled the perfume of woodsy remains, and sighed, now satisfied. She rolled up the rubbing and slipped it into her coat pocket.

❧

Nella must have been looking out her kitchen window waiting

to ambush her, because the minute Minerva pulled into her carport, her neighbor bustled out her side door.

"Wonderful," Minerva muttered. She liked her neighbor fine, but some days she wished she could hang a closed sign on her door.

"Have you been to the cemetery, Minerva?"

Nella was perpetually pleasant, which annoyed Minerva to no end.

"What can I do for you, Nella?"

"Oh, not a thing. I'm bringing you a piece of pie." She held up a plate covered in tin foil. Her smile revealed a smear of red lipstick on her teeth. Nella, still in her forties, wore too much makeup—lipstick, rouge, eyeliner, and mascara. All that for a simple weekday.

"C'mon in." She gestured with her finger to indicate that Nella should clean her teeth.

"Oh, thanks." Nella rubbed and re-smiled. Minerva nodded. "Did you hear about the house around the corner selling—the Sullivan house?"

"Huh-uh," Minerva called from the hall where she hung her coat. She noticed that Nella had gotten a new coat. A plaid involving gold, red, olive, blue, brown, and orange. Loud. Minerva wouldn't say vulgar or obnoxious, but borderline. "Who bought it?"

"Somebody moving from out of town. Somebody with the plant." Nella transferred the wedge of pie from her dish onto one of Minerva's plates and licked her finger. "Cherry rhubarb."

"Very thoughtful." Nella liked to experiment with her culinary skills, though Minerva kept trying to convince her that she preferred straightforward dishes. Exotic fare such as tuna fritters with cheese sauce, peas Juliette, or fritos veal roll did not, could not, measure up to a simple meatloaf. Minerva tolerated experimental sweet recipes better. Nella had made a chocolate cake with mayonnaise—mayonnaise!—and it had been delicious.

"I'll find out who it is at bridge club."

"Maybe so." Minerva knew Nella found out all sorts of things at bridge club, a bastion of gossip. Minerva subbed every so often because bridge kept her mind sharp. But the women cared more about what was going on in town than about playing the game. Plus, you were expected to host at some point and Minerva had no use for that. She'd have to clear off her table, find a place for all her research, disrupt her organization. She preferred crosswords to keep her mind intact.

"All-righty." Nella smiled and raised her eyebrows. "Who'd you find at the cemetery today?" She ran her hand across the back of a kitchen chair. She wouldn't find a speck of dust or grease there.

Minerva knew it would be impolite to ask Nella to leave, especially after she had brought her a piece of pie. But really. She would like to be alone to think about Margaretha the German without an inquisition. She wished she had never confided in Nella about her work.

"Oh, nobody you'd be interested in."

"Try me."

For goodness' sake. Nella was not budging.

"The epitaph was written in German and I'll have to get it translated, so I don't know much yet. I'll tell you, Nella, I'm just worn out. Could we visit another time?"

"Oh, sure. Sure." Nella's frown was almost audible, but she did gather up her coat. "Get some rest. Oh, look, I almost forgot." She turned back to pick up the plate. "I do want to hear all about the German sometime, though."

Minerva nodded, hoping she would forget about it. Why couldn't people just keep to their own affairs? A bunch of busybodies in this town. That was the problem with small towns. Everybody knew each other and believed they were entitled to know everyone's business.

Well, Minerva preferred to keep her business to herself, thank you very much. It wasn't that she didn't like people. No. Certainly not. The Bible taught that she should love everyone. And she did try to follow the Good Book's advice. She loved them. She did. In her way. At a distance. But nothing good came of letting just anybody know everything about you.

The pie urged her to sit down. Deep dish. Lattice top. Looked like a flaky crust. She stabbed a cherry with her fork.

"You couldn't call what I do meddling," she assured the pie and herself, but as she said it, she fidgeted and dropped the bite. "Oh, fiddle." When she leaned over to scrape it off the floor, she knocked her head on the table. "Aah!" She clenched her jaw and started toward the sink with a blob of pie in one hand and a fork in the other. "Forevermore, Minerva, what in the world's the matter with you?" Antsy. That's what she felt. Antsy. No reason for it at all.

No, that wasn't true. There was a reason. Every time she discovered someone new to investigate, she was anxious until she had completed the research and written the story. She ought to be used to it by now.

Then, bursting through her contemplations, came a baritone voice as real as the pie sitting in front of her. "Excuse me, Mrs. Place." The sentence rattled in her ears like a boom of thunder. Was it happening again? Her heart palpitated like a colt trotting toward an open gate. The voice came from the direction of the dining room.

Faster than she could blink, she let out a shriek—"Eee-oww"—and sprang to her feet. Catching her breath, she mustered all the authority she could and demanded, "Who's there?" Pinpricks of adrenaline spritzed through her. If there was a strange man in her house, she wasn't going to just sit there. "I'll warn you. I've got a frying pan." She scrambled for the cast-iron skillet sitting on the stove.

The man, lean and tall, dressed in an old-fashioned uniform complete with a captain's hat, appeared in the doorway between the kitchen and dining room. He grinned with the comfortable assurance that she would not assault him.

"Captain Fowler?" Minerva held the pan like a baseball bat.

"Indeed!"

"What are you doing here?"

"You let me in last night."

Minerva stuttered for a moment, breathing rapidly. She tried to order her thoughts, which were colliding like a dozen carnival bumper cars. First, she reminded herself, this man was not real. He was a product of her overactive imagination.

"Captain Fowler, you are not real; therefore, you cannot be here."

"And yet, Mrs. Place, here I am." His smile widened and he held out his arms like a welcoming host.

She inhaled deeply. He had a point, but she gripped the pan tighter as if it would fortify her position.

"You are correct." Her mind raced with a desire to make sense of this. "Let's deal with what appears to be happening now. I did allow you into my imaginings—my home if you will—last night. Perhaps I should have said, 'What are you *still* doing here?'"

His whole face seemed animated with pleasure. Oh, but he was charming. She had learned that in last night's session. "I simply have more to say."

Minerva chewed the inside of her cheek and lowered the skillet. Thank God Nella wasn't here. How would she explain this?

She studied him as if that might reveal her answer. Ropey and handsome in a scraggly way, he had a full beard that hinted at a former ginger. His small blue eyes were tucked into deep sockets of layered, weathered skin.

He was a river man. Captain Joseph H. Fowler, born 1833; died 1904; buried in the Old Section, plot 576. Here to visit Minerva in 1952.

"Is this really happening? Again?" Minerva whispered. Then, eyeing the very real man standing before her, she shrugged in defeat. She pointed Captain Fowler toward the dining room with a wave of the frying pan. "Have a seat at the table."

Real or imagined, Captain Fowler needed her full attention.

2

She knew it wasn't the first ring, but she wasn't sure how long the phone had been ringing. Minerva's focus had melted everything else away. She had become so absorbed in the world of Captain Fowler she had slipped into another zone. The phone's insistence eventually broke through, though, and when it did the sound accosted her like a swarm of wet bees.

"What is it?" Minerva asked the air around her before a brisk head shake restored her to the present. Hearing her own voice allowed her to regroup.

She picked up the phone. "Hello?"

"Hello. Is this Mrs. Place?" a young man's voice began, but Minerva didn't recognize it. She hoped someone wasn't trying to sell her life insurance.

"Yes."

"Mrs. Place, I am Robert McAlpin. We haven't met, but Mrs. Gibson referred me to you." Oh, dear. It was life insurance. Or a brush salesman. It could be about brushes. She was not interested in brushes either.

"Yes."

"Well," Mr. McAlpin began again. Minerva didn't approve of beginning a sentence with *Well*. It was lazy speech. "Mrs. Gibson tells me you—"

Attempting to head him off at the pass, as they said in the Zane Grey westerns Minerva sometimes read, she interrupted him: "Mrs. Gibson is certainly kind, but I assure you, Mr. ..."

"McAlpin."

"Yes. Mr. McAlpin. I assure you I do not need any life insurance at this—"

"Oh no! I'm not selling life insurance."

"Or brushes. I have no desire to buy brushes either. Furthermore, I do not need to see any demonstrations. My vacuum, knives, and household cleaning agents of all varieties are fully functional." There, she had covered it. Bible salesmen usually came to the door where she could present proof positive of her lack of need in that department. He wouldn't be selling Bibles over the phone.

"No. No. Mrs. Place, I'm not calling to sell you anything." Mr. McAlpin laughed.

Minerva had been certain. "You aren't?"

"No, ma'am." Here Mr. McAlpin paused so long Minerva wondered if the connection was lost. She looked at the headset as if the motion would reveal whether Mr. McAlpin was still on the line. "My son and I are new in town and I'm hoping to enroll him in piano lessons. I know you are in demand as a teacher. But you see, I wanted to take lessons as a boy and now...Mrs. Place?"

"Yes. I'm here."

"Well, Mrs. Place. I must sound foolish going on like this. It's just... Well, I hear you are quite a piano teacher."

Quite a piano teacher? Is that good or bad? Minerva frowned. Could be taken either way. The man was inarticulate.

"Of course, I mean, she said you are an excellent piano teacher." Minerva wondered for a split second if she had spoken her thought aloud, but he continued. "So, I am calling with hopes that you can work my son into your week. I'm hoping you have time to teach my boy."

Minerva did not. Her schedule was full. As full as she liked it anyway. An hour consumed with a student was an hour lost to her writing. A person needed balance. She figured the ratio of time spent working—as the church organist and a piano teacher—to the time she spent doing what she truly loved— writing—needed to remain exactly as it was in order for her to maintain good mental health.

"No, I'm sorry. I do not have any openings." She was adamant in her decision and her voice reflected it.

"Oh no." He cascaded from a hopeful tone to grief stricken.

Minerva felt a twinge of…what was it? Guilt? She could take on one more student, she supposed. In fact, she probably shouldn't turn down a chance at extra income. She knew she *ought* to but she didn't *want* to. "No time at all?" He sounded dejected, like she'd turned him down for a date to the prom, for pity's sake.

"No, I'm sorry Mr. McAlpin. Nothing." *Want to* won.

"Do you have a waiting list maybe? If someone were to drop out…"

She hesitated. Goodness gracious, why was she even considering this? She was comfortable with her schedule as it was. She didn't particularly care for little boys, either. She shocked herself with her next words. "I suppose."

"Oh, thank you," he rushed in. "I really appreciate it. I want George to have this experience so much. I've already bought the piano, and I think he'll love it."

Minerva's twinge of guilt expanded to a full-on pang. He'd already bought a piano, for crying out loud. He rambled on, but she didn't pay attention to his outpouring. She instantly regretted agreeing to consider the possibility. She should not have given him false hope. She did not want another student on her roster—especially a little boy (boys were unreliable, messy, and often uncooperative, in her experience). She stood straighter, resolved to return to her original instinct.

"It's extremely doubtful, Mr. McAlpin, but I will contact you if anything opens up. You can leave me your number."

As she put the phone back on the cradle, she stuck the scrap of paper in the phone book under M. She could hardly throw it away, now, could she?

That pesky, antsy feeling scurried back. All Minerva Place wanted was to be left alone. Was that too much to ask? People kept cluttering up her life, scrambling over her like ants on a deserted picnic. She wanted to be more charitable. She did. But forevermore, for someone who lived alone, she never got a minute's peace. First her neighbor and then the phone call, and what was that in between? Was Captain Fowler real or a figment of her imagination?

That whole episode was unsettling. He seemed real enough, but she knew he couldn't be. Could he? She considered that she might be on the verge of a nervous breakdown. She'd been hearing about more people having them. Lots of Hollywood types, but regular people too. And the prescribed cure she'd heard about was terrifying. Electroshock therapy. Awful. Minerva wanted nothing to do with that. But what if she didn't have a choice? What if she was crazy? What if someone found out she'd been seeing people who were dead?

Captain Fowler wasn't the only visitor or apparition or whatever it was she had seen. No, these episodes had happened before and were becoming more frequent. Taciturn and fixed to a casual observer, Oak Grove Cemetery had risen to ask Mrs. Minerva Place to dance. The resting place that slept beneath a canopy of stars and branches and moss and granite winked at eternal constraints and offered Mrs. Place an engraved invitation. A bevy of invitations. Each gravestone vibrated with intrigue. She was compelled to learn more.

Captain Fowler's marker was like every other marker in Oak Grove. The angel, the obelisk, the unassuming flat piece of granite—all summoned Minerva. Each spoke with a distinctive voice. And she could not rid her mind of these sounds.

"Tell my story," urged Bailys Terrell, born February 26, 1780; died October 21, 1852. "Tell mine," said Malcomb Greenleaf, who lived to be one hundred and eight. One hundred and eight! Minerva's mind raced. "Tell my story," cried Percilla Tyler, who died in 1909 of exhaustion. But when was Percilla born? The stone withheld. How old was Percilla? How exhausted was she?

Oh, the stories! The questions! Who could resist such invitations? Not Minerva. So, instead of sitting on the sofa stitching a sampler, she sat at the cherry Duncan Phyfe dining-room table in her late parents' home and wrote, her measured handwriting detailing the lives of otherwise forgotten souls.

Minerva carried a plethora of knowledge about Paducah's history in her head, and as a woman insisting her overstuffed pocketbook will do, she kept trying to wiggle one more thing in. She knew the town's myths and mysteries, its secrets and scandals. In her hours at the library she scoured newspapers line by line and then read between those lines.

With the consideration and care of a surgeon, she stitched the flesh of each character into reality. She spent hours deciding how the person would respond to what life had dealt him. Had he loved more than one woman? Whom did he dread seeing every day? What had he feared when he laid his head on the pillow at night? What had he dreamed of?

These characters were as real as anyone sitting on the church pew or standing in line at the market. And much safer. Although when he appeared, Captain Fowler did not seem safe.

"I thought we had finished," Minerva had said to him after he sat at her dining-room table. "You can't just be showing up here willy-nilly. My neighbor was just here. She'll think I've lost my marbles."

"Relax, Mrs. Place. I knew to wait. I thought of one more anecdote I thought you'd enjoy. I'll leave right after the telling."

As he spoke, she lost herself in his story. She wrote every word he said, asking him to slow down when she got behind. Real or imaginary, crazy or sane, the writing—the writing was her refuge and joy.

3

After Captain Fowler's tale of the Mexican hairless dog, during which she had to chastise him for his salty language, Minerva was in much better spirits. The sugar rush from Nella's pie and the surge from her writing encounter left her starving, but the refrigerator offered nothing except half a pear covered with plastic wrap and a questionable carton of cottage cheese.

She plucked the car keys from the hook by the back door. She'd run to the grocery.

Her car, which she had christened with the name of Spencer, required her to use her left ankle, still sore from the fall in the cemetery, to depress the clutch. She gingerly pushed it as she revved the engine. Caressing the cool, slick steering wheel for a moment, she enjoyed the power vibrating in the machine. Though she would never admit it to anyone, Minerva Place's deepest well of gratitude flowed when she drove Spencer. The car could have been the work of Robert Burns, pure poetry. The shiny black 1940 Buick Super Coupe was one of the few indulgences she allowed herself.

"A beauty," was the salesman's opener. Minerva had gone to the Buick dealership on her birthday, which fell on a Saturday that year. The whole day had been upside down. She ate a Munal's doughnut for breakfast instead of eggs and toast, for example. Craziness.

She had driven her sensible 1929 Ford Model A Coupe since she had bought it used in 1932. No reason ever presented itself with enough rationality to persuade her to trade it in for another vehicle. It still ran, after all. But on that day in 1940, her birthday, her fortieth birthday, no less, Minerva was toying with the idea of her mortality, and the salesman pressed all the right buttons.

"Look at this torpedo body. Slick." He ran his hand along the hood and stepped away from her. "No running boards to distract. Clean. Sleek."

Minerva hadn't stepped away from her own sensibility so much that she didn't suspect any salesmen of trickery. So, she watched him as if he might pull a sleight of hand. His black hair, Brylcreem stiff, peaked like meringue over pigeon eyes that darted back and forth behind black-framed glasses. He wore one of those stylish skinny ties and kept his left hand jammed in his pocket where he jingled coins. But it was a mustard stain on his frayed white shirt—a mustard stain and it wasn't lunchtime yet—that distracted Minerva the most.

"Plenty of shoulder room and hip room." He stopped and peeked through the driver's window. "A column-mounted shift lever." He patted the door. "They weren't stingy with the chrome details, either. It's practically a Cadillac."

He stopped moving, stopped bantering, and looked away. Minerva followed his gaze out the window ablaze with a whitewash of sun. What was he staring at? She thought he looked like a cowboy at the end of a good western. And indeed, with the timing of Gene Autry, the salesman paused a beat before he said, "Stylish but sensible."

The clincher. With one phrase—one word, really—he had her. "Sensible" might as well have been the name of a Border Collie herding all her suspicions and doubts into the corral.

She considered the Buick a gift from herself on her fortieth birthday, a milestone she saw as needing a tangible indicator of "achievement and meritorious honor," which was another phrase the salesman inserted in his spiel. At the time she felt reckless and frivolous spending seven hundred twenty-eight dollars and ninety-four cents on a car. But it proved an excellent investment. With careful oil checks and changes at Lou's Texaco, regular tire rotation and replacement, stringent tending to all fluid levels and lubricants, the car had rewarded Minerva with reliable companionship for more than a decade.

Mr. Buttz, who asked to be called Lou but who received

the same treatment from Mrs. Place that she extended to all, gave it superb service. Still, he encouraged her to trade for a newer model since he said any car showed signs of wear after twelve years. She ignored him on this also. She trusted Spencer completely, she told him. "Who?" he asked, wiping his nose with the blue grease rag he kept in his back pocket.

"My car," she said. "Spencer."

She assigned her car this moniker in honor of her favorite movie star, Spencer Tracy. Minerva never missed a Spencer Tracy movie. *The Power and the Glory* might have been her favorite because it was about a railroad tycoon. And she'd just seen the excellent *Adam's Rib*. But she also loved *Father of the Bride*—how could you not like pretty little Liz Taylor? She had violet eyes. Violet! And Spencer Tracy was hilarious in it, at his comedic best. Minerva smiled, remembering his expression as he was adding up the cost of the wedding.

Yes, Spencer was the perfect name. It communicated steadfastness, nobility, sensibility. Everything you desired in a man and a car—if one desired a man, that is.

Today Spencer was proving his worth once again. He was the perfect distraction. The tan interior stretched as taut as the skin of an aging Hollywood star with a fresh face-lift. Minerva's less than taut bottom sat on the driver's seat with such resolution she may as well have been Joan of Arc leading troops to war. Such power at her command. She pumped the gas pedal. Spencer roared to life, pleased to be of service. Such a gentleman. Minerva smiled with satisfaction. She rested her right arm on the back of the seat, twisted her body, and looked through the rear window to pull out of her carport.

But as she backed out of her driveway, she met with a thump and heard skin-shredding scraping.

Minerva jerked the car into park. What on earth?

A child's wagon left to fend for itself in her driveway met her with no explanation. She checked Spencer for signs of damage. The paint and chrome were unscathed, thank you, Lord. Hands on her hips, she glared at the wagon with enough contempt to melt it. Where had that come from? She surveyed the neighborhood. Nella's car was gone. No movement at the Douglas house. A dog barked at the Rhyers'. She had told them about that before, that blasted barking beast. Matter of fact, that dog had gotten loose and... Focus, Minerva. Who had left this wagon? The trees, houses, dogs, cats—useless witnesses abounded.

She hauled the oblivious, clattering wagon out of her way. Every child on the block had a Red Ryder, and it would take some investigating to find this one's owner.

෧

By the time she made it to Myrick's, she'd simmered down some. She pulled into a prime parking place, smoothed her dress, checked her list, and ventured forth. Myrick's wasn't the largest grocery in town, but it owned the best location. Right there on Broadway, in the midsection of town, bridging the expanding residential suburbs and downtown, it made for a convenient drop-in.

Minerva considered the store to be on the pricey side. But she appreciated its clean, wide aisles gleaming in a bath of blue fluorescent light, well stocked with inventory organized in neat rows. Cans of peas stood at attention beside green beans. But the butcher's case stole the show. It beckoned with cool efficiency, sporting a silver bell you could tap for prompt service if the butcher was in the back finagling fresh bovine.

A young man whose son was standing on the end of a cart holding on to the basket acknowledged Minerva as she chose her cart. People coddled their children these days, she thought. Make the boy walk, for crying out loud. She scanned her list. Lists were critical for two reasons—obviously, for efficiency, but also for avoidance. She didn't have to make eye contact with other shoppers if she was involved in reading a list. Even so, she recognized that never smiling or nodding was impolite, and so she coached herself to look up occasionally. *One must make an effort*, she could hear her mother say through her perpetually pursed lips.

When Minerva arrived at the butcher counter, four people were ahead of her. A large lady who favored Milton Berle when he did that routine dressed like a woman was ordering liverwurst. Several items wrapped in white butcher paper sat in her cart, so Minerva wagered she was almost finished. The next in line was Mrs. Anderson, a mousy thing who looked as though she might be squashed by the Milton Berle lady if an accident happened. The next two were Mrs. Dunn and Mrs. Beiderman, choir members at First Baptist, where Minerva played the organ. Not only were they choir members, they were also sopranos. Everybody knew about those sopranos. Busybodies with a spoon in every bowl in the church kitchen. From their vantage point in the choir loft, they could see each pew.

The two women, immersed in what appeared to be an intense conversation, did not hear Minerva draw near. She considered herself artful at the quiet approach, having first found it useful as a child who loved to eavesdrop on an older sister.

"But does anyone know?" Mrs. Beiderman asked Mrs. Dunn in a conspiratorial whisper.

"I haven't heard of a soul who does." Mrs. Dunn's nervous habit of wiping the tip of her nose with her first two fingers was creating a crease across it.

"Well, it's all rather mysterious." Mrs. Beiderman arched her overplucked eyebrow.

"A logical explanation must exist," Mrs. Dunn replied, swiping that nose of hers. Minerva resisted the urge to warn her that she was going to regret that habit all too soon.

"Well, undoubtedly a logical explanation for the child's behavior exists." Mrs. Beiderman emphasized the word *behavior* with enough disapproval that it was clear the mystery child was a mischief-maker. Minerva wondered if the two women would continue to repeat each other or if they would get on with their conversation. Not that she was nosy, heavens no, but she was curious whom they were discussing.

"You are right, Evelyn. Every child needs a mother. My goodness."

"Oh, hello, Mrs. Place."

Minerva stutter-stepped back, wondering if it was obvious she'd been listening. "Hello, Mrs. Dunn. Hello, Mrs. Beiderman."

"How are you?" Mrs. Dunn flipped her concerned expression into a smile. Minerva didn't care for the way Mrs. Dunn's upper lip revealed an expanse of pink gums above niblet teeth. *Now wait, Minerva, you were going to have more charitable thoughts about people.*

"I am fine. And you?"

"Lovely."

Mrs. Beiderman piped up, using Mrs. Dunn's last word as a jumping off point: "Lovely music Sunday."

"Yes," Minerva said, remembering to add, "Thank you."

The three women stood, smiled, and blinked until Mr. Reynolds called for the next in line.

"I'd better concentrate on what I need to order," Mrs. Dunn said.

"Yes," Mrs. Beiderman echoed.

These women must not prepare before shopping, Minerva surmised. People were so odd.

A loud clatter from the canned-goods section jolted her thoughts.

"My lands!" Mrs. Beiderman cried.

"My goodness!" and "Heavens to Betsy!" and "What on earth?" were all exclaimed with equal gusto from the butcher's line.

"That's all right. No problem. These things happen. It's all right," and other reassuring words quickly followed when Mr. Myrick, who had sprung from his perch to attend to the accident, made his way down the aisle. So much for the organized green beans.

From what Minerva could gather—she didn't want to wheel her cart over and gawk—a child had removed a can from a lower part of an end display, causing the many cans resting on it to tumble. If she'd said it once, she'd said it a hundred times: people today needed to discipline their children better.

Minerva saw that Mrs. Beiderman (that nosy, nosy soprano) had strolled to the end of aisle four and was now shaking her head at Mrs. Dunn. She mouthed the words, *I think that's them* or *I think that's him*—something like that. Minerva's mind snapped back to the conversation they were having in the line. Mrs. Beiderman must be talking about the new man in town with the misbehaving son. Evidently they were the ones who had caused the disturbance. Of course.

Minerva longed to get a glimpse of the pair, but she couldn't allow herself to stoop to the level of Mrs. Beiderman. After all, Mrs. Minerva Place was not nosy. So she finished up her shopping list and headed home, unrewarded with anything but her imagination to fill in the physical details.

༚

That afternoon, after she put her groceries away, Minerva sliced her pimiento cheese sandwich diagonally, speared a dill pickle, and poured herself a glass of milk. She saw Nella shaking a rug out, and darned if she didn't catch her eye. Here she came. Oh well. Maybe this wasn't so bad.

"How are you today, neighbor?" Nella said. The woman beamed. You couldn't help but like her. Minerva glanced at her lunch.

"Would you like a pimiento cheese sandwich, Nella? I just got back from Myrick's." Nella looked startled, but she recovered with a smile.

"Sure."

Minerva couldn't think of a time the two of them had sat down and had lunch together, but she was itching to talk about the grocery store incident. Nella had timed her rug cleaning perfectly.

"Mrs. Beiderman and Mrs. Dunn—do you know them?"

"I think so. Is Mrs. Beiderman married to the man who owns Beiderman Motors?"

"Mmm-hmm."

"And Mrs. Dunn is the wife of Dr. Dunn, the orthodontist?"

"That's right. We were discussing (Minerva didn't think it

was necessary to explain the logistics of the conversation) a new resident of Paducah and I wondered if he could be the same man you mentioned to me."

"You mean the new engineer?"

"Yes, the one with the young son."

"What did they say about him?"

"He isn't married. They don't know what happened to his wife. I suspect she died because he has the boy. If he were divorced, I doubt he would have their son."

"Good point."

"But this boy is a scallywag. He's nothing but an accident waiting to happen. While we were at Myrick's the pair came in and the boy knocked down an entire aisle of canned goods. You should have heard it. You would have thought the New Madrid Fault Line had split open."

"Is that right?" Nella's eyes had grown larger. She was riveted, which delighted Minerva, who for the life of her couldn't imagine why she didn't like to have lunch with her neighbor.

"Oh, my stars. Mr. Myrick was very nice, but you know he wanted to rip into that child."

"I'll swan," Nella said as she took another bite.

"You know, Nella, it strikes me that there might be a connection between what you said about somebody new moving in around the block, what Mrs. Beiderman and Mrs. Dunn were discussing, and a phone call I recently received. Did I tell you about that? I don't think I did. A man called me earlier and told me he was new in town. He wanted his son to take piano lessons from me. If I were a gambling woman, I'd bet it's the same man."

"I'll swan." Nella had finished her sandwich and leaned back from the table. Minerva had never noticed how much red was in her neighbor's hair, but the sun shining on it brought out the henna highlights, and a smattering of freckles that you don't often see on adults. She also had a chipped tooth—a tiny chip on the tooth next to the front one.

"I'm glad I turned him down. Can you imagine the trouble

that one would cause?" Minerva got up to put some Oreos she'd just bought on a plate for their dessert. She didn't have anything homemade like Nella would have.

Nella didn't say anything at first. Then she said, "I suppose." Her reply arrested Minerva.

"What do you mean by that?"

"I just think you are such a good teacher, Minerva. And it might be nice for a father who is all alone to have a little help from a strong woman like you."

Minerva sniffed. "I don't have time in my schedule."

"If you don't have time, you don't have time." Nella reached for another cookie.

"Why should I take on some young boy who's already proven himself to be trouble?"

"Oh, it was just me thinking out loud, Minerva. You don't owe that man   or that boy, for that matter—a thing. You surely don't."

"You act like I do."

"Now, Minerva, I didn't mean to get your hackles up."

"My hackles are not up."

"I wonder where they moved from." Nella ignored Minerva's irritation and dunked her Oreo into the half glass of milk. "Maybe I can find out at bridge club."

Minerva watched the milk turn brown. Now she remembered why she didn't like having lunch with anyone.

4

Minerva practiced her organ pieces each Saturday morning from eight o'clock until ten. She liked the way this behemoth brown instrument required her entire mind and body's attention. Playing this organ was the closest she came to dancing. Her feet flew athletically from one pedal to another as her hands glided with authority over the tiers of black-and-white keys. Unlike the keys of the piano which plunked with a sparkly, crisp sound, the organ keys fell like snow, as if they rounded velvet notes out of the air. She preferred songs that required muffled stops to those that were tinny and thin, and she lingered on the lowest points of the hymns when she was not under the direction of the Minister of Music, Brother Matthew Larson.

Brother Matthew Larson could be likened to a squirrel, Minerva observed. He twitched and flitted. A man shouldn't twitch and flit if he wanted to be respected. There he stood in front of the congregation, Sunday after Sunday, in the manner of a squirrel, waving his arms and wiggling his tight but rather round bottom. Minerva couldn't help noticing this bubble-shaped physical feature. He held his chin tipped up and consequently his eyelids appeared partially closed as he sang. Even if he had been the kindest, most generous man on earth, Minerva would have disliked him based on his looks and behavior when leading the assembly in song. She realized this was an unreasonable judgment, but there it was.

On this Saturday, Brother Larson entered the sanctuary while Minerva practiced her organ piece for the next day.

"Mrs. Place," he chirped (he was a tenor). "How are you this morning?"

"I am the same as always, Brother Larson." Minerva refused to use first names with those in authority. This alarming trend was on the rise among the congregants, and she may have been single-handedly fighting for the respectful traditions of those who had built this church. However, she wasn't keen on the Baptist affinity for the term "Brother" either. She didn't particularly feel like Brother Larson was her brother. Still, that was the tradition, and tradition was better than nothing.

She shifted her weight from her left hip to the right. That fall in the cemetery had bruised her tailbone, but she wasn't about to tell Brother Larson about her bottom being sore, or about a fall. Heavenly days, no!

She wondered if her current discomfort was why she was acutely aware of Brother Larson's fanny. No, she decided she had noticed that long before she fell. Still, Minerva refrained from mentioning how painful sitting on the hard organ bench was. *My mercy, this seat may as well be concrete.*

The night after the fall, she had tried to look at her bare bottom with her hand mirror. The pain caused her to imagine it would look atrocious, several shades of purples, pinks, and blues. She was disappointed that not even a trace of a bruise showed.

She had considered visiting Dr. Herbert. Upon her mother's insistence, she had seen the physician before she married Manny. All those years ago Dr. Herbert had suggested using Lysol as a douche to prevent having babies right away, which turned out not to be an issue. Heat beginning on her chest worked its way upward ever after she remembered that conversation. Minerva had rarely been sick enough to call on the doctor through the years. He'd been to see her a couple of times when she was too ill to leave her house. For the most part, she'd managed with a couple of Bayer aspirin, cod liver oil, and steam baths.

But now? Now that she was so old she was falling over? Should she see about herself? Oh, nonsense. There was no point getting worked up over an insignificant moment of gracelessness.

Was there?

She had questions about her brain too. It could not be normal—this business of seeing dead people so clearly. But how would she ever broach that subject? Dr. Herbert might just lock her up if she told him about these visitors.

She was in a pickle. That much was certain.

She rolled her eyes, set her lips firm, and jotted a note to herself to buy that cow-udder balm from Mr. Albritton at the drugstore. It was supposed to be good for arthritis and other aches and pains. As for her mind, she'd think about that later.

Right now, facing Brother Larson, she willed herself not to flex her gluteus maximus. Bobbing up and down on the bench like a cork in water was not an option.

"Well then," Brother Larson began, clearing his throat immediately after choking out these two inconsequential words. The man lacked the ability to articulate. As often as they interacted when planning the Sunday music, you would expect they would have had an amiable working relationship. Minerva supposed the relationship rated as amiable, just not comfortable. *It's about as comfortable as this darned bench. Mercy.* The man persisted in being unable to look her in the eye. He was a nervous, flitting squirrel. *Look me in the eye, man. I won't bite.*

But poor Brother Larson flitted and fussed and avoided gazing into the piercing eyes of Mrs. Minerva Place. He managed to communicate with her through the written word. He left a note with the next Sunday's plan sealed in an envelope labeled MRS. PLACE on the ledge of her organ each week. Since she came in on Saturdays, this method allowed Mrs. Place an entire week to prepare and—key point—eliminated any need for conversation. She noticed that the minister figured this out early in his tenure at First Baptist and wondered if he commended himself on having developed the system. However, on this Saturday Brother Larson had been delayed.

"Next week I am planning on Mrs. Thibodeaux providing the prelude, and you both accompanying during 'Nearer My God to Thee' and 'Rescue the Perishing,' then the choir will sing a selection with piano accompaniment, then a benediction. I thought, if you don't mind, of course, that you might play for the offertory, a selection of your choosing if, of course, that would be satisfactory with you and you would be happy to accommodate us in that regard and if not, well then, I could always ask Mrs. Thibodeaux…" He babbled a run-on sentence of squeaky urgency that seemed to have no clear ending even when it clearly ended.

"I will be glad to play the offertory next week," Minerva said. The man should take up a sport. Perhaps hunting. He should hunt squirrels. Minerva nearly shivered with pleasure at her wickedness.

"Thank you, Mrs. Place, and now I'm afraid I am late getting home. I was delayed at the barbershop—Avondale's." Why did he assume he owed Mrs. Place a detailed explanation? Besides, who would be bothered by his delay? He wasn't married either. His time was his own. As if hearing her unspoken thoughts, he reddened, placed the envelope containing his plan on the organ, and scurried out.

Minerva ignored the envelope, considered her bottom, and returned to "Prelude in C Major." The piece would do nicely for next week's offertory. Its upbeat tempo ought to lure the cash right out of the congregants' wallets. Brother Brown would thank her when he realized the organ had summoned tithes to appear in the offering plates, and no one aware he was parting with a cent. The fact that she was practicing while she was in pain brought her a flush of sainthood.

❧

At the crack of dawn Monday morning Minerva sat up in bed and cocked her ear toward the ceiling. Was that a squirrel in her attic again? Surely not. No. She decided she'd been dreaming about squirrels because of her terrible thoughts about Brother Larson. Wait, there it was again. A scurry of sharp claws directly above her head. Raccoons? The noise stopped. She waited. Nothing for what seemed like five minutes. Could there be another visitor like Captain Fowler? No, she hadn't had any encounters since he was there last week.

"For pity's sake, Minerva," she said to herself and slid into her house shoes.

Minerva enjoyed Mondays the way most people appreciated Fridays. Sundays were exhausting, with all those people at church, the smiling and nodding, the unavoidable chitchat. She valued her role as organist because she welcomed the transport of music. She treasured its protection. Sitting on that bench with her eyes focused on the sheet music rendered human interaction impossible. Still, persistent souls who insisted on engaging were at times problematic.

"Beautiful music today, Mrs. Place."

"I love 'What a Friend We Have in Jesus,' don't you, Mrs. Place?"

"My legs would never move across those pedals while my hands worked the keyboards, Mrs. Place. You have to be so coordinated!"

What was she supposed to say to these comments? Was she supposed to carry on a conversation based on these remarks alone? Apart from "Thank you," and "Yes"? And, well, how would one reply to that last remark? There was nothing more to say. She adjusted the corners of her mouth and tried to look pleasant.

Yes, Mondays were a respite, a well-earned, well-deserved break from having to think up chitchat, and Minerva put stock in earning and deserving.

Scratching at her eczema, she stood in the kitchen waiting for the coffee to perk. She glanced out the window and saw that Nella was already up too. Her neighbor had a head full of big curlers covered with a scarf she had tied under her chin. The back of her red-and-white gingham curtains glowed pink with the morning sun. She was washing dishes, Minerva guessed, and singing to the radio she kept on the window ledge. Buster, Nella's husband, sneacked up behind his wife, scaring her so that she threw up hands covered with yellow Playtex gloves and dishwater soap foam. Her mouth wide open in a squeal Minerva couldn't hear. Nella turned around and wrapped her wet arms around Buster's neck and they kissed. Minerva looked away. Kissing like that so early in the morning seemed a bit inappropriate.

Nella and Buster had moved from the window and Minerva realized she was standing there scratching the dry patch behind her ear, gazing at a blurry middle distance. She shook her head and poured a cup of coffee. Enough daydreaming.

Today's writing would focus on a woman named Emma Skillian. Minerva's curiosity about her had been piqued the last time she visited the city office that housed official records from Oak Grove. Emma died in Paducah's Great Flood of 1937. She took out her notebook and studied her meager notes. Not much had shown up about Mrs. Skillian. She hadn't been able to find Emma Skillian's obituary yet. The only fact she had was what the clerk had written about her—"the last victim of The Flood."

Minerva began her entry as she always did, by recording the basics:

Emma Skillian, born 1878; died January 24, 1937; New Section 13, Lot 298.

Though Minerva preferred to know more about one of her characters before she wrote, she was compelled today to write about Emma. For reasons she couldn't explain, she was drawn to this woman. Something about the words, "last victim of The Flood" penetrated her. How did the clerk know she was the last victim?

The Flood of 1937 was a landmark in Paducah's timeline. The Ohio River had swollen to seven miles wide. Only a fraction of the town of forty thousand remained in their homes. Thirty-two thousand people fled for higher ground. Life was unsettled for a month, and when the waters receded a filthy, stinking mess was left behind.

Minerva leaned back in her chair and let her mind drift. She had found that if she relaxed before she began writing, an image would emerge. If she could visualize whom she was writing about, the story flowed better.

A picture slowly started to form, watercolor vague, but coming. Emma Skillian seemed to be a woman a few years older than Minerva was, with glasses and short, fuzzy, salt-and-pepper hair. She wore an aqua-green apron with embroidery on the pockets over a flowered dress that hit right below her knees. Her ankles were swollen over the sturdy black lace-up shoes she wore. Her knuckles were knotty with arthritis and Minerva wondered if they gave her much pain.

She began to write.

She lost track of time, as she often did when she wrote. As the afternoon slipped away, shadows teased across the page obscuring her concentration. Stiff with the effort of sitting in one position too long, she moved slowly to flick on the light above the table. As she crossed back to sit down, she paused. Something was off.

The writing was going well. What was wrong? She hovered over the table and read the last words she had written:

> That day, January 24, 1937, turned out to be nastier than we could have imagined. By mid-morning, while the gray sky poured out its freezing rain, a team of men were knocking on doors telling us to evacuate. The water stole its frigid fingers inch by inch into our homes. I didn't know the man who stopped by our house. His bulbous nose was as red as a tomato and rain poured off his head. I offered him some hot tea, but he looked at me with wildness in his steely eyes and said, "Get out now. And, sister, I mean now." Sister. He called me sister like he knew me; knew me well. I'd never laid eyes on that man before. Cheeky. I felt entitled to ignore him.
>
> Still, the flotsam-filled river lapped at my steps like a thirsty stray. I figured I would have to take a boat out to the evacuation site, so I forced myself to consider my options if Jacob didn't come home.

Minerva tried to imagine why Emma would not have evacuated immediately. What would keep a person from leaving a dangerous situation, especially after being warned? Maybe Emma was one of those people who felt invulnerable. Or maybe she thought she could get one last thing done.

What would Minerva have done if she had been in Emma's place? She had given Emma a husband, Jacob, but she realized she had painted a picture of a woman alone. Emma's husband wasn't around. This was a hole in her story that she'd have to fix. Was he at work that day? Would he have left Emma alone on a day when the river threatened their safety? What kind of husband did that?

Minerva tried to ignore thoughts of her own marriage. *Of course*, she reminded herself, *not every marriage is like yours was*. Shaking her head, she picked the pen off the table as if holding it would answer her questions.

She studied the story, then felt the words bursting out. Feverishly she wrote what she imagined about Emma, where Jacob had been, why the poor woman had been alone, what she had been doing. The words rambled in a jumble of thoughts until finally, she wrote the last paragraph:

> The clerk listed me as "a victim of The Flood," but he might as well have listed me "a victim of her own stubbornness who died for one more thing." What's worse, Jacob got to be right. For all eternity he could silently say "I told you so." I loved the man, but no woman wants to leave that kind of legacy.

"You've got that right," Minerva said as if answering the character she had created. "No woman wants to hear 'I told you so' from her husband."

Minerva blew on the ink so it wouldn't smudge. She tapped the pages on the table to straighten them and slipped them into a folder. She allowed herself a smile. The story she had told herself about Emma delighted her. This was why she wrote.

She was so lost in her thoughts that when she heard the voice, she threw the folder up. Papers fluttered like a flock of birds.

"Hello."

"What's that?" Minerva stuttered. "Who's there?"

"I'm sorry I startled you, but I need to make a few corrections. You don't mind, do you?" A lone figure, a rail-thin woman with a gaunt expression, stood at the other end of the room.

Minerva breathed deeply through her nose and realized she was holding her palms up in a defensive gesture. She lowered them and blew a silent whistle. "Who are you?"

"I apologize again, but you have several facts incorrect." The woman ignored her question.

Minerva batted her eyes, thinking the vision—another figment of her imagination, she hoped—would disappear. But she didn't. This person, this imaginary invention—Oh dear, Minerva, are you crazy?—had pulled out a dining-room chair at the end of the table and was pushing her frameless glasses up her nose as she sat.

Minerva stared. "What? Excuse me, but how did you get in here? Who are you? I am certain we've never met. Do you make a habit of walking into people's homes without knocking?"

"What's that?"

"I said… Never mind. Who are you?" The women stared at one another until Minerva became uncomfortable with the silence. "Are you Emma?"

"I am." This small woman, painfully thin and drawn, was not the ample Emma that Minerva had written. And she wasn't flighty or boisterous. She didn't carry a hint of humor. This Emma was vulnerable, bruised. "It's true that I died in The Flood, but my real death came years earlier."

Minerva blinked and tapped her pen on the notebook. "I don't know what…" Another uncomfortable silence fell. Minerva scrambled through her thoughts for something to say. "Would you like a cup of tea?"

"No, thank you."

"I'm stumped, because…" Minerva searched for words. "I'll say it plainly, you are not real."

"I could go in the other room."

"Why would you do that?"

"It might give you time to collect your thoughts and decide what to ask me. You can ask me anything."

"No, no. I don't need time. Let's see. For one thing, what do you mean you died in The Flood, but you died years earlier? That's rather cryptic."

"You keep searching. I don't like talking about it.

"I thought you said I could ask you anything."

"I did. I didn't say I would answer."

I may have met my match here, Minerva thought. "Could you steer me in the right direction?"

"I suspect with the amount of research you do, you'll run across it." Emma turned her head and looked at Minerva from an angle, as if she were testing her.

"I don't want to be rude," Minerva said. "But you haven't told me anything except that I've gotten some things wrong."

Emma rose from the dining-room chair. A faint scent of something Minerva couldn't readily identify wafted over her. A mustiness that carried the peppery odor of geraniums.

"I didn't mean to offend you," Minerva offered, refocusing.

"No offense taken." And she was gone. Just like that. As quickly as she had materialized, she was gone.

Minerva stood. She expected the scattered papers to flutter with Emma's departure, as if disturbed by a breeze, but they didn't move. Nothing moved but the hands of the mantel clock producing an exaggerated *tick-tick-tick*. Or was that her heart?

"You have gone over the edge." Minerva's voice stumbled onto the silence. Her words thick and slow, muffled. What was happening to her mind? She smoothed her dress and picked at a tiny bit of lint. One by one, she picked up the papers and then patted The Flood folder, but despite the slowness of her movements her forearm knocked her cup over.

"Oh!" Minerva dabbed at the spill, righting the cup. "Emma is a product of your imagination." But she had looked different than in Minerva's imagination. "You imagined her. Remember, this happens when you write." Saying the words aloud gave them weight. Still, perhaps she should take a break, take an aspirin, settle down.

"Who are you talking to?" Minerva whirled around at the sound of another voice.

A boy stood in the kitchen, right inside the back door. He wore a baseball cap backward and he smelled like wet straw and forgotten laundry. His big brown eyes, framed in thick lashes, stared at her. A curly mop of blond hair poked out of his baseball cap and a dimple punctuated his grin. She was filled with an unfamiliar urge to hug him.

This was not her imagination. At least she was certain of that.

"What are you doing in my house? How long have you been standing there? Just who are you, young man?"

"I brought you this." He held up a crayon drawing of a tree. "It's my lookout tree."

Minerva was so shocked by the appearance of not only Emma Skillian, but also this, this…urchin, that she stood frozen in place.

"I thought you might want this since it's in your yard and all. Look, I signed it." He held up the drawing. "Do you have friends nobody but you can see?"

Minerva took the piece of paper but felt rooted to the floor, like the very maple in her front yard that this little boy had drawn. What did he mean by "lookout tree," she briefly wondered before he rattled on.

"It sounded like you had company, but I didn't see anybody," he continued, which prompted Minerva to shift and remember to breathe. "I have a friend my dad can't see. He's a funny kid. His name is Frank. He likes the harmonica. What does your friend like?"

Minerva stammered. "My friend…" Maybe she wasn't crazy. Maybe she was only like this child, entertained by a lively imagination. "My friend was telling me about her life."

"Does she have a name?"

"Emma. Mrs. Skillian. She is a grown-up like me." Minerva hesitated, but only a moment. Something about this conversation was such a relief. Someone who understood. Never mind that he was, she estimated, no more than seven years old. "She went through The Great Flood in Paducah. Do you know anything about that?"

The boy frowned. "You mean she was on the ark with Noah?"

His serious question took Minerva by surprise, and she laughed. It was a full-on laugh, the kind she rarely experienced. In fact, she couldn't stop laughing. She laughed so hard the boy joined her. Eventually, with tears streaming down her face, she caught hold of herself. She hadn't laughed like that since—well, she couldn't remember when.

"Oh dear!" She had completely forgotten she was annoyed. "What did you say your name is?"

"George. I'm George Robert McAlpin. I'm named after my grandfather and my daddy."

"George Robert McAlpin," Minerva repeated, thinking the name sounded familiar. "I thank you for the drawing." Then it hit her—McAlpin! Robert McAlpin was who had called her about piano lessons. This must be his son. Could this be the scallywag who knocked over the vegetable display at Myrick's? It all fell into place.

Good gracious, here he was.

"You'd better get home. Your mother's going to be..." She caught herself. If she was right about the bits and pieces she'd picked up, this boy didn't have a mother. "You'll be needed at home, I'm sure."

Once he was out, she leaned against the door and put her head in her hands. My mercy, she thought, who will that boy tell what he saw and heard? What did he see and hear, anyway? Oh, my sweet goodness. Why had she told him she had an imaginary friend—if indeed that's what she had? What had she been thinking? This was out of control. What would she do?

A dull thud started behind her eyes. She went to the bathroom to find aspirin and was confronted with her reflection in the medicine-cabinet mirror. She usually avoided looking at herself, but now she stared.

Manic white hairs escaped the bobby pins Minerva used to secure the bun she always wore. Her skin poured across her bones like warm wax. Distinct frown lines perched like commas between her brows while parentheses corralled her mouth. Had she ever had skin like George's? Had her eyes ever been that full of innocence?

"Okay." Minerva drew in a deep breath. "This will be fine. The boy will probably forget everything. And if he does happen to tell someone, nobody would believe him." Minerva Place talking to invisible beings. Why, that was just crazy.

5

Becky Parker, Jane Miller, Tammy Turner, and Vanessa Seiboldt came for Tuesday lessons and—Minerva wasn't sure how she'd managed to arrange this—all four girls were working on "Für Elise." The blasted song was doodle-doodle-doo-doo-doo-doodling through her head in a tortuous loop. She endured the two hours of calming excited poco motos and regulating spastic arpeggios.

"The right hand plays the melody, Jane. You want to emphasize what the right hand is playing." Jane was left-handed. "Let up on the pedal here, Becky. You are not trying to win a race on a speedway."

Now—finally—Minerva could get back to writing. But after adjusting her back support, cleaning her glasses, lining up her cups of pens, straightening the file folders, and rearranging them, she leaned back in her chair, unable to concentrate. The room stared at her.

By the window, a mother-in-law's tongue leaned over as if it were trying to reach its roots. Minerva knew how it felt. The plant was the only touch Minerva had added. The rest was what her mother had left behind. Wallpaper featuring a periwinkle-blue-and-yellow flower vine on a trellis. Wood trim that had mellowed with a waxy coat of age. Built-in china hutches defending her mother's dishes behind glass doors. An unadorned ecru tablecloth protected the tabletop from scratches. Her mother had been finicky about such things. When her parents were alive, they ate their meals in the kitchen because the dining-room furniture, like the china, was too nice to use.

When Minerva first started writing, she'd favored the Formica-topped kitchen table. The formal dining-room furniture was for Sundays and holidays. But as Minerva walked further away from her days as a member of the Webster family and as

her research accumulated, she tired of clearing the kitchen table
so often.

Now, instead of hoping for turkey and dressing, mashed potatoes, and green beans, the rich cherry table welcomed history
books, manila envelopes stuffed with bits and pieces of trivia,
accordion files, stacks of notes anchored by paperweights, and
crowded cups of pens and pencils. The dining table offered a
pleasant place to gather with friends from Oak Grove, who,
when they weren't shocking her with unexpected appearances,
regaled her with tales of dreams both reached and dashed and
a litany of secrets. She expected that her table was privy to the
best after-dinner conversations in Paducah.

But on this evening, she remained agitated by the Tuesday
lessons. So, she consulted the thermometer mounted outside
the kitchen window for its opinion on a walk. The October air
crackled at sixty-six degrees, leaving her no excuses. She tied a
sweater around her shoulders in case it grew chillier.

She regretted her decision before she was out of her driveway.

"Hello, Mrs. Place!"

Oh, dear. This was why she walked in the mornings.

"Hello, Mrs. Place!" Mrs. Rhyer repeated and waved from
her porch. "Hold on a minute." The eager-to-talk neighbor set
a watering can beside a yellow mum and jack-o'-lantern and
bustled down the porch steps toward Minerva. "I'm so glad to
see you. I've intended to stop over."

"Oh?" was all Minerva could muster.

"Yes. I've talked with the neighbors and everyone's agreed to
have a Halloween party together this year. It will be exactly two
weeks from today."

Minerva thought this idea sounded worse than horrible, but
she tried to arrange her face into what she hoped was its pleasant expression. "A Halloween party?" A technique she often
employed was to return words as a question. This served to buy
time until she could figure out what was proper to say.

"I know you don't have any little ones trick-or-treating,

but you'll enjoy being with all the neighbors. I'm planning on having everyone over to our backyard—if the weather cooperates—after the kids make their rounds. All the little witches and scarecrows can play, burn off some of their energy before we try to wrestle them into bed. And I'll have some adult treats for the grown-ups." Mrs. Rhyer winked as she said "adult treats" and Minerva realized she was talking about alcohol. She tried to keep her face neutral, but disapproval bubbled. Alcohol around children was inappropriate.

"You are certainly kind to think to include me, Mrs. Rhyer."

"Oh, come now, I've told you to call me Maxine." Maxine wore slim black-and-white checked slacks, a black blouse, and a cropped white sweater. It set off her black hair and green eyes. She wasn't exactly pretty, but she positively exuded confidence despite her casual apparel.

Minerva continued, "But I tend to turn in early. The older I get, the more I'm married to routine." She hoped she sounded pleasant about being older.

"Oh, I'm disappointed. I had hoped everyone on the block could come." Mrs. Rhyer—Maxine—did look disappointed. A pout and drawn eyebrows replaced her enthusiastic smile. She was an expressive one.

"Thank you so much, though." Minerva felt a need to console her because, well, she looked downright dejected. My goodness. Had she actually thought Minerva would come? "Please bring your boys by to get some candy. I'll have suckers for them."

Maxine's smile blinked back on. "Oh, we won't miss a single house." She reached out and patted Minerva's arm. Minerva noticed she had painted fingernails and wondered if she had a housekeeper too. "Enjoy your walk, Mrs. Place."

☙

Minerva did enjoy her walk. She thought she'd handled Mrs. Rhyer—Maxine—deftly. What a nightmare a Halloween party would be. Bad enough having to answer the door time after time. But never mind that right now. She wanted to think about her lunch at Kresge's. She'd eaten there yesterday and what she had overheard stuck in her mind like a repetitive song. Like "Für Elise," in fact.

Kresge's blue-plate special on Tuesdays was fried chicken livers, a dish she preferred not to make for herself. Too much trouble for one person. But boy, oh boy, did she love liver. She'd hung her coat on the coatrack between booths and sat with her back to the entrance.

Minerva wasn't sure when the conversation occurring in the booth behind her had caught her attention, but at some point she couldn't help listening. Minerva wasn't being nosy. No. But one woman had spoken in a squeaky voice no one could possibly ignore.

"So, nobody knows what happened? He came here with a little boy, but no wife?" said the squeaker. Minerva had been certain that if she'd looked, the woman would have had food in her mouth.

"That's right. He's supposed to be a widower."

"Oh, how peculiar. You know a man doesn't stay single long—especially if he's raising a child. They always snag a mother for children as fast as possible. I wonder how long he's been on his own."

"I wish I'd asked."

"It's so sad." Squeaker must have paused to swig her drink or scarf down another bite. Minerva had itched to turn around and see what the women looked like but restrained herself.

"It is. It is. I wonder why he's never remarried. Do you know if there's something wrong with him? Did he have a war injury?"

"Who's to say? Some of those men returned damaged in the head, you know."

"Oh, don't I know it. My husband's cousin Floyd sits in his truck all day reading girlie magazines ever since he got back. He wasn't perverted before he went. He can't keep a job or anything. He's not right."

"Well, this man seems normal. He works at the plant as an engineer. Ted Gibson's his boss."

Minerva sat up straighter. She knew the Gibsons. She taught the Gibson children—Helen and the twins, what were their names? Tommy and Timmy or something silly—nice enough girl, but wretched boys.

"Yes, Janet Gibson told me all this. She hosted the young man for dinner. She is the sweetest thing, isn't she? Having her husband's new employee over to eat just to welcome him to a new town? So sweet."

Minerva had rolled her eyes. Sweet. Yes. Get on with it. But the women had finished talking about the mysterious single father and had moved on to Cousin Lois's bursitis.

Minerva had been crunching on another liver when she heard, "Why, hello, Mrs. Place."

Minerva tongued the liver to one side of her mouth, covered her lips with her napkin, and gave a nod. "Miss Boswell." Thankfully, the little librarian passed. But reverie disrupted, she had felt rushed to eat the rest of her lunch before she saw anyone else. That is why she didn't like to eat out. Who wanted to converse with a mouth full of food, when you could guarantee that someone would ask you a question just as you took a bite? Then you'd swallow prematurely, leading to hiccups immediately or indigestion later. Social eating was a nightmare. A nightmare.

So, now on her walk she was able to reflect on the conversation she had heard in Kresge's. The one she couldn't help but overhear. Their voices had carried. People couldn't expect you to plug your ears up with your fingers or some such. If you talked loudly, your conversation broadcasted itself. It was hardly Minerva's fault.

Anyway.

She wondered if this fellow was the same one who had called her. Robert McAlpin. That would make sense. He lined up with the description of the pair who had been at Myrick's and with the man Nella thought was their new neighbor. This could not all be coincidence. Paducah wasn't that big.

When she got home, though, the walk's refreshment

blanched. A child was in her maple tree. Forevermore! It was George, perched in the branches of the black maple in her front yard!

"George McAlpin," she called. "What are you doing there?" He was at least fifteen feet above her head, leaning on the trunk of the tree with his legs cocked so that his sneakers gripped the bark, one foot in front of the other. A crow could knock him off.

"I'm checking for enemies," the boy yelled back. He put his hand over his brow as if to shade his vision from the sun and surveyed the area.

"What enemies?" Minerva could see him taking a dive out of that tree and the whole town holding her responsible. Why was she asking him about enemies? "Get down this instant."

"But they're coming. I see them."

"You do not see anyone. Get down. Now." The boy didn't move. "Now!"

He lowered his legs and straddled the limb. Then Minerva understood why he hadn't immediately obeyed. Getting down looked tricky. He would have to hug the trunk, reach with his foot to a sturdy branch on the other side of it, and then rely on a couple of puny branches to swing his body around. First, he had to turn around on the branch where he sat.

"Be careful. Don't fall!"

"What?"

"I said do not fall."

He leaned away from the trunk and swung one leg over so that he was facing Minerva and his feet were dangling. Minerva inhaled. "Oh, please be careful."

"I think I can jump."

"No! Don't jump!" Minerva threw her arms up in the air. "Just come back down the same way you got up there."

Now he hugged the trunk and reached around it to a branch about a third of the way from him. He grabbed what he could and kept rubbing the trunk with his foot, trying to find the branch he wanted.

"Oh, heavens, watch yourself." He stretched. Almost. He slipped and Minerva gasped. "Oh!" But his foot found purchase and in what seemed like one fluid motion he lowered himself onto the next branch down. From there he scampered like a monkey.

"Child, what on earth did you think you were doing?" Minerva felt her face heat up and a headache erupt. "You could have fallen and hurt yourself. You could have broken your neck or your arm or a leg."

"I've never fallen before." George stared at her with those round brown eyes; doe eyes, she thought.

"What do you mean? You've climbed this tree before?" Minerva felt a wash of alarm tingle.

"Sure. It's my lookout tree—the one I drew you a picture of."

"George, you cannot keep climbing this tree. It's too dangerous. In fact, under no circumstances are you to come into my yard unsupervised. Do you understand? That could have been a very serious accident."

"Do you have any cookies?"

"Cookies?" Minerva drew her head back with a jerk. Had he heard a word she'd said? "*Cookies?*"

George blinked. He scratched his neck. A tear in his jacket caught his attention and he stuck his finger in the hole.

"No, I don't have any cookies. Now get on home. Your father and I will have a conversation about this."

George picked up a stick that had fallen out of the tree with him. "I'm sorry I made you mad, Mrs. Place. I just wanted to make sure no bad guys came." His lower lip pooched out. Oh, dear, she had hurt his feelings. But he could not be allowed to climb the tree in her yard without supervision. He just could not do that. He needed to know she was serious.

As she watched him amble away with an almost visible cloud of dejection hovering over him, Minerva took a breath and blinked with purpose. There was no reason to let this episode get under her skin. The boy needed better supervision. The boy needed a mother.

Oh, Minerva, did you have to be so hard on him? He doesn't have a mother, for pity's sake. She stewed over the whole ordeal for a good hour before she got a grip. She must let this incident go. Absolutely no reason to remain upset. The child was out of the tree and was gone. She would continue with her day.

Right now, she believed she had most certainly earned the right to sit down and write.

The moment she hit the chair she relaxed. Ahh. The joy of it. Submerging in another's life. Stringing words together to shape that life into whatever she wanted it to be. Not that there weren't rules. She did have parameters. She hung her imagination on a skeleton of facts. She leaped from the research she had done to what might have been, and in doing so, developed friends who crossed the boundaries of time.

Today she was exploring the life of Margaretha, the woman whose headstone she'd made the rubbing of. The German teacher at the high school had easily translated the epitaph for her, and now she rubbed her hand over the words as if they had the same texture as the engraved stone.

The young woman's voice began in a thick accent and all thoughts of boys in trees fluttered away like the autumn leaves.

Margaretha Stuck Retter, born July 6, 1819; died Jan. 1845; Old Addition, Section 9, Lot 142

Margaretha
Stuck
Retter
For the love and friendship
Of his early deceased wife,
Margaretha Retter, maiden name,
Stuck, this monument was dedicated
by her grieving husband and children.
She was born in Siebeldingen, Germany, on July 6, 1819
And passed away after a short sickness in January 1845.
Soft and Peaceful in the Lord
Rest her ashes.
(The last line could also be translated "Rest her soul.")

They sent for a doctor, but he didn't arrive at our place in time. I suppose I might have had any number of diseases, but the doctor wrote influenza on my death certificate. I was twenty-five.

When death comes for you odd scraps wander through your awareness—Will Gertie remember to feed Otto? Will Papa catch those moles? Did I tell Lutz to marry Anna after I died? Will Gertie's blond hair dull with age? The fever melted the compartments of my mind until everything from moles to marriage took on equal importance.

I carried vivid memories of Siebeldingen, a tiny village in the Südliche Weinstraße district, in Rhineland-Palatinate, western Germany, when I was Papa's kleine prinzessin, Daddy's little princess.

Minerva paused and checked the spelling of the German words. She tried to pronounce *prinzessin,* but the middle turned to mush in her mouth, and she sounded like she had a lisp. She chuckled trying to spit the word out with no success. No wonder she loved doing this. Always something interesting to tweak her mind. She got back to it.

Papa was a farmer and like every farmer, he wanted land of his own to grow his crops. He attended a reading club at our church where our pastor read from the *Leatherstocking Tales* and from Herr Gottfried Duden's writings on America. Papa learned that in America you had meat on your table every night—so much meat you could never eat it all. He obsessed about moving.

When Papa discovered land at a good price in Kentucky, he celebrated as if it was Christmas. Once we saved enough money for the trip, we said goodbye to our neighbors and began our adventure. After weeks of arduous travel, we landed at the tangle of trees knotted on the muddy river called Ohio.

Soon we discovered what we didn't want to know— Herr Duden was deceptive. Oh, he hadn't exaggerated the country's beauty. Kentucky was vibrant with greens and rich soil, and its rivers teemed with life. But the reality of our lives stood in harsh contrast to nature's richness. Papa soon called Herr Duden "Duden der Lugenhund"—Duden the lying dog.

Still, what choice did we have? The money bought several acres of land outside a settlement called Paducah. Our lot was cast. Kentucky was now our home.

Minerva stopped and thought about the day her father had told her they were moving to Kentucky. Not a day of celebration for her. She never had felt such rage before. She tapped her pen and let her mind wander back to her girlhood days.

Minerva would have preferred a different sort of childhood. She deplored moving, but that was the nature of her father's work.

"I don't understand what is so difficult about finding a friend," Geneva would say. "You just pick out a girl in your class who seems nice and start talking to her."

Minerva's stomach churned. Besides, she wasn't convinced that having friends was necessary. Minerva was content with a book. But her mother (and father and sister) kept insisting.

"Who did you talk to at school today?" became a standard dinner question. *Why don't they ask me what I learned today?* Minerva thought resentfully.

She did acquire a best friend once, in Chicago. Catherine Gray.

"Call me Cat," the girl with the strong northeastern accent had said when Minerva met her. This was during the Websters' Chicago years between 1913 and 1915. Cat's exoticness intrigued Minerva. She looked at Minerva with unnerving frankness through one brown eye and one blue eye. The brown a rich, deep brown and the blue the color of a cornflower, each possessing a startling crispness. And then to have such a name. Her full name was Catherine Eleanor Leone Gray. Minerva had been breathless with the prospect of this friendship.

Her mother had been breathless with the prospect as well.

Cat's father was William Gray, and he served on the Board of Education. The Websters were firm believers in education—though they had daughters—and they relished the thought of friendship with someone who had influence.

Minerva rarely made friends, but when she did, my goodness.

Minerva and Cat did not care about the state of education in Chicago at all, however. They were thirteen. They talked about more significant matters. Boys. Other girls. Their mothers. Their teachers. What a real kiss might feel like (Minerva spoke of her kiss with Luke in the fourth grade, but Cat declared that kisses were supposed to last longer.) That magician named Houdini. What would happen if one of them contracted polio.

"I know what I would want you to do for me," Cat said as she sucked on a cigar they had snuck out of her father's study.

"What?" Minerva, already woozy though she hadn't smoked yet, watched the cigar smoke curl around Cat's head.

"I would want you to read me *Little Women*. What about you?"

"Yes, I'd definitely want *Little Women*, but I love *The Red Badge of Courage* and *Huckleberry Finn* too."

Cat coughed and handed Minerva the cigar, which Minerva put in her mouth but did not inhale.

"I wish Louisa May Alcott had written more books."

"More grown-up books. I didn't like *Jo's Boys*."

The girls thought that over.

"Minerva?"

"What?"

"I'm going to be sick."

They'd vowed to be blood sisters by pricking their thumbs with pins and rubbing the two bubbles of red together. They wrote each other notes in class. They shared root beer floats.

So, the worst day of Minerva's life was born at the family dinner when her father announced that Burlington had a new assignment for him in Cairo, a fledgling town in southern Illinois. Far, far away from Cat.

Minerva had responded with shocking force.

"You cannot do this to me." Minerva surprised herself with the volume and force of her words. She surprised her parents, too, who were accustomed to a silent, solemn teenage girl who rarely pushed back.

"Minerva, sit down." Her mother frowned at her. Her displeasure did not dissuade her, though.

"I will not sit down." Minerva felt emboldened. A rarely felt burst of confidence coursed through her. How could her parents do this to her? She was finally settled, happy. She finally fit somewhere.

"Minerva, do not speak to your mother with such disrespect." Her father could usually control his youngest with a stern look of disapproval. He was off-kilter now. Both of her parents' expressions contained equal amounts of displeasure and confusion.

"You have made me move and move and you have insisted I have friends and now that I finally have a friend I love, you are taking her away from me." Minerva's voice grew louder with every word. She felt like a runaway train. The collision course she had set for herself was rapidly approaching. "It's not fair!"

Those last three words out of Minerva's mouth were the most often-repeated phrase in the lexicon of children through the ages, and that night as Minerva's torment lit the room, her astonished parents were rendered speechless by them. She dismissed herself from the meal by throwing her napkin on the plate of steaming food and stomping out of the room. By this time Geneva was married and so was not witness to her younger sister's shocking coming-of-age scene. She, too, would have been dumbstruck by the intensity of Minerva's reaction, though. None of the Websters ever had heard Minerva raise her voice.

Despite her protests, the Websters moved. And Minerva determined never again to allow herself to become vulnerable to such loss.

The friends she made at Oak Grove Cemetery were perfect. She could discuss her heart with them without fear of losing them. They were completely trustworthy and forever hers.

She refocused on Margaretha, whose voice she imagined carried a German accent.

> I can't paint the entire picture in bleak hues, though, because we had each other, which was a blessing. And Papa bought land, another blessing because through farming he supported the family.
>
> As I grew up and times improved, Mama let me work alongside her in the kitchen. Here I learned to create the tastes of my memories. Oh, the Hase im Topf I made when Papa and the boys brought home rabbits and we harvested fresh carrots, turnips, and onions. And I made countless loaves of sauerteig. In late summer we enjoyed apfelstrudel hot out of the oven, made with apples from our backyard. Mama taught me to knead and stretch the dough until it was as thin as a butterfly wing.
>
> I married Lutz Retter—Luther—when I was eighteen. I had loved him since I was fourteen and he was sixteen. He was tall and blond with crystal-blue eyes that crinkled at the corners when he smiled. The day we married I wore a dress my sister Anna made for me from a tablecloth Mama brought from home. Anna stitched doilies on it so that it looked fit for royalty.
>
> Then, just ten months after we married, God began to bless us with children. By the time I was twenty-four, I had given birth to six—one a year since I married. A desperate sorrow filled me when my second boy and third girl died before I weaned them, but life refused to stop for me.

Minerva looked at what she had written and hitched her nose up on one side as if smelling rotten eggs.

"You're dull, Frau," Minerva announced, flicking her pen back and forth so quickly it looked like an arc in the air. She marked through a line at the beginning of Margaretha's story and replaced *Will Gertie's blond hair dull with age?* with *Did Lutz think I didn't know he loved her?*

There—Minerva smacked her lips with approval—you're more interesting now. She continued to write:

> I may sound as though I remain sorrowful in the afterlife, and I struggle to explain how a soul undresses when she's crossed to glory. I'll suggest this: you remember without sadness.
>
> Lutz loved my sister, but he loved me too—at least enough to give me children. And two of my children died, but four lived. Do you see? You're unaware of everything happening on earth, but events that bring you peace command your attention. Does this make sense? Of course not. You're still there.
>
> Anyway, though my life wasn't long or impressive, it was blessed. I crossed a vast, turbulent ocean and traveled into a wilderness thick with stretching trees and rivers, wildflowers, and wild folks. The land challenged my spirit and flesh. I cried in frustration when my hands bled and my back ached, and I gave thanks when it yielded results. The man I married filled me with love and desire. Our babies held the freshness of heaven's dew behind their ears. I laughed and danced and cried with friends. The scent of bread baking perfumed our home. I lived my life, each day a gift.

Minerva stopped writing. She felt someone watching her. Her pulse quickened as she looked up to see a woman staring at her without a smile. The short German woman was flanked by solemn children and a handsome man. An older man and woman stood beside them. Someone who looked a lot like the woman in the front stood by this couple. Minerva had never encountered more than one person coming alive before.

She considered the group. This must be Margaretha. And her papa who called her "his little princess" and her mama who taught her to cook. The one who resembled Margaretha must be Anna, her sweet sewing sister. Their thick bodies filled the archway between the kitchen and the dining-room. They had made themselves at home. Minerva smelled a pungent odor. Sauerkraut?

Here again were real people, who could not be living and breathing, standing in her house. Living and breathing. She was having another episode. But it was—*they were*—so real. She scratched her scalp and scowled. Each person stood before her alive with individuality. Anna's hair blond and braided, pulled across the top of her head and pinned like a halo. Luther's blue eyes and square shoulders, standing between the sisters. Margaretha, pretty and plump, with lips and cheeks so rosy she didn't need rouge or lipstick.

"Hello there," Minerva finally said.

"Hello, Mrs. Place." Margaretha took a step toward the table. She smoothed her apron and smiled shyly. "Do you have some questions for me?"

"No. I think I understand your life just fine." Minerva heard prickliness in her voice. She felt sorry for Margaretha, but she didn't want to tell her so. Nobody wanted you to feel sorry for them. Pity smacked of vulnerability and Minerva knew vulnerability was a place she preferred to avoid.

"I'm not sure you do," Margaretha rejoined.

"You birthed babies and baked bread," Minerva said to Margaretha, aware she might be bordering on rudeness. Still, she continued what she had started. "Nothing special. Offer one morsel to separate you from other women." She tried to check her anger, baffled by why, after writing a charming profile of a harmless young woman who had endured so much, she was angry.

Luther stepped forward. "I don't like the way you are speaking to my wife," he said.

Minerva felt a ripple of anxiety. She had been abrupt. "I apologize. I do. It's a problem I have—being too blunt at times. I've been told that."

Margaretha turned to Luther. "It's all right, dear." She patted his forearm. "I understand her confusion." She returned her attention to Minerva, whose pulse had quickened with her outburst. These encounters couldn't be good for her health. She needed to get herself in check or she was going to have a heart attack. Or stroke. Maybe she was having mini strokes. Could that be? Could that be the reason for these visions? Some sort of neurological malfunction?

"You wonder why I seem so cheerful when my husband loved my sister and my life seemed to amount to nothing?"

Minerva glanced at Luther and Anna. Neither of them seemed perturbed, but this was discomfiting. The truth like that. Just hanging out in the air like a sheet on the line.

"I…uh…yes." Minerva cleared her throat and sat up a little straighter. "I do wonder."

Minerva was no stranger to feeling unloved. Her own parents hadn't seemed to love her much, and as she wrote about Margaretha, bothersome memories surfaced about her own marriage. She liked to keep those tucked away. It was over. Why tread on painful territory? It was as useless as picking a scab. She wasn't a masochist.

Margaretha began, but Minerva didn't let her get past "I."

"And tell me this—why do women's stories all sound alike? Babies and bread. Husbands and home. Just because he gave you babies, you give thanks. Didn't you want his love too? Didn't you want to be loved?" Minerva scooted away from the table and ignored the Germans as she hurried to the light switch. She could feel their eyes follow her, and she whipped around. She felt like that teenage Minerva, the one whose emotions controlled her words instead of the current Minerva, who was direct but controlled. The blunt outpouring continued.

"Margaretha, rabbit stew does not make for a fulfilling life, I don't care how blue your husband's eyes are—were. And what was the silly name he called you? Dumpling? My eye. You are fat." She blanched as the words tumbled loose.

But now the room, awash in the yellow light above the table, ignored Minerva's accusations. The Germans had left.

Minerva rubbed her aching hand. Her heart continued to pump a notch too fast. It's just imagination, she reminded herself. Imagination. *You're not a lunatic.*

6

Wednesday woke Minerva with such vivid sunshine, she groaned and rolled her eyes. This autumn day had dressed up in blues, yellows, and reds. People would toss out "what a perfect day!" and "wish we could bottle this weather and keep it all year long!" and other such comments. Lots of exclamation marks would fly around on the ends of people's greetings. But the cemetery waited in gray, never minding the fiasco of color. At least there was that.

Today she walked down Faith Avenue, pad and pen in her right hand, a camel cardigan around her shoulders, top button buttoned. Minerva had walked Faith Avenue so many times she'd memorized that there were twenty-seven rows of headstones between the streets. She counted the markers as she passed in the same way she counted every step in a set of stairs (most household flights had thirteen).

Her mother and father, Lucille and Earl, were buried in Old Section, Lot 516, Section 35, next to the plot Howard Pleasant came to occupy two years after the Websters died. Minerva didn't know Mr. Pleasant, but she appreciated his name. Her father should be glad to be interred alongside someone who must have developed a sunny disposition by the sheer force of hearing himself called "Pleasant" day after day.

As the sole Webster in Paducah, Minerva felt obliged to visit and groom the plot. She was uncertain about the details of her obligation to her deceased parents, but assumed she was overlooking something. Her entire life until their death had revolved around fulfilling duties to them while simultaneously coming up short.

Both of her parents were thirty-five and her sister, Geneva, was ten in 1900, when Minerva was born. The Websters had thought their childbearing days were over.

"Minerva's arrival was a shock to the system," Earl had said to Dr. Gray the first time those two families had met. Earl was a big fellow with a big voice. Minerva got her height from his side of the family. He ordered all of his pants from special men's store in Chicago that carried his size. He wore suspenders—he called them braces—to keep his pants from settling below his waist. (He continued wearing these well after suspenders were no longer the style because they were sensible.)

Minerva, twelve at this time, could hear her parents in the parlor while she and her new friend, Cat, finished their tapiocas in the kitchen.

Lucille agreed with Earl: "We were set and happy as could be with our precious Geneva and then, boom, like a clap of thunder on a clear day" (and Lucille slapped her hands together with much bravado, as if slamming cymbals together for a marching band), "here comes Minerva Jean. Why, none of us got any sleep for the first eighteen months of her life. She was colicky."

Dr. and Mrs. Gray understood. Colicky babies were the worst.

Of course, Minerva had always known she was a disruption to the happy family of three, but her discomfort with this knowledge bloomed as her parents shared the information with the world at large.

How ironic that it turned out to be she, rather than Geneva, who cared for them at the end of their lives. She knew they would have preferred to have had Geneva, but at the same time, they were thrilled that her sister had made such a fine match and was living an exotic life in Texas. ("The sky is so big in the Lone Star state," Geneva was fond of saying. Is it really bigger than the sky in Kentucky? Minerva thought. And anyway, does a big sky make a state superior? That sky business irked her.)

Household chores and their nightly dinner became her responsibilities when they both decided—prematurely—they'd had enough of life. Though they were capable of driving and not, when she reflected on it, elderly yet, she accompanied them to doctor appointments and ran errands for them. She organized their medical and financial records, though her father still balanced the checkbook. And of course, when they became legitimately ill, she nursed them around the clock.

After they died, Minerva wondered if their attitudes had invited their illnesses or if they had subconsciously known they were programmed to be ill. Perhaps they had felt an alteration in their physiology that had signaled the end was coming and that this sensing caused them to forfeit a more normal state of living.

Either way, she had been their caretaker then, and surely something as ethereal as death didn't suspend obligations. So, after their burial Minerva began checking in with her father and then her mother each Wednesday morning. She'd take flowers from her yard when they were in bloom, jonquils in the spring, and zinnias in the summer. Sometimes she'd write a poem and read it to them when she got there. Some days she'd just tell them what she'd been eating for dinner that week. Conversing with them was easier now that they were dead.

She arrived at their plots empty-handed today. She hadn't gotten around to going to Rhew Henley for flowers. Her familiar companion, guilt, hovered around her like fog.

"Hello, Mother. Hello, Father." She had so much she'd rather be doing. Writing. Reading. Almost anything else.

"I've had an interesting week," she continued. "A couple of—more accurately, a young father and his son—have moved into the neighborhood. The little boy, George is his name, he's a little spitfire, but his big brown eyes will swallow your heart whole. And his father, Robert, he seems very sweet, but—I don't know what to call it—a little naive. Clueless. I think his wife must have passed on. I've only heard speculation about that. Anyway, he's asked me to take George on as a student. You might be surprised to hear that I'm considering it."

When she looked up she saw Tiny Johnson rolling a wheelbarrow in her direction. *Oh, dear.*

"Hey, Mrs. Place!" The lumbering man's face was lit with delight. She dreaded talking to him.

"What are you doing here?" His overalls were caked in mud and the wheelbarrow was loaded with dead branches. Minerva's jaw clenched with the prospect of fending him off.

She would keep it brief. "I'm making my usual visit to Mother and Father. I'm finished now."

"You talk to them?" Tiny's eager eyes told of his yearning for companionship. He looked like an overgrown basset hound, droopy eyes, sagging belly.

"Yes."

"Do you think they can hear you?" Tiny wiped his face with the bandanna he always carried.

"I don't know." Minerva had turned as if she was leaving, but Tiny continued.

"I think they can. I talk to the people here all the time. I think they go back and forth between heaven and here. I think they want to check up on their loved ones here."

My goodness, Tiny might be slow, but he had thought through a complex subject. His conclusion was childlike, but it just might be right. Except, what about the souls who do not go to heaven? Minerva swallowed hard at that thought.

"I don't know," she repeated. "Nobody knows, Mr. Johnson. Nobody." Tiny nodded. She hurried on to say, "I must be on my way now. See you later."

"See you, Mrs. Place."

Minerva was buoyed by the conversation. Despite Tiny Johnson's lack of intelligence, his conclusion intrigued her. Maybe there was something to what he said. Maybe souls traveled back and forth. Maybe she was seeing real people who had simply stepped out of one dimension and into another for a moment. Maybe they still had something to say that death couldn't extinguish.

7

Minerva was still thinking about what Tiny had said when she sat down to write that night. The memory of her first encounter crept back into her mind. She was startled every time it happened, but that first time—whew! Talk about unnerving.

It had unfolded in such an unlikely way; a city celebration honoring the past achievements of some of its residents was to blame.

Minerva avoided affairs involving crowds, but Jamey Heath, one of her Wednesday piano students who possessed unusual charisma for a child of eleven, had invited her. He was to play the part of Irvin Cobb, which meant he was to have a significant role since Mr. Cobb had achieved stardom beyond the confines of western Kentucky.

Cobb was one of many bringing Paducah prestige these days. Why, right now their own Alben Barkley, Jr., served as the vice president of the United States of America alongside President Harry S. Truman. Yes, everyone agreed Paducah had come into her own. No longer would the town sit idly by, an ignored old maid, while the cities of Lexington and Frankfort and Louisville marched toward the altar. No, sir. They had produced a vice president and a famous author. Even if you didn't care for the Democratic Party, you stood proud. Even if you didn't like one of the sixty-some-odd books Cobb wrote, you were obliged to credit the man, Minerva reasoned.

Yes, success unified unlikely cohorts.

So Minerva had found herself attending the festivities to report to Jamey that she had indeed heard him recite his lines as Irvin Shrewsbury Cobb. She hadn't paid this Cobb man much attention, but since she learned Jamey would portray him and since she knew many considered Cobb a "brilliant humorist," she had checked out one of his books prior to the performance. She wasn't impressed. Although she did like the Judge Priest character. No accounting for popular tastes.

The late afternoon of the celebration threatened rain. But someone must have been on God's good side, because the black clouds had held their store and now shuffled along like grumpy old men heading off to an early bedtime. Minerva found a wooden folding chair—too small for her hips, but at least it had back support. And it was either that or negotiate a stand of bleachers already bulging with a passel of folks.

People everywhere. She regretted coming.

"Mrs. Place! Hello, how are you?"

Harriett Boswell. Terrific. Just terrific. She was dressed to the nines, of course. Minerva shifted in her seat, aware that her bottom hung over the sides of the chair.

"Hello, Miss Boswell."

"Isn't it a delectable evening? We're simply delighted the storm passed through without consequence. The committee has worked diligently, and our cast has prepared and practiced unceasingly. It would have been grievous had a summer shower rained on our parade, so to speak."

"Indeed." Minerva couldn't think of another single word to say. Harriett Boswell was so articulate. Such a vocabulary. The little librarian seemed to shut Minerva down every time. Minerva felt like Tiny Johnson around her—large and not too bright. Not a pleasant feeling. Minerva tried to overcome it, recognizing she was being ridiculous, but that wave of insecurity washed over her despite her self-pep-talks.

"Enjoy the festivities, Mrs. Place. Thank you for coming."

Minerva smiled and mumbled, "Thank you."

Jamey was in rare form, his voice booming to where she sat. She was impressed with his ability to memorize such a lengthy speech and didn't lose interest once.

The boy was dressed in a brown pinstriped suit and wore a fedora. She smiled when he paused and gulped a breath. He carried a large cigar in his hands and Minerva guessed he was itching to chomp on the forbidden prop just once, for effect. But he fought the temptation and concluded his soliloquy:

"I passed away March 10, 1944, in New York City, but I left instructions in a letter for Edwin Paxton Sr. and Mr. Fred Neuman that all I wanted was for my ashes to fertilize a dogwood in Paducah. If you happen to wander by my burial place in Oak Grove Cemetery, you'll see that although I was a word aficionado, the granite boulder that marks my resting place is simple."

Minerva perked up. Oak Grove? Irvin Cobb was buried there? Well, now. How interesting. Both Cobb and some of the Barkleys were buried in the same cemetery where her parents were laid to rest. At this realization, Minerva experienced a wave of pride. These men were Paducahans. She was familiar with stories of Cobb's fame and Barkley's accomplishments before the play, of course. But now, their achievements seemed linked to her family. She decided to check the office of public records to locate Mr. Cobb's burial plot so she could visit it the next time she went to Oak Grove.

She wondered if Jamey's speech was true, and Cobb's headstone only displayed the words "Back Home" on it. Her curiosity about his epitaph was partly due to an argument she and Geneva had tangled in when they were making various funereal decisions. Geneva said:

"On Father's headstone let's put,
As the bird free of its cage seeks the heights,
So, the Christian soul in death flies home to God."

Minerva was combining two half-full bowls of potato salad into one smaller container to gain real estate in the refrigerator. She whacked the spoon on the side of the container while Geneva continued.

"And for Mother's let's use,
It Broke Our Hearts to Lose You
But You Did Not Go Alone
For Part of Us Went with You
The Day God Called You Home."

Minerva thought that twaddle. Names, date of birth, date of death, period. No "Beloved Mother," "Beloved Father." No lines of verse. No scripture. She stirred the two salads together, noting that one was more mustard-y than the other. She licked the blend from the spoon.

"Are you serious?" she asked her sister. Geneva and Minerva looked like sisters, but genetics tweaked Geneva's features toward dainty. Where Minerva's pronounced jaw gave her a look of stubbornness, Geneva's face balanced strength and delicacy. Geneva's eyes were oval, larger than Minerva's, and her lips turned up at the corners, allowing people to feel loved and admired in her presence. Minerva's gaze was intense and her mouth turned down at the corners. Minerva, whose thick hair tended to be frizzy, dealt with a cowlick. Geneva, whose thick, wavy hair was (of course) frizz free, didn't fight. Minerva's eyebrows were just slightly lower than Geneva's, inviting what seemed to be a scowl when she felt perfectly pleasant. Minerva's cheekbones were ever so slightly sharper than Geneva's, casting her as edgy in the minds of onlookers, however unfairly. And of course, Geneva was smaller than average, a remarkable (and, yes, many remarked) contrast to Minerva's size.

"Yes, I'm serious. Why? What do you propose?"

"I propose their names, the dates of their births and deaths." Minerva wiped the counters with a sudsy rag.

"But that's so stark." Geneva now stood with her hands on her hips as if Minerva needed to be warned off.

Minerva considered what Geneva had said and narrowed her eyes, as if the action would help her understand. Death was death. Poetic words wouldn't change the facts and Minerva guessed the more words, the more the headstone would cost.

"I suppose we could put a brief scripture," she conceded. She recognized Geneva's determination and thought better of confronting it. No point, really. Geneva would get what she wanted. She always did.

&

Because the folderol of the Paducah festival plucked at Minerva, she sought Mr. Cobb's marker one day after she'd picked stray leaves off her father's gravesite. Mr. Cobb's ashes did indeed "fertilize a dogwood." A granite boulder engraved with elegant simplicity paid tribute to him: "Irvin Shrewsbury Cobb, 1876-1944, Back Home." Minerva appreciated his nod to humble beginnings.

On the day she found Mr. Cobb's marker, she also ran across a life-size marble figure of a young woman. The figure's aura of sadness meted out such grief Minerva half expected to see a tear running down the girl's stone cheek. The engraved name read: Della Barnes, June 27, 1897. She noted that she was in Old Section 9, Lot 136, at Myrtle Street and Rest Avenue.

Who was this Della Barnes, now a mere name marked by a noble work of art? What caused the girl to die so young? Quite mysterious.

So, Minerva began her writing career. She supposed *career* wasn't the word. But neither was it a hobby like building model airplanes or embroidering. And her pursuit of these people was weighty. The more she explored Oak Grove, the more intrigued she became.

She developed a system for research, but allowed herself some freedom because one couldn't oppose spontaneity all the time, now could one? Still, Mrs. Place preferred first to visit the office of public records and peruse the population of Oak Grove. She relished scouring the older records, handwritten in flowery flourishes. She noted unusual deaths and their burial addresses.

Her next stop would be the cemetery, to visit the actual site and take a rubbing. Then it was on to the library to conduct meticulous research. By the time she finished, she believed she knew the person well.

But Della Barnes was the first voice that had called to her with the irresistible urgency of a siren. And she had called directly from the cemetery: "Mrs. Place? Do you see me here? I cannot let go. I have something yet to say. Mrs. Place? Mrs. Place? Don't you hear me?"

To decipher Della Barnes's mystery, Minerva found herself in new territory, the city library's research section.

Minerva was no stranger to Carnegie Public Library. She kept her library card in her pocketbook and read choice picks from the *New York Times* best-seller list. That year she had read *The Caine Mutiny* (didn't care for it; more of a man's book), *My Cousin Rachel, Green Dolphin Country, Raintree County, The Parasites,* and *Steamboat Gothic,* the last of which prompted her to go back and read all of Frances Parkinson Keyes's earlier books. But apart from an occasional biography—she appreciated quality work about any First Lady—she rarely ventured outside the fiction shelves. The research department intimidated her with its strange filing system.

So, when Minerva determined to learn more about Della Barnes, she set about overcoming her reservations. With a confident set to her jaw belying the discomfort she felt, she headed for the desk under a sign hanging from the ceiling by two brass chains.

Here sat none other than Miss Harriett Boswell herself. The Sentry of Sacred Scripts. The Regent of Research. The Docent of Undecipherable Dewey Decimal Systems. The librarian, engrossed in filing, leaned over a drawer of hundreds of index cards. A bud vase with a pink carnation nodding out of it sat on the corner of a desk arranged with neat stacks of papers and books. "Excuse me," Minerva said, clearing her throat to get the words out.

Miss Boswell, who had a perfectly coiffed, unnaturally blond head of hair (done weekly at the beauty shop) and a tightly cinched waist, smiled at Minerva.

"Yes? Oh, hello, Mrs. Place, nice to see you again," she said in a practiced hush. "May I help you?"

My goodness, such vivid lipstick! Minerva worked to replace that thought with a proper greeting.

"Hello, Miss Boswell, nice to see you too. Your committee did an excellent job with the city celebration. I'm here to research Della Barnes." Minerva felt like she was speaking in staccato and wondered, not for the first time, why it seemed like some conversations were made up of broken shards of glass rather than words.

"Thank you. You are most kind. And of course I can help you with that," Miss Boswell said as she left her filing, clapped her hands in a silent gesture of enthusiasm, and returned to her guard post. She came to Minerva's shoulder. For such a small person she had a large presence. The little librarian was like a special police force, appearing to be friendly but capable of calling you out for disobedience at any moment. Minerva fought the urge to step back.

"Right this way. I'll show you where the microfilm files are and how to operate the machine."

Irritation spread over Minerva like a rash. Machine? She wanted nothing to do with a machine. Machines were trouble. But although her neck tensed up and she gritted her teeth, she caught on quickly. The contraption made a lot of noise, but it was easier to operate than a sewing machine. Thank the Lord for small favors.

She had originally written the information from Della Barnes's tombstone on a receipt from Myrick's, but she couldn't bear the note's flimsiness and the prospect of losing it. So she'd found a notebook in a desk drawer and transferred the information. Now in the library, she checked the dates of Della's death in her notebook and found the correct microfilm reel. After several starts and stops and being distracted by many fascinating but unrelated stories, she ran across this headline:

ACCIDENT BRINGS WOE, A MISTAKE SUDDENLY ENDS THE YOUNG LIFE OF MISS DELLA BARNES. MORPHINE TAKEN FOR CALOMEL. SCORES OF SORROWING FRIENDS ATTEND THE SAD INTERMENT AT OAK GROVE CEMETERY.

Minerva's pulse fluttered as she continued to read:

A most unfortunate death occurred in the city yesterday morning. The victim was Miss Della Barnes, the youngest daughter of Maj. George F. Barnes, the well-known councilman and coal merchant. The death was brought about through a dose of morphine accidentally taken for calomel.

"Evidently her fiancé wanted his valuable engagement ring back when he learned of her affair." Miss Boswell had walked up behind her without Minerva knowing it. Minerva jumped, causing her notebook and pen to fly off the table and somersault through the air.

"Oh, I am sorry, dear," Miss Boswell continued whispering. "I didn't mean to startle you. Are you all right?" She bent and retrieved the notebook and pen, handing them to Minerva with an earnest expression that embarrassed Minerva. Or maybe it was her own reaction that embarrassed her. Either way, Miss Boswell was the source of the problem. "The truth behind Miss Barnes's death may never be uncovered."

Was she implying murder? Minerva wondered. Just because you're in charge of a department at the library doesn't make you an authority. Minerva nodded, choosing not to reply. She had learned that many situations called for silence. Often this moved people along much more quickly, and sure enough, Miss Boswell moved on to the next table to inquire if that researcher needed assistance.

Minerva took copious notes, writing some sentences from the newspaper account word for word. Then she rewound the microfilm, alarmed when the tape flapped like a flag in the wind as it finished.

That night she wrote her first story.

Della Barnes, born—unknown; died—unknown; Old Section 9, Lot 36, Myrtle and Rest Ave.

The question that lingered after my passing disturbed later generations more than it did my contemporaries. Family and friends develop a portrait of you in their minds painted with brush strokes particular to their views. They see you from their unique positions and the portrait they paint becomes their truth. They assume their knowledge is fact—why wouldn't they?

Then time sifts suppositions and winnows assumptions.

At my death, my loved ones thought they knew. They insisted they knew. Later, uncertainty arrived, carrying baggage no one knew how to unpack. At first, shadows of doubts crept into the telling of my story, but then the doubts seasoned and darkened. After enough years passed, a gruesome edge hung round my tale.

I'll tell you the truth, but you still must make your own choice. Was it murder or suicide? Or, was it an accident? You decide…

Minerva heard a rustle, what sounded like a ruffle in the curtains, a faint something. A nervous ripple passed through her.

"Nella, is that you?" No reply. Must have been the radio. Minerva got up and checked it. The radio was off. She must be imagining things, she assured herself. She leaned back over her paper and picked up the pen. The words flowed into sentences and the voice began again.

How all consuming, how glorious and passionate is one's first love. This emotion is a being unto itself. It wakes you in the middle of the night and wants to discuss itself. It consumes your daily thoughts, interrupting the most mundane aspects of living with infusions of joy and light. It introduces itself into every conversation you have with others, as if they too are interested in it and cherish it as you do. First love is an aching hunger that requires constant attention and care.

Another stirring caused Minerva to pause, her pen in midair. "Yes? Someone there?" Her heart accelerated but, she reassured herself, she had checked. No one, nothing was there. Still, the distraction continued.

She scooted her chair out. "Hello?"

"When I met him, I fell into such a spiral of emotions I was incapable of recovery." A young woman's voice floated into Minerva's awareness. It sounded as if she were in the next room. "At the time I called it love. Now I'm unsure."

"Who is that? Who's there?" Minerva said as she leaned back in her chair and looked down the dark hallway toward where she thought she'd heard the voice.

She craned her neck, squinting to see through the shadows. Her breath came quicker. She licked her lips, trying to moisten her mouth. A shadow stepped into the light at the end of the hall. Minerva's heart palpitated.

"Are you who I think you are?" Her own voice sounded unfamiliar, disconnected from herself.

"I'm Della Barnes."

Minerva struggled with the collision of logic and what she was seeing. "But you can't be here. You're deceased. You've passed on."

"Some might say that."

Minerva thought her heart was going to explode, it beat so fast. Blooms of perspiration burst out all over her body. She might as well have been climbing a mountain.

"I don't understand." Minerva thought her words sounded slurred. Was she dreaming this? She pinched her arm and felt pain. She bit her lip. That hurt too. Did that prove she was awake? Was she having some sort of stroke? Was she hallucinating?

"The day I met you in the cemetery, I knew you were the one to tell my story," Della continued. She now was almost in the dining-room. Younger than Minerva had imagined, the girl wore a creamy dress of lace and bows, and her blond hair was upswept with a pink satin ribbon. Ringlets floated around her fair face, giving her the look of a cherub in a Reuben painting.

"Me? Why me? Why should I be the one to tell your story?"

"You understand what it's like to be carried away with love."

"What? Me? No..." Minerva's protest caught in her throat.

Minerva's brief marriage might have happened to someone else. She had placed that sliver of time in an inaccessible closet in her mind and locked the door. The result was that now she sometimes wondered if the relationship had happened at all. She couldn't always bring Manny into focus.

And she couldn't go back, could she? She couldn't untangle the honeysuckle vines that had smelled so sweet as she and Manny had swung in that wooden swing on her parents' front porch. The vines that grew up her ankles and into her womb. Vines that twisted their way into her heart, where they choked it until only a tiny part of it lived and beat anymore.

Minerva swallowed the hard memory as Della began again.

"Jack carried me away," she said as if it were a simple inevitability. "I'm not sure it was even real love. I may have been swept up in an emotion that I never had experienced before. I was moved. But was it love? I was a young girl dreading the prospect of marrying an older man. Perhaps the feelings that assaulted me when Jack came into my life, well, perhaps they were born of desperation."

The uncertainty of understanding what real love felt like resonated with Minerva. Over the years she had doubted that what she had felt for Manny was ever love. But instead of revealing her thoughts to Della, she asked, "Who is Jack?"

Della's smile caused Minerva's heart to clench.

"Jack Green." Della clasped her hands together under her chin, making her seem even younger. "He was such a handsome man. Taller than Father by six inches at least, lean but muscular. His thick brown hair never stayed tame, and his lively hazel eyes didn't either. We met quite by chance on a day I was strolling alone, overcome with the enormity of what my engagement meant for my future. I admit that I was crying because I simply saw no way out. Jack saw me after I had dried my tears, but he must have sensed the heaviness in my soul because he knew instinctively that I needed cheering. We struck up a conversation that lasted until the dinner hour, and I found myself shocked that a man I had so recently met could see through me so well and reach into my heart with such grace and ease. We ended that first day staring into each other's eyes as if we were reading each other's souls."

Minerva thought about the first time she had seen Manny. He had been a big man, like Della's Jack. His imposing presence filled a room. She had met Manny through her father. Earl Webster, who was a supervisor for the Chicago Burlington & Quincy Railroad before he became a vice president, had noticed Manny at work. The young army veteran, stationed in France during the Great War, had caught shrapnel in his leg, leaving him with a permanent limp. However, he bulged with upper body strength, ambition, and a ready smile—a trifecta that, when combined with his military service, made him the perfect hero to Earl. Despite the age disparity, the men found they shared a great deal.

"Fishing and hunting, you can't beat either one," Earl might say.

"That's right," Manny would reply with a nod.

"Take a look at this, Manny," Earl would mutter, bent over an engine he had taken apart. "Can you get this jumble back together?"

Manny would laugh and slap Earl on the back. "Faster than you, old man, in the dark, with my left hand, standing on one foot."

"Stay for dinner," Earl would urge. "Lucille, what are we having? Pork roast? Perfect."

Pork was better than chicken. And venison trumped rabbit; quail topped squirrel; beef won over all, the men agreed.

"What are your views on the president, son?"

"Couldn't be prouder," Manny would say. "Democrats—the only party that makes any sense."

Southern Baptists, of course.

Pro-Prohibition around the women, but happy to take a nip (or more, as it turned out, much more) of home brew with the boys.

Marry one woman for life, and the man's king of his castle.

Cars would never replace horses completely.

"Manny, I swear, if I ever had a son, I'd be proud if he were the man you are."

And to Minerva, "That Manny Place. Now, there's a fine young man. Some young woman…"

Minerva understood his meaning.

Minerva would have been interested without her father's heavy hinting. Her scalp tingled and the fine hairs on her forearms stood up like toy soldiers marching into imaginary battle when she was with Manny. At eighteen she'd never been kissed. Not really kissed. There was Luke Werner in fourth grade, but an experience in primary school shouldn't count.

So when Manny came to dinner that first time, with flowers for her mother and a smile for her, she was cautious but hopeful. She tried not to allow any expectations to rally behind those goosebumps. Still, how could she not be attracted? For Minerva, the fact that he was a big man was his first asset. Leaning on his gimp leg, he was still taller than she was by at least three inches, unusual since Minerva was five feet, ten and a half inches (with no shoes on). He seemed chiseled out of a piece of west Kentucky clay—ruddy, earthy, and brick-like. The scent of machine oil and iron and the woods lingered on him.

The attraction mingled with forces stronger than the inexperienced Minerva. Earl wanted a son like Manny, and Lucille saw a prime (the one and only?) opportunity to nab the title of "Mrs." for her youngest. Both went to work to help Minerva. For the first time in her life, Minerva felt the fierceness of her parents' desire on her behalf. This was something she'd observed in the life of her sister, but had not, until then, experienced. She liked it.

And after a year of the elder Websters arranging get-togethers, encouraging Minerva in the ways of courting, and hinting at promising futures for Manny, he proposed. The evening when he struggled down to one knee and looked up at her while he held her hand between his, she fell headlong into his cavernous hazel eyes. This was love. This had to be love. Surely this was the voice of God himself whispering, *This is my way. Walk in it.*

Minerva's musings had distracted her from what Della was saying.

"To say that I fell in love with Jack upon sight would be wrong. I felt as if I had always loved Jack and merely met him one day. My mother was the first to sense a difference in me.

"One day as the seamstress took her leave after more measuring for my wedding gown, Mother asked me if I was happily anticipating the arrival of my wedding day. I had traversed an emotional mountain from being ecstatic, having secretly seen Jack, to being despondent after my fitting.

"I cried to her that I could not go through with the wedding. I poured out the contents of my clandestine life to an unsuspecting parent whose face revealed she was experiencing layered emotions of betrayal, shock, horror, and pity. I threw myself into her arms and sobbed, telling her that I loved Jack. I loved him so. I could not—would not—marry another. I felt my mother's body alter from the tender instinct to comfort her suffering child to the stiff realization of now knowing why her child was suffering. I drew back upon recognition of this coldness."

Della's words triggered Minerva's sympathy. She knew what a mother's stiffening felt like. Her own mother had insisted many times that Minerva ignore her feelings and "be strong." Mrs. Webster often told Minerva, with a trace of scorn, that she was too sensitive. So, Minerva learned to cordon off any tenderness, which her mother associated with weakness, and present an impenetrable image to the world.

"She told me I had no choice." Della's eyes glistened with the hint of tears. "I must cut the relationship with Jack off right away, never see him again, and move forward toward the day of my wedding. I could not and would not embarrass the family, drag our good name to demise, ruining the reputation of my father, a city commissioner. I was to get hold of myself and stop behaving as if I were a foolish schoolgirl.

"After that day, I was never left alone. Mother ensured that I was escorted everywhere; she occupied my every waking hour and I half expected her to post a guard at my bedroom door at night. I never saw Jack again, and I fancied that a piece of my spirit had flown away, leaving an unfillable, gaping hole. My health deteriorated alongside my waning spirits. Dr. Elliott prescribed some calomel to boost my system, and Mother warned me to perk up.

"She said, 'We cannot have people questioning if you are happy, Della. This should be a joyous time in your life and Mr. X would be embarrassed if news of your dalliance ever were to get out. You must get yourself in order. That means putting on a cheerful countenance when you make your calls. Now, take the calomel to restore your system and resolve yourself to a happy disposition.'"

Minerva perked up when she heard Della reference calomel. She had read that Della had mistaken morphine for calomel, thus accidentally killing herself.

"So, was it an accident, Della?" Minerva walked back into the dining-room and picked up the copy of the newspaper article detailing Della's death. "Here's the headline: *Accident Brings Woe, a Mistake Suddenly Ends the Young Life of Miss Della Barnes. Morphine Taken for Calomel. Scores of Sorrowing Friends Attend the Sad Interment at Oak Grove Cemetery.*"

Della lowered her head into her hands and continued quietly. Minerva concentrated on her small voice, dusty with emotion.

"Cousin Clara Blair came to stay with us during this period, and she slept in my room. I was tempted to confess my affair to her, but I checked myself from doing so when I considered Mr. X's reputation. I did not despise this man. I simply didn't love him. I could see that his feelings for me were quite different, and this gave me grief. How unfair to live in union with one who loved you when you did not return those affections. Yet this is what my parents (because I had no doubt that Mother had told Father) were requiring of me.

"One night, after I could hear Clara's breathing signal sleep, I found myself in the familiar place of mourning. I could not sleep, and as the night hours wore on I grew more agitated. My mind filled with the torment of losing Jack, of having to live in a loveless union, of facing a physical relationship with such an old man, one for whom I had no feelings at all. I was repulsed on this account. I got up in the moonless room and made my way to the bureau where the calomel was. Another dose of the medicine would calm my nerves and cause me to sleep. When I saw the bottle of calomel standing next to a bottle of morphine, I hesitated, but only for an instant.

"Who can say why Clara awoke when she did, but she noticed my breathing was labored. She knew something was wrong, and she alerted my parents. They called for Dr. Elliott, but he was too late to save my life.

"The newspaper erred in their report. I'm not sure why my father recounted the facts as he did. I suppose he fashioned events to sound more acceptable."

Minerva couldn't help but ask again, "So you did deliberately take the morphine?"

Della didn't reply immediately. She looked at Minerva a long time. The dark room cast away any color to her and she looked like an image on Minerva's black-and-white television, a spectrum of grays.

Minerva couldn't stand the silence. "There are rumors today that speculate that you were murdered." She considered what Miss Boswell had implied.

"I know about the rumors."

Minerva turned her head away and looked at Della sideways. "People say your fiancé snuck into the house to retrieve his ring and when he couldn't get it off your finger, he cut it off."

"I mean no disrespect, Mrs. Place, but think about that," Della said. The morbid theory seemed to perk her up. "That idea makes no sense. My intended did not know about the affair."

"Some say he found out."

"No." She fanned her hand as if to inspect it for completeness. "Besides, I'm afraid he didn't have enough of a backbone for something so daring." The dead girl's voice shifted. Though she was calm and genteel, syrupy with a Southern drawl, Minerva could hear that she had a will of her own.

"So, did you kill yourself, or was it a mistake?"

Della again ignored Minerva's question. "I projected much

more masculinity and honor onto Jack than I should have. I was quite naive."

Minerva remembered herself at that age. All seventeen-year-olds carried some naïveté about love, didn't they? Minerva herself had imagined a tall, handsome man, quiet and firm, discovering her hidden intelligence and untapped potential and rescuing her from a family who did not appreciate her. She thought a man would appear one day and love her. He would see what no one else could see. He would bring out what she herself did not know was there. Minerva was sure. At seventeen.

"Your memorial in Oak Grove is missing a finger, and teenagers like to scare each other by saying they see you walking there late at night."

"I admit to spying on young lovers, but I don't know how that finger broke off the statue. Strange, I grant you that. But despite the legend, my fiancé did not chop it off. That's a gruesome story. It makes no sense at all. You need to make sure the truth is told." Della's face hardened.

"Do you regret what you did?" Minerva asked, because something about their conversation had convinced her that Della had taken her life. An air of sadness draped over the young woman like a mantilla.

Minerva understood the weight of such sadness, the pain that tempts you to snuff it out. Minerva had considered what it might be like to end this life. She had concluded that pills were the way to go. A gun was loud and messy. Jumping off a bridge seemed terrifying and subject to last-minute retreat. Exhaust from a car may or may not work. Pills—you take a bunch and fall asleep. She approved of Della's choice.

"No." Della took a step away from the window. Minerva leaned forward, wishing she would come closer. "I would have been miserable in the wrong marriage."

"I think you nurtured the wrong idea about what love is, though," Minerva said.

"Perhaps I misunderstood what love is. But I knew—I know—what it isn't."

Then she was gone. Minerva couldn't say she left. It was more like the air absorbed her. She was, and she wasn't. A trace of lavender was all that remained.

After Minerva went to bed that night, she lay awake thinking about her experience. Why did Della kill herself? She didn't have to. The situation wasn't so dire that it warranted taking one's life. At worst, she would have been forced to marry a wealthy older man who was a respected member of society, who would have provided for her the rest of her life, someone she could have shared a place in the world with.

Minerva had squared off with much worse in life and had held her own. She might have considered death, but only at her lowest, only after the grief had multiplied many times over, and even then she didn't. No, even then she didn't. She tried to brace herself against sorrow for Della, but her slow dance with depression wouldn't let her ignore such desperation.

In the twenty-nine years since Manny had died, Minerva's anger toward him had evened out. If Della had stayed, she thought about what she would have told her.

Love isn't perfect, is where Minerva would start. *No one we love is going to love us the way we want them to all the time. You can't expect that.*

At fifty-two, Minerva Place would have gladly traded the ecstasy of falling in love for the warmth of remaining in love, however imperfect the state.

All I wanted was a gentle man who let me be. Someone I could have a conversation with. Someone to share a history with.

The dark room seemed to sigh with her.

꙰

In the light of the next day, Minerva debated what had happened with Della Barnes. She reasoned that she became so engrossed in the deceased's story, the character seemed real to her. She told herself regularly that day and for many following that ghosts do not exist. An unseen, but real veil separated the living and the dead. Still, she never got over the jarring sense of corporeality that accompanied the visits.

Della was her first visit, but not her last. She got to know every friend, as she came to think of each character, in the same way. What had begun as a curiosity grew into a need. She needed to get to know these people to find herself.

First their stone and then the research. Minerva always started by gathering as many facts as she could find, but there was so much she didn't, couldn't, know. And since she was not writing for a newspaper or for an encyclopedia, she gave herself permission to sprinkle in bits of her own speculation. With every stroke of her pen, she became more aware of the individual voices speaking to her from the shadows.

Real voices. Real people. Real friends exposing who they were. Exposing who she was. Like friends do.

But along with her journey through these lives came the uncomfortable question of her sanity. She wanted to speak to someone about it, but she couldn't take that risk. What if word got out there was a crazy lady living on Harahan Boulevard? She'd lose her piano students. The church would let her go. She'd become a scary story kids talked about around a campfire.

No. Nobody could know.

8

Minerva Place did not tolerate bad moods. While Minerva had never been one to showcase her emotions, Manny had cured her from the temptation to surrender to the frustrations of a day gone south. When you get a bee in your bonnet, you take the bonnet off and chase the bee away. Simple as that. Today, though, Minerva woke up crabby and noted that she didn't have a bonnet to take off. She slipped her bunion-vexed, calloused feet into worn house shoes and cinched her powder-blue flannel robe around her waist. Flimsy defense against the cold morning, the first day of November.

Maybe that was why Minerva was out of sorts. Though she had avoided the neighborhood party, October 31 had brought all sorts of witches and scarecrows and pirates and ghosts to her door, and frankly, all those people had worn her down. She had managed variously aged children with aplomb, and she had handed out suckers in an orderly fashion. One important lesson she had learned over the years was not to allow the children to choose the sucker's color. A free will system took much too long. Their sticky hands rooted through the pile of cellophane-wrapped candy looking for a red—no, green, no, orange—until she teetered on screaming. And she knew screaming would be wrong, totally unacceptable, and she would have been mortified if she had lost control in front of children, not to mention their parents.

So, to avoid a scene she dropped one treat into each child's bag with such decisiveness no one dared negotiate. Almost without exception, the children said thank you and returned to mothers who were chatting at the end of the sidewalk. The mothers waved merry greetings to Mrs. Place and, if they were fellow church members or piano students, called out, "Happy Halloween" or "Thank you" in sing-song voices.

The one exception to the polite trick-or-treaters was a little one clad in a white sheet with two eye holes cut out. Mrs. Place opened the door to find the ghost accompanied by a man she assumed was his father. As she reached in the basket to distribute a red sucker, the child darted past her and down the hall. He came right into her house. What in the world?

The father leaped into action, calling for the hooligan to stop. But in his quest to collect his child, he entered her house too. Minerva stood stunned, blinking rapidly, holding the basket of candy high with one hand and the red sucker with the other. The father snagged the little scamp by his arm before he got too far and pulled him out, scolding with each step.

Minerva lowered the basket of suckers but continued to be speechless.

"I am so sorry," the man said. "So sorry. Please excuse us."

Just as she was about to offer the expected forgiveness, the ghost spoke up.

"It's me, Mrs. Place! George!" He threw the sheet off and beamed at her.

"George, why did you do that?" Minerva resisted her urge to pop him on the head and looked to his father to discipline him.

But Mr. McAlpin only looked confused. "You're Mrs. Place?" he asked. "The Mrs. Place who teaches piano? I don't understand how George knows you."

"Your son has been here before," Minerva said curtly.

"Yeah, Dad. I drew her a picture of my lookout tree."

"So you are the woman George told me he had met." Robert McAlpin broke into a wide, toothy grin, dropped his son's arm, and made his way to her with his hand extended. He seemed to want to shake her hand. Odd. When Minerva didn't move, he lost his momentum and began to sputter.

"I, well, I, uh…I'm happy to meet you in person."

Minerva didn't budge.

"I'm sorry to have intruded this evening." He laughed. George chewed the inside of his cheek.

"Yes. Tonight makes George's third trip to my house." Minerva figured she would lay it on the line and get matters straightened out before the child made these visits a habit. By pointing out his lack of decorum (even a child should have some sense of boundaries), Minerva tried to imply the inappropriateness of George's behavior without being too harsh.

Mr. McAlpin looked confused. "Three times?"

"Once he climbed that tree," Minerva nodded toward the maple, "and once he simply walked into my house. Tonight makes his third appearance."

"Oh dear." The man looked at George. "Why would you do that?"

"I had a picture for her. A picture of the lookout tree. And I thought she might have cookies."

"George." Mr. McAlpin frowned at him and turned his attention back toward Minerva. "Mrs. Place, I apologize. I can assure you it won't happen again. I am sorry. This is embarrassing. He's just six and, well, his mother's not around, and we're trying to settle into the neighborhood. But... Well, we'll get out of your way. Sorry again—for all the intrusions." He laughed, but when she didn't, he went on. "George got into his candy and the sugar seems to have energized him. But still. Anyway. Sorry. Well, have a good evening."

"Here's a sucker." She offered a sucker to George when she saw that Mr. McAlpin had taken her seriously.

"Thank you," Mr. McAlpin said. He nudged his son. "Say thank you, George."

"Thank you."

"You're welcome."

All in all, it had been a most unpleasant confrontation and it had set Minerva to thinking about her decision not to teach young George. On the one hand, she didn't need the added exasperation of a student who was too young and too wild. And a boy. On the other hand, maybe Nella was right. Maybe she could make a difference in his life. He needed a firm hand and she had that. His father seemed earnest. Bless his heart. He couldn't help it if he was a man.

Today, though, Minerva was less concerned with Halloween

than with the arrival of November, the dreadful month that ushered in the holiday gateway. Thanksgiving—Thanksgiving, which danced into Christmas, which frolicked its way to New Year's. Stomach-acid-inducing, routine-interrupting, musically challenged days of weariness. Call her Scrooge. Bah, humbug. No one could convince her "Fa-la-la-la-la" was a worthy lyric. And what is the point of bringing a tree into your house only to have the needles fall off and fill your vacuum cleaner bag, or, more serious, catch fire when you forget to water it?

Now, Minerva. She caught herself. Take a lesson from the birds. This morning, house finches were swarming the feeder, jabbering every detail to one another, leaving nothing unsaid, nothing to chance. Look how those birds get along. Such cheery things. But with her thought a blue jay swooped in with a squawk. The yellow birds scattered like confetti. How rude, she thought. Lesson learned. Don't be a grumpy blue jay.

She hunted for her reading glasses to peruse today's *Paducah Sun-Democrat* until she found them on the table where she had abandoned them last night after losing patience with Emma Skillian's story. After Emma visited her, Minerva decided to dig deeper into old newspapers to find a scrap of news, even a morsel, about the flood victim.

Donny Wasson, the paper boy, had thrown the paper into her holly again. She set her jaw and leaned into the prickly green leaves to retrieve the darned thing. It was hard, this not being grumpy business. Her robe caught on a branch and she glanced around to make sure no neighbors were witnessing her outside unclothed. She usually dressed before she got the paper, but today she was tired. Her throat was scratchy, and her head hurt. She could be coming down with a cold, or worse, the flu. The flu. The thought of having it filled Minerva with dread. She couldn't afford to be sick.

Missy Youngblood no doubt had been the carrier. She just knew it. Missy had brought her that revolting caramel apple.

"My mother made these for Halloween and said to bring you one," Missy explained when she plopped the waxed-paper-wrapped confection onto the top of the piano. Missy was soft on her "r" and sounded younger than she was. Minerva felt sorry for the girl, but for the life of her could not imagine why someone would send her a sticky, gooey caramel apple.

"Wash your hands before we begin our lesson today, Missy," Minerva responded, "and I'll put the apple in the refrigerator for later."

Now she peered in the kitchen wastebasket at the apple she had never bothered to unwrap. The fruit's bulky brown body remained covered in the crinkled waxed paper, a Popsicle stick handle poking through coffee grounds and last night's dinner napkin. She suspected the messy gift had somehow been the vehicle for this pesky virus that was coming on.

Fortunately, she had gone to the grocery store yesterday and bought orange juice. She'd have an extra glass of vitamin C with breakfast. By the time today's first student arrived, she'd have this bug licked.

But by the afternoon Minerva struggled to swallow and felt lumps of swollen glands on her neck. Her head throbbed. She endured one lesson before she conceded and taped a note to the front door. What else could she do? She didn't have enough energy to phone her students' mothers. She crept back to her bedroom, careful not to jar her head, pulled down the bed-spread, slipped off her shoes, and slid between the sheets. She'd rest a couple of minutes before changing into her nightgown.

Twelve hours later, close to three a.m., Minerva woke up but didn't recognize where she was. Her closet door was half open and the moon glow streaming through the window bent the dresser and the framed pictures and bottles of lotion and perfume clustered on top into a wavy pattern up the wall. She studied the distorted shadows, trying to make sense of them, trying to connect them to the open door. She shut her eyes to clear her brain. This time when she opened her eyes, she made sense out of the shadows and door, but the pain in her head registered too.

A moment lapsed before she realized she'd slept for twelve

hours. Vague concern over missing an entire day of piano lessons drifted to the edge of her thoughts. Such a lapse was so unlike her. Then she remembered the note must still be taped to the front door. That wouldn't do. Anyone could read it. A door-to-door salesman might happen on it. Some unsavory sort. You never knew about these men. He might take advantage of her.

She arose from bed too fast and reeled, dizzy; and back down she went. Oh my, this was not good. Not good at all. Her second attempt was slower and gentler. She eased up, bracing herself on her nightstand. Then, hand on the wall, she walked to the front door (unlocked, oh my) and removed the note. She padded to the kitchen and made herself a cup of tea, spooned in two teaspoons of honey, and returned to the bedroom, where she placed the steaming cup on a folded napkin on the nightstand to avoid making a ring on the wood. Leaving her clothes on the chair in the corner, she pulled on the pink cotton gown she preferred when she needed comfort. It slipped on like a hug. Sighing, she returned to bed, where she plumped up her feather pillow, reached for her cup of tea, now the perfect temperature, and sighed again.

At times like these Minerva wished for a mate or at least a companion. She longed to say to someone, "I feel awful. You cannot imagine how my throat hurts. Would you mind looking at it with a flashlight?" She ached to hear, "Oh dear. I see bright red covered in white streaks. You are extremely ill, and we should call a doctor." Then she would reply, "No, I'll be all right. I can make it."

The companion: No, I insist. You are too unwell.

Minerva: You are sweet to care about me so much.

Companion: Oh, how you are suffering. I don't know how you have endured this much, being so sick. You are brave and strong. You haven't said a word until now, and you must have been in such pain.

Minerva: I didn't want to worry you.

Companion: You are selfless.

Minerva: No.

Companion: You are. Truly, you are the bravest, most selfless person I have ever known. We are calling the doctor. I couldn't live with myself if something more serious developed. Please allow me to call him.

Minerva: If you must.

But Minerva knew this was not realistic. Not even close. Other people's marriages might travel such a route. Maybe Nella and Buster's. Her parents seemed to have had a happy marriage, if her mother cooperated with everything her father wanted. But Manny would never have told her she was selfless. According to him, she was the problem. Stop fantasizing, Minerva. Better to be alone. Never mind you don't have anyone to complain to when you're feeling poorly. Doesn't matter. The Bible was clear about complainers anyway.

Minerva sipped her tea and wondered about her temperature. She should have taken it before she drank her tea. Well, never mind. She wasn't going to die. She needed sleep. She finished her tea, used the bathroom, and settled into her bed, fluffing the pillow and turning it over to the cool side before laying her throbbing head down.

"Minerva?" A woman's voice slipped through her thoughts.

"What?" Minerva turned toward the voice, propping herself up on her elbow. Had Nella come to check on her?

"Do you mind if I sit with you while you sleep?"

Minerva scooted up in the bed, pulling the covers up to her chin. It wasn't Nella. "What are you doing here?"

Emma Skillian sat in the chair in the corner of the room by the closet with her hands clasped in her lap. Shadows hung over the woman's deep-set eyes and chiseled the bones of her cheeks, giving her a skeletal look. She wore a bottle-green dress reduced to gray in the scant light. She reminded Minerva of a schoolgirl waiting to receive punishment.

"I came to keep you company." Emma spoke as if she were trying to soothe a dying soul. Was she here to escort Minerva to the afterlife? Was Minerva dying after all? Minerva laid her head back down. The contents of the room began floating. First the smaller items lifted off the bedside table and drifted away, then the table itself. Minerva watched the tissues dissolve and the cup of tea bobble over and spill its contents into the colorless waters. Emma's dress grew darker and ballooned around her waist, carrying her like a raft in mesmerizing dips and bobs as if the gentlest breeze were controlling the waves.

"You aren't real," Minerva managed to say. Emma smiled. "Are you?"

Then Minerva realized it wasn't Emma, but her mother. "Mother? Is that you?"

"Yes, it's me, Minerva Jean. You're very sick, dear."

"I am, Mother. My head is throbbing. Nothing seems right. The vase is floating." She longed for her mother to come to the bed and hold her, to stroke her forehead with cool fingertips.

"Oh, Minerva, don't be like that. You always were a dreamer when you were a child, always making things up, your head in the clouds. Your father and I could never get you to focus."

"But, Mother, I took care of you later. I was the one who was here. Geneva left. I stayed."

"Darling, you let us die."

"No! I did all I could." Minerva felt as though her mother's disapproval was going to strangle her. "I swear I did. I—"

"Minerva, you always were such a disappointment." Her mother drifted off like a mist of rain.

∂

Minerva woke up the next morning to the sound of her bathroom faucet dripping. She stared at the empty chair in the corner, the one Emma and her mother had occupied during the night.

She groaned from the pain in her head. Her eyes moved like wads of cotton soaked in a viscous chemical. Razor blades seemed to have scraped her throat. The thought of calling everyone to cancel the day's lessons made her drop her head into her hands.

But she did it. That was the thing about Minerva. She did what she thought she couldn't do.

After hearing "get well soon, Mrs. Place," "can I do anything for you, Mrs. Place?" and "sorry to hear that, Mrs. Place" in various ways, Minerva crawled back into bed with a sleeve of Saltines and a glass of orange juice. She didn't even have the strength to brew a cup of tea.

9

It took four full days for Minerva to feel like she might manage to live. When she woke up on day five, she decided she could at least try to write. This illness had gone on long enough.

Wrapped in her favorite gray sweater, the one with pockets where she could stash her tissues, Minerva sat at the dining table and fanned out the folders. A page was cocked out of one, catching her attention. The random folder turned out to be connected to the Civil War.

So far away. So unattached to her. The perfect distraction. She looked at the information for the longest time. Finally, an idea sprouted and she scratched away, but her pen burped and left an ink blob in the first paragraph.

"Oh, forevermore." Minerva tried to dab the blot of ink, making it worse, smearing the ink across the words in a blue wash.

She fidgeted in her chair. Her thoughts still seemed murky, jumbled, as though they'd been shuffled by the fever. She was getting nowhere.

This wouldn't do—she might as well put her coat on and go to the cemetery. She had missed her day to visit her parents, and some fresh air would do her good. Clear the cobwebs and such. Whatever fresh air was supposed to do.

Mindful she was still peaked, Minerva layered an extra sweater and scarf under her coat, stuffed cotton in her ears, wrapped her head in a muffler, and cranked up the heat on Spencer's dashboard. By the time she got to Oak Grove she was hotter than a steamed frankfurter and considered peeling off some layers. But knowing she was seeing her mother, she fought the temptation. She'd never hear the end of it if she ended up with pneumonia that sent her to the Great Beyond.

Her mother would be waiting for her on the other side of the
Pearly Gates with her hands on her hips saying, "Minerva Jean
Webster Place, you knew better."

Minerva moved some stray leaves away from her mother's
gravesite with her toe. That dream of hers stuck in her craw.
She knew she had been a disappointment to her parents, but
did her mother have to continue to tell her so after she was
gone on to the other side? Minerva had hoped Heaven would
temper her mother's criticisms. On the other hand, maybe her
mother wasn't in Heaven.

Minerva couldn't help but chuckle at that thought. "Oh,
Minerva, you are awful," she whispered as a confession. But she
felt justified holding on to a splinter of vindictiveness. Forevermore, she had been sick, and her mother was still accusing her.

"Mother, you still know the way under my skin, don't you?"
She directed her attention to the gravestone. A few more leaves
blew back. Oh, but she was a terrible daughter for saying such
a thing. She whisked at the leaves with her foot again as if to
clear her thoughts.

"Hi, Mrs. Place!"

Minerva jumped and, despite her sore throat, let out a shriek
that could have raised the dead.

"Oh, I'm so sorry!" Mr. McAlpin reached for her with one
hand. His other held a small bouquet of carnations. George
stood beside him grinning.

"What on earth?" Minerva cried. "Mr. McAlpin, why would
you sneak up on a person like that?"

"Well, I wasn't sneaking up on you," he began. "We were
just—"

"You could have given me a heart attack," she continued.
"I've been sick." It crossed her mind that the two were not
remotely related, but that's what had popped out of her mouth
and she let it stand.

Mr. McAlpin's face registered alarm. Now he did grab her
arm. "Oh, please let me help you. I am so very sorry. Really. I
thought you must have heard us. We were crunching through

the leaves. We weren't trying to be quiet at all. No one ever accuses us of being quiet." He laughed and the tension in his face relaxed a bit.

Minerva's heart slowed and she regained her composure. "No, no. I'm sure you weren't trying to startle me."

"We upend your life every time we show up. Again, I am sorry. Are you okay? Is there any way I can help you?"

"No. I'm fine. Fine." Minerva sniffed and took a tissue out of her pocket. She held it to her nose and tried to wipe it without making any noises. Snorting and sniffling were so unbecoming.

Mr. McAlpin smiled at her and said, "We'll leave you in peace." He cocked his head at the boy. "Let's go." The two walked away, the boy intent on kicking at a rock.

What could those two be doing at the cemetery? Minerva had heard the pair had moved to Paducah from back east somewhere, so she didn't think his wife was buried here. That would make no sense. She didn't think the McAlpins who used to live in Paducah were related to him, and besides, they were still alive as far as she knew. Another mystery. So odd how the pair kept showing up in her world.

Maybe God was trying to tell her something. Maybe she was supposed to teach that ornery little boy. Perhaps God wanted her to instill some old-fashioned discipline in him. On the other hand, she'd had trouble discerning God's "voice" in the past. His "still, small voice" was something she didn't trust herself to know anymore.

Take her understanding about Manny, for instance. She had thought he was God-sent.

He had seemed so sweet when she met him, so tenderhearted. He had brought her mother a bouquet of flowers that first time he came to their house. A bouquet like what Mr. McAlpin was carrying, except white daisies instead of white carnations. She could still see it.

After Minerva got home from the cemetery she couldn't stop thinking about Manny. That young man—Robert McAlpin— who had scared the bejeebers out of her had triggered her memories. He didn't look anything like Manny. He didn't sound or behave like Manny. He was simply young like Manny. So young. Holding that bouquet as though it was his ticket to something he'd always longed for.

She might just call him and tell him she'd teach George. It couldn't hurt. Well, it might, but how bad could it be? She laughed to herself. "The visions might indicate you're crazy, Minerva Place, but this truly proves it."

10

Minerva could not help herself. The next Tuesday when she opened the door she blurted out, "Heavenly days!" and stood with one hand on the doorjamb and one on the doorknob as if barricading the entrance. Her new student stood on the front porch with his father. This was a fine how-do-you-do. George's shirt was untucked, and Minerva spotted filth under his fingernails. That might be grape jelly on his mouth.

This is what you get, Minerva, for sidestepping due diligence.

A typical exchange with a parent would have been much more involved than her conversation with Mr. McAlpin had been. She had broken down and called him, pulling out that slip of paper tucked in the *Ms* of her phone directory, because guilt had welled up and choked her. Nella's direct challenge to her had weighed on her. Then she kept running into the pair, surely a sign. Not wanting to make God mad, she had given in.

She was so nervous about calling a man that she failed to give him her requirements for students—proper clothing (a tucked-in shirt, for one) and general tidiness and, perhaps more important, clean, clipped nails. In addition, arrive promptly and practice thirty minutes each day. She also typically asked questions about maturity, grades in school, and behavioral issues.

But their conversation had been limited. Minerva had phoned him to say, "Mr. McAlpin, a spot has opened up at 5:30 on Tuesdays if George would like to take piano lessons then." And after he gratefully accepted, they hung up.

Now, here stood the reason she should have asked those questions—a hoodlum in the making, this, this urchin. Her own piano teacher, Mrs. Ruewena Sinclair, had required written applications for students. Minerva already felt lax because she only asked questions. Mrs. Sinclair knew what she was doing.

Never mind that she was a terrifying behemoth of a woman. She knew what she was doing.

"Hi, Mrs. Place. We're here. Right on time." Mr. McAlpin had his shirt tucked in. You'd think he'd teach his son to do the same. He had that grin glowing, white teeth lined up and shining. He was not classically handsome—gray eyes a little squinty, nose crooked as though it had been broken—but there was such a happy attitude about him, he fooled you into thinking he was.

Minerva lowered her chin and glared over the top of her readers. "Yes. Come in. You know the way."

"Yes. George, you know the way, don't you, son?" The young man's laugh percolated as he referenced his son's foray into her house. But when he caught Mrs. Place's expression, he blushed. Minerva gave him points for having the sense to know his child's behavior had been inappropriate.

"I hope you won't hold that against us. You know, George busting into your house. That was quite a night." The gangly young father smiled (he certainly smiled a lot), and Minerva worried he would say something stupid like, "Aww, shucks." He looked like that kind of person. Eager. Earnest. Painfully sincere.

"I'm afraid George had already dipped into his candy before we arrived at your house on Halloween. Sometimes when he eats sugar, he gets rambunctious. Do you think the two could be related?"

"I'm no expert, but I suppose they could be related." Minerva wished he would stop smiling. "Come in."

George wasn't as eager to enter Mrs. Place's house this afternoon. Robert tugged his son's jacket, urging him forward.

"Hello, George." Minerva pursed her lips and frowned. Upon closer inspection, it was worse than she initially thought. Some sort of loot overflowed George's front pockets and a stain—chocolate milk?—resided on the chest of his T-shirt.

"Hi," George offered.

She held the door open and made a sweeping gesture with

her arm. Mr. McAlpin didn't break eye contact with Mrs. Place as he pulled on George's jacket more forcefully. George wiped his nose with the back of his hand, then sniffed with gusto.

Minerva froze. "Are you sick, George?"

"No. No, no, no. He's not sick, Mrs. Place. Here, George." Mr. McAlpin handed his son a handkerchief.

"If a student is ill, I understand he may miss a lesson."

"He's fine. Aren't you fine, George?" George didn't say anything. The three continued to stand there as if waiting for a cue from the imaginary stage manager of life. Then Robert eyed the sofa and Minerva regained control.

"I ask parents to return for their children at the end of the lesson. This is a one-on-one session."

"Oh, of course. Of course." He started for the door but turned as he was halfway out. "How should I pay you?"

"I will send a statement home with George at the end of every month."

"Good. Good. Thank you. Yes. Thank you." And with that, Robert McAlpin and his eager smile finally left.

Minerva watched him lope down her sidewalk. He was a strange one, Mr. McAlpin; he was outgoing and friendly, but so easily embarrassed, such a "gosh darn" kind of guy.

He reminded her of—and then, clear as new spectacles fresh off the shelf, there was her fourth-grade sweetheart—Luke Werner. Luke had been like that—sweet and guileless despite a bent toward trouble.

∂

The alphabet had assigned them seats next to each other.

"Minerva?"

"Shh, Luke. Mrs. Saxon will get mad." Minerva sat still and talked out of the corner of her mouth, tucking her chin, and turning her head just enough to send her voice to the boy who constantly tapped her on the shoulder asking questions.

"Minerva, did you get sixty-five for the answer?"

"Be quiet, Luke."

"Did you?"

"Yes."

"Minerva Webster. Luke Werner. Tend to your own business." The teacher turned around from writing on the blackboard and leveled a stern look at the pair. Minerva teetered between nervous and angry. Luke! She had half a mind to tell the teacher what he was up to, but she'd only get in more trouble. Still, Minerva couldn't help but like Luke. His crooked grin and bright eyes spoke of mischief, and he was often standing in the corner or holding out his hand for a slap from the ruler.

Plus, she knew his secret.

Though they couldn't have been less alike, Luke and Minerva shared one thing. Neither could count many friends. Minerva because she kept to herself. Luke because of his sister. The other children whispered about her, but Minerva couldn't quite grasp what was wrong. They seemed to think there might be something to fear from the entire Werner family because of her.

Minerva saw Luke with this sister once. The day was one of those surprise gifts of early spring. After a long, hard Chicago winter cooped up, families were eager to get outdoors, so the park bulged with picnickers and strollers. Minerva trailed her parents and Geneva by a few paces. Geneva swung a bag of bread crumbs and yammered to their mother about something or other. Minerva didn't care. Geneva talked a lot. She was no doubt talking about what color the ducks would be this year, or something else equally ignorant.

A glint of sunlight off the pond caught her eye first. When she looked, Minerva saw a boy bent over a girl seated in the small wooden chair by the water. The thin girl listed to the side and her head lolled toward her shoulder. Her stick arms crossed over her chest and her hands were drawn up like claws. Jerky spasms punctuated her movements. Minerva knew she shouldn't stare, but she couldn't help herself. She was ashamed that she felt repulsed and was horrified that she couldn't stop watching. The boy wiped the girl's mouth, then he reached in and tickled her, which surprised Minerva.

Minerva watched the girl's face contort into a sort of grimace and heard her gasp a laugh. The boy stopped tickling her and leaned in to kiss her on the forehead. When he stood up, Minerva realized the boy was Luke. She quickened her pace so he wouldn't see her, and as far as she knew, he hadn't. Minerva tucked this piece of information about Luke away, never telling anyone; but now she told the kids who called his sister "retard" to stop.

On the playground the day he kissed her they were playing hide-and-seek. Her stomach lurched when he found her behind the huge forsythia and kissed her quickly, but soundly, on the lips. She could still smell the spring-washed air of that day and remember the small smacking sound the kiss made. She stayed hidden behind the forsythia for the rest of recess after he ran away. She remained hidden so she could think more about Luke Werner—a boy who would be kind to his feeble sister, a boy who would kiss her.

Yes, something about Mr. McAlpin's way reminded her of Luke. Was it nonsense for a grown man to remind her of a fourth-grade boy?

❧

"George?" George wandered down the same hall he had sprinted down on Halloween. "George, come back in here, please. You are not here to explore my home. Sit." Minerva patted the wooden bench.

"It smells funny in here."

Mrs. Place slapped the bench more slowly, but with more force, her ring clicking against the hard wood. He climbed up. His feet dangled. Suddenly he splayed both hands and brought them down on the keyboard in a cacophonic eruption.

"George!" He yanked his hands down to his lap. He had startled himself. "That is not the proper way to address the piano." The shadow of disharmonious notes clung to the quiet, volleying in Minerva's sensitive ears.

"I'm sorry."

"You should be." The vibration echoed. "Now, correct posture."

George scratched his chest as if allergic to the word "posture." He wore a beige, orange, and brown striped shirt sporting, along with the milk stain, a grubby ring inside the neckline, and his brown corduroys were frayed at the cuffs. His mop-top of blond hair was overdue for a trim. And was that earwax?

"What do I mean by posture?"

He stared at her with those dark brown eyes, fringed in extraordinary lashes (what a waste on a boy) and said nothing.

"Posture is the way you hold your body when you sit at the instrument. The instrument being the piano. Sit up straight, squarely face the keyboard—do not swing your legs—and place your arms over the keys as such."

She joined him on the bench and demonstrated. George pulled his shoulders back, tucked his chin down, and held his arms over the keyboard, mimicking Minerva.

"Scoot off the bench for a moment." Minerva retrieved a Baptist hymnal from the seat and told him to sit on it. "Very good. Now, this is how you hold your hands."

Mrs. Place allowed him to play middle C with the forefinger of each hand several times and promised him the opportunity to play more notes if he mastered his posture and hand position over the next week. "You must establish the habit of practicing every day, George. A few minutes every day." She wasn't sure he heard her. He was off the bench and heading down the hall.

"George!"

"I've got to go."

"Go where?"

"Bathroom."

҂

When she opened the door for Robert McAlpin she got straight to the point. "George flushed a pine cone down the toilet today."

Mr. McAlpin's eyes widened. "Oh, Mrs. Place. I am so sorry." He looked at his son with such disappointment, Minerva almost felt bad.

"George."

The boy avoided eye contact with his father.

"You know better. I spanked you when you flushed the army men."

George looked at the ceiling.

"George. Look at me. George!"

George rolled his eyes back toward his dad. He chewed the inside of his lip, making his mouth scrunch to one side.

"George, you know not to flush things down the toilet."

"Yes, sir."

"Then why did you do it?"

George shrugged his shoulders and hummed, "I don't know."

"You need a better answer."

George's eyes rolled back toward the ceiling.

"Apologize to Mrs. Place."

"I'm sorry, Mrs. Place."

Minerva stood with her hands on her hips. She wasn't convinced George was sorry, but at least he'd said it. Mr. McAlpin gripped his son's upper arm.

"I can assure you I will deal with this further at home, Mrs. Place. Is your toilet stopped up? Do I need to get the pine cone out? Where did he get a pine cone anyway?"

His last question bordered on impertinence. Why does the origin of the pine cone matter? She happened to have a jar of potpourri on the back of the toilet. The mixture contained a few scented pine cones. She knew if she explained this, the pine cone's size would be in question, and she had implied that the pine cone was full-sized. So, she ignored the question and said, "Being a widow, I have learned to fend for myself in situations such as these."

Mr. McAlpin nodded.

"Well, I apologize again."

Minerva closed the door behind the pair and shook her

head. Why on earth did she agree to teach such a ragamuffin? She wondered if she had the starch to bring this boy around.

☙

Although the clock read five thirty, losing daylight savings time had kicked shadows up an hour. Minerva turned out the lights and closed the drapes beside her chair. Through a slim bit of uncovered window, she watched Mr. McAlpin and George walk down her sidewalk.

"I'll bet that boy doesn't get more than a stern talking to," she said to no one. "What he needs is a spanking and to be put to bed with no dinner."

Charmaine Douglas was at the corner of her driveway like a spider waiting to catch a fly. Minerva watched her neighbor smile at Mr. McAlpin and saw the pair engage.

"I'll bet she's telling him what a mean old lady I am, and he's telling her I got mad at his precious son for nothing."

Charmaine dyed her hair platinum blond and, it seemed to Minerva, wore only slacks and tight sweaters. She liked to wear a headband with a little bow and was fond of pastels and polka dots.

Minerva stood so her curtains concealed her from view. She watched Mrs. Douglas's chubby cheeks lift her cat-eye-framed glasses off the bridge of her nose. She was rolling a child's bicycle out of Minerva's driveway when Mr. McAlpin and George came along.

Minerva had conducted numerous conversations with the parents on this street about their children's toys. Just last week Mrs. Douglas had said, "We have told Danny time and time again to be more careful with his possessions, but I'm always lugging it (Danny's bicycle, Minerva inferred) home for him from somewhere."

Minerva wanted to say, "If you wouldn't lug his bicycle home for him, he might learn to care for his possessions himself." But she didn't. She simply thought what a crass word *lug* was and what a crass person Mrs. Douglas was and how you never could straighten out crass. It was a birth problem.

What were those two saying now? They turned and looked in her direction. She pulled her head back, though they couldn't have seen her. Mrs. Douglas was now pointing at her house. The woman was talking about her. She knew she was. Minerva knew what people thought.

She had overheard Doris Marlin talking about her once.

"She's practically a recluse," Mrs. Marlin had said to some new neighbors at a neighborhood safety meeting. Minerva had just arrived and was giving her coat to the host. Mrs. Marlin had her back to the door. "Nobody in the neighborhood ever sees her." She leaned in as if this were serious, classified information, and the new neighbor stretched her neck out to move closer too.

Then Mrs. Marlin started up again quickly. "But I understand she is very talented. All artistic-type people tend to be a little odd. Mozart would blurt out curse words in the middle of conversations. His condition is called Toulane's syndrome today."

Minerva was 99 percent sure Mozart did not have *Tourette's* syndrome, and she considered giving away the fact that she'd overheard the conversation for the pleasure of correcting this mistake. But she hadn't, and Mrs. Marlin continued. "Talented people are often strange. Frankly, she scares the pants off my kids." Mrs. Marlin's laugh bubbled, and she returned to full volume.

Then, as now, Minerva's nostrils flared with emotion. She was certain Mr. McAlpin and Mrs. Douglas were having a similar conversation. Just then Mr. McAlpin waved at Charmaine and walked on, George still in his grip.

11

A nasty batch of weather visited Paducah like a disagreeable aunt. Minerva feared a relapse of that vicious virus if she ventured out, so she opted for the library over the cemetery.

Minerva would claim the library as a second home if she could. (And if not for Miss Boswell, who was so petite and self assured.) She breathed in the decaying smell of leather and paper, the mingling of perfumes and aftershaves, and the pine-scented soap the janitors used to clean the floors. Hushed air floated the buzz of a filament about to go out in a ceiling light, the muffled coughs and throat clearing, the scraping of a chair as someone pushed back from a desk.

Minerva basked in the rustle of pages being turned, the dull thud of the librarian stamping the return date on books being checked out. She even enjoyed the occasional outburst from a child who couldn't bear the silence another minute. The air was different in the library. Dust motes and magic danced here. Possibility of discovery, mystery, and music resided in this place. Untold stories lingered. Tales anticipated revelation. Presents from travels abroad waited to be unwrapped and experienced.

Minerva had discovered that the oldest marker at Oak Grove belonged to a Revolutionary War army officer. Major Charles Ewell was born September 29, 1758, and died May 10, 1830. She was eager to learn everything she could about this weathered stone. Miss Boswell perched in her usual chair at the entrance to the Special Collections section, with her beady little eyes watching everything. Okay, they weren't beady. They were large and an interesting shade of blue, almost aqua.

"Hello, Mrs. Place."

"Hello, Miss Boswell." If they were cowboys in a movie, they'd both have hands on holstered guns. What would two

women in a movie do? Minerva wondered. Probably just scowl
and then steal each other's men. Movies were all about men.
Life was all about men. Minerva batted her eyes to regain focus.

"How may I help you?" Everything this woman said sounded insulting. Her hushed way of speaking irked Minerva. Never
mind that they were in a library. She recognized she was being
petty but couldn't manage to put the lid on her simmering pot
of irritation.

"I am on a quest for information about Major Charles Ewell.
Can you steer me toward helpful sources?"

"I see." I see what? Minerva clenched her jaw. You didn't answer my question, she thought. Miss Boswell continued. "With
which war was the major associated?"

"The Revolutionary War."

"I see," Miss Boswell repeated. Minerva was about to pop. I
see what? The word *vexing* sprang to mind.

"Let me see what I can find." Miss Boswell smiled and nodded, which provoked Minerva further. "For now, I'll steer you
to information that may help you understand that period."

Minerva fumed. Help me understand, huh? Miss Boswell's
snooty-patootie, holier-than-thou attitude niggled her to her
core. This petite pedigreed Paducahan thought she was so
smart, knew something about everything, thought she would
illuminate Minerva. Well. They'd just see about that.

"Thank you, Miss Boswell."

When she got home and situated herself to write, Minerva
wrote the names at the tops of two pages:

**Major Charles Ewell, born September 29, 1758; died
May 10, 1830; Old Section 6, Lot 82, Peace Ave.**

**Maria D. Ewell, born June 30, 1788; died February 27,
1863; Old Section 6, Lot 82, Peace Ave.**

Then she waited. And waited.

Today she had read articles about the Revolutionary War,
lost herself in tales about pioneers forging through the Cum-
berland Gap, and found snippets about what life could have

been like in Paducah's early days. But Major Ewell still wasn't speaking to her.

His wife, Maria, was buried beside him, so she listened for her voice. Surely one of them would have something to say. How did their family come to America? Didn't the major have a comment or memory about the Revolutionary War? Or the dangerous journey to Kentucky? Or forming Paducah? Was the man mute? What kind of war hero was mute?

She leaned back in her dining-room chair. Manny. Manny was mute. Whenever Minerva had asked him about his nightmares, he clammed up and brooded.

Minerva had tried to talk to her mother about it. After all, her mother had been married forever. She must know about men. But the conversation didn't illuminate much.

They had been sitting on the Websters' front porch one summer afternoon when Minerva screwed up her courage to talk to her mother about Manny. She wanted to "do" her marriage right. She wanted to be a successful wife. But her husband, whom she thought she knew before she married him—forevermore, they had rocked on this very same porch for a year—her husband was a mystery. He had such moods.

Yes, the moods were worse after he'd been drinking, but sometimes he got worked up in the middle of the night. He'd throw the sheets off in a rage, screaming and crying. He looked like he was awake, but he didn't respond to her voice. He would finally settle down on his own. She learned it was best to leave him be because once when she tried to wake him up, he'd batted her with those beefy arms of his. She'd gotten a bloody nose.

So Minerva had questions. How do I handle this? Should I say something to him about it? He gets angry if I bring it up, but maybe I should insist? Why does he drink so much? Is it…you know…supposed to be so uncomfortable? These questions and more rattled around Minerva's mind. She wanted to do it right.

But as they sat on the porch shelling peas, she didn't learn much.

Minerva snapped the fiftieth tip off the fiftieth pod (she knew because she counted as she worked) before she had enough courage to begin the conversation.

"Mother, did Father ever have bad dreams?" That seemed like a good way to start. They could get to her most burning question in time.

"I'm sure he did, Minerva. What a strange question."

Minerva wasn't going to retreat now, though.

"Manny has awful dreams and I get scared sometimes." There it was. She had admitted her fear.

"He was in the war, Minerva. I'm sure every man who fought in the war has bad dreams from time to time. I wouldn't worry about it. Feed him a nice meal and make sure your home is clean. You want a pleasant environment for him. In time I'm sure that will override his stress."

Minerva thought about this as she continued to shell. That made sense. She needed to try harder to make their home comfortable and peaceful. She bit her lip as she thought about asking more questions. A flitter fluttered in her stomach. But she took a deep breath and asked anyway.

"Mother, what about marital relations?"

Her mother never blinked an eye, and certainly didn't look her in the eye. She went right on with her work saying, "Yes. You must never resist your husband's advances. Men are driven by nature in a way unfamiliar to women."

What did that mean?

"It is your responsibility." Mrs. Webster's shoulders bunched around her ears. She spoke with a clipped decisiveness, as if she were instructing a schoolchild. "It is a woman's job to provide children to the home. After that you'll see a change in your husband, I can assure you. Now, let's talk about something else. Your marriage is a personal topic, and you really shouldn't discuss it with anyone."

For a while, month after month passed in the same fashion and no amount of intercourse (an altogether uncomfortable, messy, and sticky proposition that her mother had not prepared her for at all) seemed to turn the young Place's fortune toward a future outside their discordant duet. Through all of this, Manny never mentioned children and they never, never discussed what went on in the bedroom.

Then one day in April two months before their second anniversary, miraculously it seemed to Minerva, she got pregnant. This was what she'd waited for, the turning point for both. A baby. A child. An answer to the awkwardness of their union. But just as quickly as the answer came, the hope stole away one afternoon in a cramping loss. Minerva filled with a rush of such sorrow she couldn't get out of bed for the next month.

And Manny's drinking increased. Minerva, an expert in living quietly, now tried to become invisible. But somehow she was unable to avoid the mug of beer he threw into her face. She also inspired him to throw five china plates across the room when she burned a roast. The backhand he popped her with when she interrupted his concentration could have been avoided for sure, she thought, but somehow it wasn't.

The next two pregnancies resulted in a miscarriage and a premature birth. Manny told her she was hopeless when she lost the premature baby, a boy. Tiny, little more than four pounds. He didn't have to tell her that. She knew hopelessness.

After her third loss the doctor suggested they not try anymore. "It's too hard on you physically and emotionally, Minerva," Dr. Herbert said. "Please stop torturing yourself...and Manny, for that matter. Many women are happy adopting. Have you considered that as an option?"

Manny snorted disapproval when she approached him with the doctor's suggestion.

"Adoption is out of the question," he bellowed. "No telling what you might get," as if adopting a child was like playing Russian roulette with genetics. Minerva knew better than to cry in front of him. Tears would make him angrier.

So, on that day in late March, when the messenger from the railroad yards knocked on Minerva's door as she was peeling carrots for their dinner, Minerva experienced several layers of emotion and struggled to grasp the appropriate one before this courier might spot the others. She was appalled that a moment of—what was it? Relief? Gratitude?—showed up when she heard the words "your husband has been in a serious accident and may not live." The presence of those feelings proved her wickedness. She was a sinner needing more forgiveness than God might be willing to offer.

Her shameful burst of relief transformed into genuine grief because she had loved Manny, or at least what the idea of being married meant. He was all she could have expected in a husband. Faithful, as far as she knew. A hard worker. A delight to her father. For nearly three years she had held the honorable rank of married woman, a status she was surprised to have achieved at all. ("You're too tall, dear," her mother had often said. "Boys don't want girls taller than they are." And then, what they thought was behind her back, "Minerva's awkward." And "Minerva needs to learn how to carry on a conversation." And "If Minerva were more like Geneva…").

After Manny's death, Minerva returned to her parents' home, expecting to grow old there, caring for them as they aged, teaching piano to children in the afternoons to contribute her part. Manny had given her more than she had hoped for. She grieved that she had never made him happy. He deserved a wife who could have made him happy.

But failure was Minerva's familiar companion.

12

It was six twelve, but Minerva's back ached and her eyes stung, and she speculated that if she sank into a hot bath, she might not be able to get out. Not only had she negotiated the four "Für Elises," she had endured George. That child would be enough to consume an entire afternoon's portion of energy. She could tell his father that George should wait until he's at least nine, but she never had fired a student. Minerva Place was no quitter. She would persevere.

Though the season's early onset of darkness confused her system, Minerva preferred this time of year. When daylight dawdled, she felt compelled to pick up stray sticks, pull weeds, clip back the ivy, or at least walk around the block. Dr. Herbert said walking would keep the pounds off her hips. The activity hadn't seemed to do much for her hips so far, but who knew? She might be wider than a house trailer if she didn't take a regular constitution.

In darkness, however, she owed no onus to outdoors. There was no pressure to enjoy the warm temperatures, no coercion to eradicate garden pests. She lingered free and guiltless at her dining-room table where she wrote and wrote. And tonight, as soon as she cleaned up the kitchen following her dinner of ham hock and beans, onion, cornbread, and homemade chow-chow (another gift from Nella—was there no end to the woman's generosity and determination to be neighborly and friendly?), she planned to settle in for a night with one of her friends. She had earned and deserved such a treat.

But just as she sat down with her folders, pens, and paper, a knock at the door startled her.

"Who on earth? Why would anybody be knocking on my door at this time of night?" She peered through the curtains before she went to the door. "What on earth!" she repeated, this time with full-blown incredulity.

"Mr. McAlpin." Puzzlement, tinged with annoyance, carried her greeting. She could hardly help it.

Robert McAlpin and George stood on her dark porch with grins that seemed to say, "Aren't you glad we're here?"

Minerva thought fast, attempting to be more civil, but couldn't come up with anything other than "How can I help you?"

"No, Mrs. Place, it's how can we help *you*." Mr. McAlpin's grin broadened to show those teeth. Oh dear. She might have to invite these two in. At the very least she was going to have to turn on the porch light.

"Excuse me? I don't quite understand."

George came alive. "I'm a Cub Scout!"

"You are?" Minerva wondered what this had to do with her.

"Yes! A Tiger!" George inserted a growl.

"George," his father said. "Say 'Yes, ma'am,' and do not growl, please."

"Yes, ma'am."

"That sounds like a nice activity for you, George." She waited for more information.

"George is learning about loyalty and friendship and responsibility and all sorts of wonderful virtues, but this month they are concentrating on honesty. Go ahead and tell Mrs. Place what we discussed about honesty, George."

Minerva realized she could no longer hold them at bay. "Please come in." Surely they wouldn't.

"Thank you." Mr. McAlpin ushered George in, where the boy stood in the middle of her living room flapping his arms like a bird. The child could not be still. "George, stop waving your arms." At least Mr. McAlpin tried.

"It smells funny in here."

"George, that's impolite." Mr. McAlpin smiled and cocked his head to one side as if shrugging.

"Dad, I'm being honest."

Mr. McAlpin ignored George and addressed Minerva. "We've yet to instill tact into his honesty."

Now Minerva ignored Mr. McAlpin. "I suppose you're smelling my dinner. I just cleaned up. I had ham and beans. Do you like that meal, young man?"

"Noooo."

"I do, but I'm afraid it does tend to cause an odor in the house." Minerva chuckled over George's screwed-up face. She had to admit the child was not lacking personality. "Have a seat. You'll get used to it before long."

"George and I were talking about honesty after he came home from his Cub Scout meeting. As we talked, I realized George had not been truthful about several things lately. And some of those things involved you."

"Is that right?" Minerva fidgeted with the button of her sweater. She wasn't sure she wanted anyone to be totally honest with her. Much less a child.

"George." The boy looked at the floor and began to twist side to side. "George, please talk to Mrs. Place about what we discussed and tell her the truth."

George took a big breath and looked at his father with a final plea. Mr. McAlpin said, "You can do this."

After a long minute, George, more meekly than she'd ever heard him, said, "Mrs. Place, I told you I practiced every day, but I don't."

Minerva almost felt sorry for him. Seeing him subdued was a new experience. His lashes rested on his cheeks as he looked at the floor with shame. A part of her wanted to tell him it was all right, that she knew little boys had other business to attend to. But she appreciated what Mr. McAlpin was trying to accomplish and she didn't want to undermine him.

"I see."

"Last week I missed Saturday and Sunday."

"And…" Mr. McAlpin urged his son along.

"And I might have practiced for twenty minutes instead of thirty on all the other days."

"Might have?" Mr. McAlpin wasn't going to let him off the hook.

"I practiced for twenty minutes on the other days. And I'm sorry I lied. And I'll try to be honest from now on." The last words tumbled over themselves like a pile of puppies trying to get to a shared bowl of food.

"George, I'm glad to hear you tell me the truth." Minerva tried not to smile. "It takes a lot of courage to be honest."

George blew out as if he'd set down five-hundred-pound barbells.

"Would you and your father like to have a bite of dessert with me?" Minerva startled herself with the invitation. She supposed she was overcome with unexpected tenderness for the fact this unruly child showed a glimmer of hope.

George lifted his eyebrows and looked at Robert.

"Oh, we wouldn't want to impose," Mr. McAlpin said.

"You wouldn't be imposing."

"Well, all right." Robert McAlpin looked as relieved as George.

The threesome sat at the kitchen table. Minerva cracked the door and laughed about how those beans were not much of a welcoming scent for guests. She served them Oreos and milk and apologized for not having something homemade. "That would be my neighbor's forte," she explained. She was surprised at how comfortable she felt. It didn't matter that the kitchen stank or that she didn't have a proper dessert. The pair of them seemed content with an invitation to sit and visit. But now that they were there, what on earth was she going to talk to them about?

The conversation didn't seem to lag, though. Mr. McAlpin— "Please call me Robert," he said—talked easily. A little too easily. Minerva was ready for them to go a notch before they left. But still and all, it was a pleasant way to spend an evening, though she hadn't gotten to write.

If nothing else, the visit had distracted her from her backache. She twisted back and forth like George had. Hmm, that felt pretty good. That little boy was a character.

☙

Minerva Jean Webster had tried hard not to be a character. For as long as she could remember, Minerva had longed to blend in as quietly as a whisper in a crowd. Her goal remained achievable in a family of extroverts. While dinner conversations revolved around her father's day at the office and Geneva's day at school, Minerva contented herself with the role of head nodder.

Minerva grew up in what her mother called "upper middle class," landing hard on the word *upper* whenever she said the phrase. Her father was some kind of boss—Minerva didn't understand what the supervisor did—for Chicago Burlington & Quincy.

"The Websters are part of the Railroad Family," her father often said, as if this were an actual family with grandparents, cousins, uncles, and aunts. Minerva did not call anyone her father worked with Uncle or Aunt, so this talk of the Railroad Family confused her.

The Websters' actual family was already confusing enough. They were unlike most families who lived on property passed from one generation to the next. The Websters moved often. From what Minerva could piece together, her father "got things started" wherever they went. This frequent uprooting meant she knew her actual relatives, but not well. She was foggy on who was who for the longest time.

Her father's family roster was simple. There was Grandma, Uncle William, Aunt Viola (an old maid with a lisp), Uncle Frank, and, of course, her father.

But her mother's family was more complicated. Grandfather Court and Grandmother Court had five daughters: Lucille (Minerva's mother), Lanoma, Lorena, Lavonia, and Loretta. Try keeping those names straight. Plus, they all produced passels of children.

"You are Lorena made over," Lucille often told Minerva, who longed for photographs she could label, because what did her mother's statement mean? Which one was Lorena?

All the aunts' names sounded alike and all of them looked

alike. The resemblances were eerie. Grandmother Court and Grandfather Court must have only known how to reproduce one version of a person. Since Minerva didn't look like any of them, she deduced that her mother meant she behaved like Aunt Lorena.

Minerva noticed that her mother's lips pressed into a hard line and her eyes narrowed when Aunt Lorena came to visit. Minerva recognized the expression. It was the same one she turned on Minerva when she was trying to make Minerva do something.

"Lorena, why do you insist on calling yourself a suffragette? It's beneath you. It's crass. Carrying signs. Marching up and down streets. Such behavior is common." Her mother sniffed as if the air had become foul.

"Lucille, women deserve to vote. If I must put on a pair of pants and jump up and down on the lawn of the White House to achieve that, I will."

"Women have a vote. Their voices are heard through their husbands' votes."

"Hogwash."

"Please watch your language in my home."

"Hogwash?"

Lucille Webster threw up her hands and stomped into the kitchen, where Minerva was lapping up every word of their conversation.

"Minerva, it's rude to eavesdrop."

Minerva didn't reply.

"Go on." Her mother shooed her out. Minerva took the back stairway up to her room, where she continued to listen through the vent.

Another time Minerva caught the end of what she imagined had been a juicy conversation. "You told me yourself you'd prefer I not bring Bruno." Aunt Lorena's voice projected right through the ceiling, but Minerva had a harder time making out the other voices in the room below her. Uncle Bruno, Aunt Lorena's husband, rarely came with her to visit. Minerva knew her mother detested him. She caught snatches, then Aunt Lorena again: "He's not a German. He happens to have a German name."

After every Aunt Lorena visit, Minerva's mother decompressed at dinner. "Lorena is as stubborn as a day-old splinter. If she decides the sky is orange instead of blue, then the matter is not up for discussion. The sky is orange. Nobody could convince her otherwise."

"Every family has one," Minerva's father replied, buttering his bread. "A maverick, set on doing things her way. You wouldn't know it by looking at her, would you? She doesn't say that much, but when she does, it's loaded with gunpowder."

"She's just so wrong and insists she's right. She always insists she's right. Stubborn. And unseemly."

So, bit by bit, conversation by conversation, Minerva pieced together why her family thought she was like Aunt Lorena.

Aunt Lorena was a woman who knew her mind.

Minerva preferred "determined, persevering, and stalwart" to "willful, mulish, and intractable," which were some of the other words her mother threw out about Aunt Lorena. But whatever adjective was applied once Minerva's conclusions gelled about something—or someone—the subject was closed. She would grant that.

Minerva would never forget the one occasion when she spent time alone with her aunt Lorena.

"It's her sixteenth birthday, Lucille," Aunt Lorena had said to her mother the day before Minerva's birthday. The sisters didn't know Minerva was in the hall. "You treat her like a stepchild. When Geneva turned sixteen, I recall you had a special party for her and bought her a new dress and shoes, and probably a fancy gift. Sometimes I think you don't know your younger daughter exists."

"I resent that, Lorena." Minerva's mother's voice was low. Minerva could hear her anger and defensiveness. "Minerva does not care for attention. She would rather we not make a fuss. She's a quiet, studious girl who would rather read a book than go to a party. I believe I know my daughters better than you."

"All I know is that there isn't a girl alive who doesn't long to feel special. If you're not going to do it, I am."

"Do what?"

"Make her feel special tomorrow." Minerva ducked into the kitchen so Aunt Lorena wouldn't see her when she came swooshing out of the parlor. She felt simultaneously thrilled and nervous. Someone had spoken up on her behalf, but she wasn't sure she would be up to any plans Aunt Lorena might make. The sisters were both right.

Although Minerva fretted that night about what Aunt Lorena might do, she did not need to worry. Her plans were stellar, as it turned out. Minerva couldn't have planned it better herself.

They went out to eat lunch and then to the bookstore.

"Here you will find your gift," Aunt Lorena said to her when they walked into Wilson's Bookstore. Lorena made the small store seem expansive as she swept her arm in front of them. Minerva smiled and considered what book she might buy. "I want you to choose a book for every year you've lived on this earth. Sixteen books that you can enjoy." Aunt Lorena tilted her chin up as if she were defying someone. Minerva could imagine her marching down the street holding a suffragette sign.

"Oh no!" Minerva knew that she could not accept her aunt's grandiose gesture. "Aunt Lorena, sixteen books are too many. That's outlandish. I don't know that I could do that."

"Of course you can. And you will. We'll stay here all afternoon and you'll take as long as you like to choose the very ones you want the most." Lorena was plucking off her gloves, fingertip by fingertip as if she were preparing to go to work.

Minerva could see that her aunt would not be persuaded otherwise. She had made up her mind and that was that. Minerva couldn't remember the titles of all sixteen books anymore, but she would never forget that day. And she never remembered that day without a warm smile. She knew then, if she hadn't been sure before, that if Aunt Lorena was a problem, then she wanted to be one too.

13

Mr. McAlpin and George were in her line of sight at church on Sunday morning. George fidgeted, but at least Mr. McAlpin had attempted to make him look presentable. His typically wild head of hair glistened, slick with water or Brylcreem—she wasn't sure which—as the sun shone through the stained-glass window. A beam of orange highlighted him. He wore a white shirt, but she couldn't see his pants. Not for the first time, Minerva thought *oh dear,* about this pair. On the closing refrain of "At the Cross," George noticed her and waved. She ignored him. Though this had never happened (who would think to wave at Mrs. Minerva Place when she sat at the organ of First Baptist Church?) she concluded that waving back would be unprofessional.

When the invitation was given for those in attendance either to commit themselves to follow Jesus or, if they had already done so, to join the church by statement of letter, Mrs. Place bowed her head to pray with the rest of the congregation. Mrs. Thibodeaux pounded out the invitation. Minerva, distracted by Mrs. Thibodeaux's enthusiasm, kept her eyes open during the prayer time, so she noticed movement. Ever so slightly, she turned her head to the left to see who was coming forward. Someone joining the church always intrigued.

What do you know? Mr. McAlpin and George were moving down the aisle.

She looked back down at her folded hands and prayed, "Lord, give me a right heart toward these two," because, though she had enjoyed their brief visit, she was not at all sure she approved of them. They were both rather crude. In fact, she had been thinking it over and she knew she must come right out and tell Mr. McAlpin to clip George's fingernails. They were so dirty. So long. Why, they made a scratchy sound on the keys.

Brother Brown patted Mr. McAlpin on the back. He was all smiles and "glad-to-have-you's" as he introduced the pair. "Won't you come by and shake Robert's hand and welcome him into our church family?" Brother Brown said. This was Minerva's cue. She attacked the keyboard and pumped the pedals with vigor. A rousing version of "Joyful, Joyful We Adore Thee" swelled. If Mrs. Thibodeaux would play with such enthusiasm today, so would she.

After the last person in line shook Mr. McAlpin's hand—George stretched his entire body out on the front pew and tried to balance a pencil on his nose—Minerva realized she was alone with them in the sanctuary.

"Welcome to our fellowship, Mr. McAlpin," she offered, hoping these words would suffice. She was tired after her Sunday morning and didn't want to be drawn into a long ordeal. It would be nice if he said thank you, and they could be on their way.

"Oh, thank you, Mrs. Place. I knew when I saw you sitting at the organ, this was the church for George and me."

What was she supposed to say?

"Ah." It had been a mistake inviting them in for Oreos. Now they were going to think she was one of those grandmotherly types.

"I am comfortable here, I mean."

He doesn't appear to be comfortable, she thought.

"It's just…I want to…George…I need to get settled somewhere quickly. I need for this to feel like home for George."

"Uh-huh." She gathered her music, trying to break free of eye contact.

"Well." There was that word again.

He was not going away. She had no choice but to respond. To do otherwise would be rude. Minerva was not rude. She straightened the music on the organ bench and squared her shoulders. "You will be comfortable here, Mr. McAlpin. There are many fine people who attend this church. But now you have a son who needs to go home."

George had given up balancing pencils. He was asleep. His mouth was open. His shirt was untucked, and his hair had dried (so it *had* been slicked with water).

"Come on, buddy," Robert McAlpin said as he leaned over the flushed, limp body of his son.

&

All afternoon Minerva thought—obsessed?—about the McAlpins. She had so many questions: What had happened to his wife? Why hadn't he remarried? Where had they moved here from? But she would never ask them. She wasn't nosy.

She wished everyone were required to keep a public record of their comings and goings. Then you wouldn't have to ask; you could go to the library, check out that person's material, and read up on him. Simple. No questions. No intrusions. No one the wiser. On second thought, such a system would give Miss Boswell an awful lot of power.

Minerva thought about the way Robert McAlpin held his head tilted to one side when he spoke, as if the world was off-kilter and he was trying to set it straight. She considered his lanky arms and legs and how he seemed too young to have a boy George's age. His brown eyes, fringed with thick lashes, blinked like warning lights. His Adam's apple bobbed goofily. His hasty blush. His crooked nose. Such a ready laugh. He was a pleasant-looking young man. His attempts at conversation dripped with eagerness and sincerity. Genuineness. She could hear authenticity stamped into every word.

Then there was George. Not the sort of child she preferred. For one, he was a male and she would take a girl over a boy every single time. Girls were more interested in learning, more conscientious, better at practicing during the week, less likely to waste Minerva's time. Rarely did she have a girl with dirty fingernails. Those fingernails. Disgusting. The child might have worms. And his hair. Unruly was the only word. She must come up with a way to steer Mr. McAlpin to Avondale's Barber Shop. The boy was too old to be sporting such a mop of hair.

Not to mention the matter of his clothing. A simple plaid

shirt and pair of pants, which would be tame enough on most children, became out of control on George. His church wardrobe—white shirt and navy pants—was fine in theory, but on George, a disaster. He should never wear white. There was always a stain.

The matter of a wife and mother baffled her most of all. What about her? Minerva leaned back in the nubby club chair with an excellent view of Harahan Street. This was her reading chair, her pondering chair, and truth be told, her observation chair. Here was where she could see the comings and goings of the entire street. Hidden by her curtains, she could see through the crack and keep up with the neighbors' lives. She considered herself interested. Nosy people asked questions. She never asked questions. She was not nosy.

But back to the serious matter of Mrs. McAlpin. Was Mr. McAlpin a widower as she had heard? She wondered how the woman had died. Did George see his young, beautiful mother die a long, slow death to cancer? Every day becoming bleaker and bleaker? Had George sat by her bedside and cried?

I'll bet he lost his energy and desire to play, Minerva thought. He developed dark circles under his sad brown eyes. Now, a year later, his energy has returned, and he is acting out because he is angry. He is angry because he doesn't understand that death is permanent. He calls out for his mother to come home. At night he longs for her to tuck him into bed, but he must settle for his father, a man who comforted with awkward long arms. Yes, Minerva decided, this might be the explanation.

She reached over to the coffee table where she kept a candy jar full of butterscotch wrapped in gold foil. She allowed herself one at night when she read. Today she decided to have one right after supper. She felt a little rebellious. You only live once, she'd heard someone say on television. What if she died before she could eat her next piece of candy? She'd better enjoy the moment. Yes, life was short. Poor, poor Mrs. McAlpin. She would be nicer to George. She would try to have nicer thoughts about people in general.

14

Miss Harriett Boswell is a snob, thought Minerva.
Actually, Miss Harriett Boswell carried an impressive
Paducah pedigree, and this, Minerva could never admit, annoyed her. Her grandparents were pioneer families who were among the first to call Paducah home. Hmph. Big deal. Also, Miss Boswell was too pretty, with those slanted feline-like green eyes and high, arched eyebrows, and even a beauty mark tucked under the right side of her mouth. Such beauty made Minerva suspicious. Beautiful women and handsome men got by on their looks. They were never forced to develop their character. Thus, shallow. The whole part and parcel of them. All good-looking people were subject to character weakness. That's how Minerva saw it.

And now, imagine, Paducah gossip said pretty Miss Boswell, Paducah royalty, raconteuse, controller of all things sacred at the library, was seeing Brother Larson, Minerva's Brother Larson. Her minister. Miss Boswell wasn't even a Baptist, either!

Late Friday afternoon, after her last piano student received a gold star, Minerva dug into research at the library. Since Emma Skillian had visited her to correct her facts and also had returned in a dream, Minerva decided she should focus on finding more information about her. She knew Emma had died in The Flood, so she started there. But she couldn't stop watching Miss Boswell.

Miss Boswell wore her hair in a fashion requiring weekly trips to the beauty shop. Minerva didn't want to get roped into such a routine. Number one, having your hair fixed cost too much. Why would you pay someone to shampoo and dry your hair when you were capable of doing this yourself? And number two, all sorts of lip wagging went on at the beauty shop. A bunch of women sitting around waiting for their looks to be improved. Why, of course that's a breeding ground for idle chitchat.

Minerva surmised that a good 75 percent of the untruths perpetuated in this town originated in beauty shops. The other 25 percent began in barber shops, because she knew men gossiped too. Since men's haircuts didn't last as long, they didn't spend as much time in the shops as women; therefore, they did not generate as much gossip. This was how Minerva arrived at the seventy-five, twenty-five split. Simple logic.

Minerva picked up the confirming information about Harriett and Brother Larson at her last hair appointment. Though Minerva didn't have a standing appointment like some women—unnecessary and excessive—she did go in on occasion to have her hair shaped up. While she was in curlers under the dryer, a woman from the Presbyterian church (Mrs. Dolby, whom Minerva knew to have overseen their church's cookbook. She had done an excellent job, in fact) told the manicurist all about the latest goings-on. Harriett Boswell and Brother Larson included.

Now as she sat analyzing the tiny librarian, Minerva noted, not for the first time, that Miss Boswell possessed expensive taste. Today she wore a smart twin sweater set—pink cashmere, no less—and a camel pencil skirt. A strand of pearls. Pearl earrings. But of course, no wedding ring. She wondered anew why an attractive, petite, intelligent (Miss Boswell graduated from one of those Seven Sisters colleges) woman like Harriett Boswell had never married. Maybe she was too smart for her own good.

Concentrate, Minerva. For pity's sake, concentrate. Think about Emma Skillian. Minerva scratched at the patch of psoriasis on her scalp and watched a wispy flurry of white flakes settle on the table. She flicked them away and glanced at her shoulder. She scratched her right shoulder, trying to clear the dusting, then cut her eyes around to see if anyone was watching.

Minerva hunkered down and scanned her notes. A Negro had found Emma and her sister dead in their house weeks after

The Flood. She was buried in Oak Grove. Two people were at her funeral—the undertakers from Lindsey's Funeral Home. The date of her death was listed as the day she was found. Oh, how sad, Minerva thought, scratching again. Nobody knows the day she died. There was not much else.

Minerva didn't want to waste a trip to the library though, so she decided to read newspapers stored on microfilm. She was curious about what had happened in Paducah the year the Websters moved here. The teenaged Minerva had been so distraught about her new environment she ignored the rest of the world. She did remember December 1917. Nobody in Paducah would ever forget that winter.

Minerva found the right cartridge of microfilm, threaded the amber strip through the machine, and flipped it on. The hum of the fan gave her a tingle as if she were beginning a journey. She whirled the film through, stopping periodically until she landed on December 1917.

The snow had been relentless all month that year. By January 8, 1918, record keepers had registered sixteen inches. She remembered that the river had frozen, so she looked for pictures but couldn't find any. She pulled the cartridge for January 1918. She scanned more stories and noted that by this month twenty inches of snow had fallen, and the thermometer was showing eleven degrees below zero.

She looked until she found a photograph of people walking, skating, and sledding on the river. Soon Minerva disappeared into the past. One paper on film led to another and another and yet another, like eating Christmas cookies. One would not do. She had to sample several. So, time ticked away; but unlike overindulging in cookies, this feast resulted in something other than an upset stomach.

Minerva slapped the table when she read the tiny type. She cried, "Oh!" so fiercely that everyone around her whispered "shh" in unison, relieving Miss Boswell of the chore.

The headline screamed at her:

ALLEGED BLAST MURDERESS
MAY BE TRIED MAY 5

Mrs. Wagner and Mrs. Skillian Likely
To Be Brought Back for Hearing

POLICE HAVE MASS OF
DAMAGING EVIDENCE
County Officials Still Considering
Summoning Special Jury

The examining trials of Mrs. Henrietta Wagner
and Mrs. Emma Peters Skillian, who are held on
warrants charging them with the murder of Mrs.
Rosetta Warren by the explosion of dynamite
Monday morning at dawn, have been set for Saturday morning at 9 o'clock before County Judge
James M. Lang.

Unless the right of the two women to face
the prosecuting witnesses is waived, they will be
brought to Paducah from Princeton, where they
were taken Monday afternoon, as a precaution
against possible mob violence.

Mrs. Wagner was represented by Attorneys Reed
and Burns, but it was understood that counsel has
not been retained by Mrs. Skillian.

Emma Skillian's name was on the front page of the
News-Democrat. Was she truly seeing this? Was this *her* Emma
Skillian? Others in the library now stared at Minerva gestic-
ulating with agitation. Her hand flitted between covering her
mouth and using her pointer finger to read the paper's print on
the screen.

The police have announced that they have all
the evidence necessary to ensure a conviction, but
they are still at work clearing up some of the clues.
Detective Jack W. Nelson and Deputy Sheriff
Robert Vannerson went to Princeton yesterday and
interviewed Mrs. Wagner and Mrs. Skillian.

Some of the county officials are still considering
the advisability of making a request for a special
grand jury to consider the evidence and if suffi-
cient to obtain an indictment. The officials also are
desirous of an immediate trial, but it was assured
that the attorneys for the defense would oppose
any such hurry.

Minerva sat on the edge of the library chair, her eyes bug-
gy. Her shoulders bunched around her ears and she kept her
hands glued to the microfilm machine. She took a deep breath
through her nose. Her heart pounded. A murderess. Dynamite.
Mob riots in Paducah. This was Emma. She had found Emma.

But just one minute. Why did she not remember this? She
should remember the most sensational murder trial Paducah
ever witnessed. She looked at the date again. May 1923. Ah, her
parents. She was up to her eyeballs in taking care of them that
year. She hadn't known what day of the week it was most of the
time. She never read the paper or left the house except to get
groceries. She seldom attended church during those months.
If someone had mentioned this trial to her, she would have
ignored the news. She didn't retain much of anything from that
period. A bucket of white paint might as well have been poured
over that section of her memory. No, she did not remember
this sensational trial of Emma Skillian and her friend Henrietta
Wagner at all.

Now she couldn't wait to dig in and learn more. She knew
the facts of this trial would uncover the meaning of Emma's
words "it's true that I died in The Flood, but my real death
came years earlier."

"Mrs. Place?" At first Minerva didn't hear Miss Boswell behind her whispering her name. "Mrs. Place?"

Minerva jumped and screamed. "Eeeoooww!"

Miss Boswell did a quick two-step backward. "My goodness,
Mrs. Place, I didn't mean to startle you."

Minerva's voice had penetrated the sacred quiet of the library and she was aware that she had become the center of attention.

But Miss Boswell continued unfazed. "Have you found something interesting?"

She was so nosy.

"Yes. As a matter of fact, I have."

Miss Boswell waited. Minerva hated to admit she could see why Brother Larson would find Harriett Boswell an interesting woman to pursue. Minerva continued to look at her inquiring face, wondering what she was waiting for.

"What was it?" So nosy!

"Oh, history about an event that occurred in the early '20s." Minerva wasn't about to tell her.

"I see. Well, if there is any way I might aid you in your project (she may have placed special emphasis on the word *project*, Minerva thought. Could she be sarcastic?), I would be delighted to do so. I do know a great deal about Paducah's history."

Minerva thought, *I am sure you do and I'm sure you would love to aid me. You are itching to know what I am doing.* But she only said, "Thank you."

"You are welcome. However, this evening's closing time for the library has arrived."

This flustered Minerva, who felt reprimanded, and who was already self-conscious about having screamed.

"Yes. Certainly. I apologize. I will rewind the microfilm."

"No need to apologize and I will be glad to take care of putting the materials away for you. You are one of our most dedicated researchers, and I admire your investment of time."

What does she mean? Minerva blinked rapidly, scooted her chair back, and stood, towering over Miss Boswell, who was so small and self assured. "I'll get my things, then." She gathered her legal pad and pocketbook from the table. Her pen dropped, but she didn't bend to retrieve it.

❧

On her way home Minerva wondered about Emma Skillian

and Henrietta Wagner. A friendship that led to murder. My goodness. Another reason you should keep your distance from people. So many manipulators. She would have to do more research, but Henrietta seemed to have been a bad influence on Emma. Emma must have been a weak person to have allowed herself to be drawn into such immoral behavior. Or was Emma the wicked one?

She was deliberating these things when she turned onto Harahan and was greeted with an abysmal sight. The red wagon. She saw from all the way down the block that the wretched toy laid claim to the foot of her driveway. Between her agitation leaving the library and this, Minerva sensed the tentacles of one of her headaches creeping in to take hold. She pulled Spencer to the curb in front of her house, got out, and crossed the street to the errant wagon. She considered kicking the blasted toy. She wanted to rear back, jam her toe into the stupid thing, and send it flying. Instead, she rolled her eyes, grabbed the handle (which was sticky) and pulled the culprit into her yard. She vowed to talk to Nella to see if she could identify the transgressor.

As she got in her car to pull into her driveway, though, the mystery was solved. Here came George. Of course. The offender was George. The little ruffian. If the boy's mother hadn't died, he would be better cared for. (Minerva's version of George's history, which was somewhat correct, had morphed into fact for her.) So here he was now, running down the sidewalk, toward her yard and his wagon, because the wayward toy must be his. No other child on this street would leave a wagon parked unattended and blocking her driveway.

George sported a straw cowboy hat on his blond mop. A holster dangled around his waist, threatening to slip off and trip him. He carried silver toy guns in each hand. His cowboy boots discouraged him from reaching full speed, but he clattered on. Minerva rolled her window down to confront him.

"George, is that your wagon?" She could hear stridency in her voice that she regretted. She didn't want to scare the child. Streaks of dirt—or was it chocolate milk?—framed his mouth.

But those eyes. Such beautiful eyes, Minerva thought, angelic. She cocked her head to one side. Maybe *angelic* was too generous.

He held the guns at his sides, then tried to holster them, struggling with the left one.

"George, please do not leave your wagon in my driveway again. This is the second time you've been so careless. I would hate to run over your wagon and ruin it. You should always put your toys away, so they stay nice."

"Yes, ma'am." Oh, for goodness' sake. This sudden arrival of good manners irritated her for reasons she couldn't pinpoint.

"Get along, then. Take your wagon home."

George shuffled to the wagon and picked up the handle. He looked back at Minerva.

"Are you practicing your piano?" she asked. "Every day for thirty minutes?"

George nodded his head vigorously. "And I'm telling the truth."

"Good. All right, then. Get along."

As she watched George walk the wagon down the street, a blend of melancholy and aggravation washed over her. The mixture of emotions tweaked her nose. *Am I going to cry? For pity's sake. This is ridiculous. Why am I so prone to tears these days?*

She pulled Spencer into the carport and turned off the ignition. For a while she sat there, her hands in her lap.

15

Thanksgiving loomed. That was the only way to put it. Nella and Buster would insist she join them. They would have their three children, seven grandchildren, Nella's younger brother and sister-in-law, whose children may or may not be there, and Buster's mother. Minerva would have no good reason to say no. She couldn't say, "I don't want to," though she didn't want to.

She would offer to bring a dish. Pumpkin pie? Sweet potatoes? "No. No," Nella would say. "You know how much I enjoy cooking Thanksgiving dinner. You just bring yourself." But Minerva would not be able to bear arriving empty-handed, so she would make a batch of her Forgotten Cookies and a new Jell-O recipe she had seen in *Good Housekeeping* involving lime Jell-O and cottage cheese. Sounded delicious.

Holidays were upsetting because of what others projected on to her. She figured they assumed she hovered between sad and lonely like a moth trying to get out of a closed window. Why couldn't someone who was alone be content? Why did everyone suppose she was unhappy? She was happy being alone. She was fine. She could pick the lettuce out of her teeth without having to excuse herself. She could pass gas in the bed without having to apologize. She could burp after a meal and not be embarrassed. All of these were positives.

Besides, she was not alone. She knew Margaretha and Della and Emma, among others.

She wondered what Brother Larson and Miss Boswell would think if they knew how she spent her time. Nella had confirmed the scuttlebutt that they were indeed a couple. Minerva realized that he seemed unusually perky these days. Whistling when he came into the sanctuary the last time she practiced. Whistling in the sanctuary! And Miss Boswell—was she a shade brighter than normal?

"It's obscene," Minerva said to the empty living room. "Two old fogies gallivanting around. I should think a minister would have more sense than to get involved with a woman—a Presbyterian at that."

The thought of the two of them sitting at the Columbia Theater watching Spencer Tracy together disturbed her. Did they hold hands in public? In private? Had he tried to kiss her? Oh, my stars.

Why did she care? She didn't.

Minerva's thoughts turned back to George. She wondered what kind of life he was having without a mama. She shook her head as if to shake the sad thought away and stood, stretching her back. From her dining-room window, she could see the light glowing from Nella's kitchen window.

Walk in the light so shalt thou know
That fellowship of love
His Spirit only can bestow
Who reigns in light above.

The hymn they sang last Sunday trickled through her mind. Brother Larson seemed to be choosing the more obscure ones lately. Maybe Harriett Boswell had lent him a Presbyterian hymnal.

Get a grip on your thoughts, Minerva Place. Forevermore. Minerva could hear her mother's voice reprimand her.

Minerva straightened files as she sat at the dining-room table preparing to write. Every so often she "spring cleaned" her research. She picked up her notes and tapped the loose pages on the table. After she put the papers away in their proper folders, she rubbed her hand over the closed file. The manilla paper was as smooth as a child's cheek.

She opened a folder labeled "Barkley, Alben" and skimmed a few pages. She hadn't done any writing about the Barkley family, but after her fall at the cemetery put her face to face, so to speak, with Eliza Barkley, she had been thinking about this illustrious Paducah family. Goodness, they were related to the vice president of the United States. Such pedigree could not be overlooked. She was trailing her finger down her list of possible Barkley candidates when the telephone rang.

"Hello."

"May I speak with Mrs. Place?"

"Yes. This is she." The voice was familiar. She was always a little suspicious when a man called her.

"Mrs. Place, this is Robert McAlpin." Why on earth was he calling? Maybe George wants to quit lessons. Wouldn't that be something? A couple weeks in and he was ready to give up. Was she happy about this or aggravated? Mr. McAlpin should insist the boy finish what he started, no doubt. A youngster should not be allowed to quit at the first sign of difficulty. He must learn discipline and perseverance. "Mrs. Place, I was wondering if George and I could extend you an invitation."

"What?" Oh dear, Minerva did not intend to speak aloud. "Excuse me, Mr. McAlpin. I do not wish to appear rude."

"Oh no. You don't appear rude at all. I can understand your surprise." He laughed. Was he laughing at her? "George and I want to invite you to Thanksgiving dinner. That is, if you do not have prior plans."

"Thanksgiving." Another word slipped out with unintended force. "Mr. McAlpin, you are inviting me to Thanksgiving dinner?" Yes, Minerva, that was what the man said. Get hold of yourself.

"Yes. Well, you see, since we are so new to Paducah and since George and I don't have any relatives here, I thought it might be nice to sort of…well…kind of…well, please take this in the way I intend it… It might be nice to adopt a relative. George could use a grandmother and you live alone, and I do not want to presume anything, and you probably have plans and you may not want to, but I thought—"

"How kind of you, Mr. McAlpin." What was she saying? Minerva could not believe these words were issuing from her mouth. "I would enjoy dinner with you two." She didn't particularly like boys, certainly not men, and she was agreeing to spend Thanksgiving with a boy and a man. What had gotten into her?

"Oh, well, wonderful. George will be so happy. I'm delighted. Good. Okay, then, we will plan on an early afternoon meal if that's okay with you."

"Early afternoon will be fine, Mr. McAlpin. And what can I bring?"

"Could you bring a pumpkin pie? I'm not sure I can bake a pie, but I can put together a turkey and all the vegetables."

Quite sensible, Minerva thought, thankful she didn't have to do the back-and-forth exchange. A pumpkin pie was such a relief.

"I will be glad to bring a pumpkin pie."

"Let's say four o'clock."

Minerva held the phone in the middle of her chest after the conversation ended and tried to interpret her feelings. Her eyes scanned the kitchen as if she would find a clue on the stove or the countertops.

Wonk-Wonk-Wonk. The noise indicating the phone was off the hook screeched and she placed the earpiece back on the receiver.

What on earth have I done?

A queasy rolling danced in her gut. She kept her hand on the phone, standing still, stunned, as if avoiding a hunter's keen eye. A shaky breath in and out, in and out, in and held. A burp. Minerva returned to the dining-room table and sat in her writing chair. She studied her trimmed fingernails and well-groomed cuticles. She twisted her gold wedding band. She placed her hands palms down on the tablecloth. She flicked her tongue against the back of her teeth making a tsk-tsk-tsking sound.

"I'll call him back," she blurted to the list of Barkleys who were waiting for her pen to revive them. "Yes. I'll say I'd forgotten Nella had already asked me." But that would be a lie. She could not outright lie. "All right. I'll wait a couple of days and figure something else out." *Oh dear. Oh my. Oh dear. This was awful. Distract. I must distract myself.*

৵

So that was how Minerva ended up downtown at Kresge's on a Saturday afternoon, all in all a most unusual place to find herself on a weekend. She could count on her toes the number of times she had visited downtown on a weekend as an adult. If she simply could not avoid visiting Bright's or Driver's or Paducah Dry Goods or J.C. Penney's, she preferred to go during the week, when the crowd was slim. Saturdays buzzed like a beehive. Adults, teenagers, and children congested the stores. Couples out for a movie matinee lingered and wandered around a department store. Teenaged girls, arms interlocked, giggled and tested perfume samples. Boys pestered their mothers to stop by Kresge's toy department so they could spend their allowance on airplane models or plastic army men.

Cardboard cutouts of pumpkins and turkeys decorated store windows, which did not help distract Minerva from her current dilemma one bit. She pressed on, though, past the display of Halloween candy marked 50 percent off, past the colorful bins of toys marked a dime each, and into the ladies' section. Here she fingered balls of yarn and picked up a shot glass with the word "Kentucky" and outlines of racehorses etched on it.

She opened the lid of a small pink music box and listened to the dainty, tinny tune of—what else? Für Elise—while a miniature ballerina twirled. She slapped the lid shut the minute she recognized the tune, then looked around to make sure no one had noticed her slamming an innocent music box with such force.

She rummaged through kitchen tools until she came upon a turkey baster that, of course, reminded her of Thanksgiving. So she moved on. Fuzzy house shoes, a rack of housecoats, a bin of brassieres swimming together, a shelf of decorative items for the home—a ceramic unicorn figurine, a Dutch boy and girl wearing wooden clogs that were a set of salt-and-pepper shakers, an orange glass ashtray, glass trying to pass as crystal candle holders. Who buys these things?

A woman with either a fresh perm or unnaturally tight, curly hair stood beside Minerva. Where had she come from? "Isn't this precious?" The woman must have been asking Minerva because no one else was nearby.

Minerva cleared her throat. "Excuse me?"

"This." The woman held a paperweight—or was it a snow globe?—and smiled with the gentleness of a magazine advertisement mother.

"Ah," Minerva tilted her head back like she was going to present her throat to the doctor. "Yes." She lied now with no compunction.

"Daddy used to bring these home to us from wherever he traveled." The woman, who was older than Minerva, took her glasses off and dabbed at her eyes with a handkerchief. Minerva noticed it was embroidered with tiny blue flowers.

"Oh." She kept her response short to discourage further talk. Minerva often wondered why people didn't pick up on the fact that she was not interested in random conversations, idle chitchat. What is there to say about a snow globe?

The woman sighed so big her ample chest heaved up as if it was inflating. "Yes, Daddy traveled all over for his job. All over the tri-state area, that is. He was a salesman."

Minerva batted her eyes as if she could blink her away. How old was this woman? Sixty-five? Older? And she still calls her father Daddy? Minerva had never used that word. *Father* was how she had addressed him. She couldn't imagine her father bringing a trinket of such little value home. He wasn't that kind of father. He placed a great deal of value on worth. A snow globe would not rank as worthy.

"I'll buy this for old times' sake." She held it up to the light and shook it. A flurry of glittery white swirled.

Minerva smiled at her, not knowing what to say. The woman patted her on her forearm as she passed. Why would you reach out and touch a perfect stranger? Shopping was proving to be anxiety inducing rather than distracting. She remembered why she didn't often go. The activity's uselessness annoyed her.

There was only one option.

16

Minerva left Kresge's and headed to Oak Grove. Today's warm November sun chased away the week's gray, so Minerva took off her scarf and gloves and stuffed them into the pocket of her unbuttoned coat. Her shoulders dropped from their scrunch and she rolled her head round and round, listening to the soft crackles and pops in her neck. The peace and stillness soothed her. She strolled along Tranquility, taking in the markers as she went.

Hello there, Drury Dunaway, born September 30, 1789; died September 10, 1878. And good day to you, William H. Gourieux, born October 17, 1806, and died April 8, 1872, and wife Sarah, who was born November 16, 1801 (hmm, five years older than her husband) and died June 25, 1872 (so they died the same year—maybe he was brokenhearted). Here's Hezekiah Stout, born November 15, 1817, died November 17, 1875 (almost fifty-eight years old to the day). Oh, here's a good name—Albert Zertha Hamock—you don't hear of anyone named Zertha anymore. He was born August 26, 1891, and died December 25, 1949 (What a shame to die on Christmas Day. I could have known him.)

Minerva returned to the Barkley plots, the scene of her fall, down Ivy Street in the Old Section. Here was John Wilson Barkley and Electra Eliza Barkley, the parents of Alben Barkley. And here was Harry Smith Barkley. Was he one of Alben's brothers? She calculated that Harry was twenty-four when he died. Why so young? What happened to him?

This bore research, but without a pad she would have to burn his name into her brain. Harry Barkley. Harry Barkley. Harry Barkley. She repeated each syllable with every step she took.

"Hello, Mrs. Place. What a surprise, and how apropos."

Minerva had become so engrossed in finding new names, she'd let her guard down and now look what had happened. She was cornered, and by Harriett Boswell at that.

"Miss Boswell." Minerva nodded, biting her tongue to keep from saying, "Apropos? Couldn't you simply say appropriate?"

"You piqued my curiosity about the Revolutionary War hero you were researching, Major Charles Ewell. I wanted to see his marker for myself. So, I came on my first day off." She wore a smart cotillion blue poodle coat over navy, red, and yellow plaid slacks. Minerva noted that she'd never seen her wear anything but a dress or skirt. She gave her credit with the low-heeled Cuban pumps she wore. Much more sensible than those heels she wore at the library. Of course, these low heels did emphasize her size, which always put Minerva off. Minerva would have given her eye teeth to be smaller. On second thought, maybe she'd just give one tooth. Two seemed extreme.

"Quite intriguing," Miss Boswell continued. "I was considering the fact that it is the oldest gravestone in the cemetery, making it a true historic relic vulnerable to climatic elements. It's a shame it can't be sheltered in a museum."

Minerva nodded again. What do you say to that?

"Yes," Miss Boswell said. "What am I saying? I'm sure you've given that some thought. While I'm here and have the pleasure of your expertise, could you direct me toward other interesting historic markers?"

Minerva blinked rapidly. "I suppose you're familiar with the Barkley plots?" she managed to say.

"I knew several family members were interred here, but I have no idea where. If I'm not inconveniencing you, could you show me?"

Minerva saw no way out. "Of course. They're right here." She gestured toward a row of headstones.

"Is this the vice president's brother?" Miss Boswell was standing at the end of Harry's grave.

"I was going to research that. I'm assuming it is."

"I know Bernice, the veep's sister." Miss Boswell raised her arched eyebrows. "Innuendos fluttered about that indicated a heartbreaking tale regarding one of her brothers, but I never knew the entire account. I'd be interested to see what you uncover."

Minerva tried not to grind her teeth. "I may or may not pursue the research." She'd rather not be drawn into any more conversations about her cemetery work. She tried to sound nonchalant to throw Miss Boswell off the scent.

The women looked at the gravesite rather than each other. The stillness felt oppressive now. Minerva would have given anything for a squirrel to scamper by or a bird to settle on a branch—anything to interrupt this silence. Funny how much she valued the silence until another person was with her. Then it became distracting, uncomfortable.

Minerva couldn't stand it another second. "It's been nice seeing you, Miss Boswell. I'll be on my way now."

Harriett Boswell, who hadn't seemed the least bit discomfited by the lack of conversation, looked up with surprise on her face at Minerva's words. "Oh," she said. "My mind drifted off, Mrs. Place. Forgive me. I was thinking about—never mind."

Minerva, for the first time, felt the briefest of kinship with this little librarian. Minerva understood what it was to get lost in your thoughts when standing at a graveside. Yes, she did.

"Before you go, will you point me toward some other interesting markers? If you don't mind. While I'm here, I might as well look."

Minerva debated whether it would be rude to insist she had to go. Especially since she didn't have to go. Her conscience won. "Major Ewell's marker is on Peace Avenue. You mentioned wanting to see that."

Miss Boswell perked right up. "Yes! I do. Any others of particular interest?"

Minerva scratched her head, then caught herself. She didn't want Miss Boswell to notice her scalp flaking. "Have you heard of Reverend Pappy Dupee?"

"No. Pappy is an unusual name."

Miss Boswell adjusted her hat. She was a stylish one, Minerva observed, not for the first time. "His given name was George Washington Dupee, but everyone called him Pappy. He was a slave who became a preacher. He was the pastor of the Washington Street Baptist Church in the 1860s." Minerva was on a roll. "He launched The *Baptist Herald*, which we now call *The American Baptist*. You may not be familiar with that since you're a Presbyterian." She hoped that comment didn't sound judgmental. Harriet Boswell could not help it that she was Presbyterian. She'd grown up that way. Maybe Brother Larson could help her with that. "He also became the Grand Senior Warden and Grand Master of the Kentucky Grand Lodge of Masons, which was a tremendous honor."

Minerva felt a faint rush in spilling all these facts to someone. Nella was the only person who knew a whiff of what Minerva had discovered.

"Mrs. Place, you know so much. What do you do with all the valuable research you unearth?" She twittered a laugh. "No pun intended."

Minerva didn't understand what pun could have been intended and she paused a beat before realizing she didn't want to answer. "I..." she began. How could she avoid telling Miss Boswell that she wrote about them? Did it matter that she knew? Could that bring Minerva trouble? Would Miss Boswell ask to read something she'd written? And, if she did, how would Minerva get out of letting her? The thoughts tumbled over themselves like a circus clown's juggling act.

"I hope you keep fastidious records," Miss Boswell continued, oblivious to Minerva's unease. "You know, we would love to run a column about your findings in our monthly newsletter at the library. Would you consider writing about the people you've researched?" Miss Boswell couldn't know how fast the alarm signals in Minerva's brain were being pumped to every fiber of her body.

"I..." Minerva began again.

"Oh, I don't mean to put you on the spot. You might think about that, though. I'm sure our readers would eat it up with a spoon. Now, where is Reverend Dupee located?"

17

She sat straight in the wooden dining chair today as if playing the organ. The Barkleys were legendary in Paducah what with Alben being the veep, a nickname that people around town liked to volley about. Harriett Boswell calling him the veep. Like she knew him so well.

She didn't want to think about Harriett Boswell, though, neither the fact that she was dating (dating at her age!) Brother Larson or the proposal she'd made to Minerva at the cemetery. At least Minerva hadn't given away the fact that she'd already written dozens of histories. No, she banished Harriett Boswell thoughts.

Back to the Barkleys. Everybody seemed to be able to trace a personal connection to the Barkleys since he was now somebody important. Miss Boswell acted like since she knew his sister, she was practically a White House adviser. Oh, that woman. She would not be sharing one whit of information about any of the Barkleys with her—fact or fiction.

She skimmed her notes. The radiators hissed. A buzzing from the refrigerator. A creak in the foundation. Minerva waited, and then it came—John Barkley, a verbose, barrel-chested baritone.

John Wilson Barkley, born March 25, 1854; died July 11, 1932; Old Section 36, Lot 525

Sometimes as I walked behind the plow, I daydreamed about my ancestors. An ancient aunt of mine once told me we could trace our roots back to Roger de Berchelai, a follower of William the Conqueror. She wove tales of a feudal baron, a family castle in Gloucestershire, battles, and royal descendants. That formidable spirit carried through our line right to my son Alben.

One year an uncharacteristic snow hit before my annual trip to town to purchase the children's boots. Alben had outgrown his boots, but he wasn't about to be deterred. He walked to school barefoot. He hopped like a blue jay following a plow in the tracks of the older boys ahead of him. That's how determined he was to get to his classroom to learn.

Minerva paused and considered this bit of information she'd gleaned from a biography about Alben. She squinted. Walking barefoot in the snow? She had a hard time believing this was anything but hyperbole. Surely the biographer exaggerated to make a point about how tough Alben was, and his father perpetuated the myth. The boy must have at least had a pair of shoes he could have worn.

She concentrated on the notes again and heard John Barkley's voice explain.

Alben had set his mind to get an education. Whatever it took. Whatever hardship he encountered, he faced with the same conquering determination his ancestors had.

He worked as a janitor to put himself through Marvin College, located in Clinton. Earlier he learned the three Rs in country schools where his teachers predicted he might become president of the United States. Of course, Alben served the public in a long career, beginning with the post of prosecuting attorney of McCracken County, then county judge, congressman, senator, and as you well know, vice president.

Minerva stopped again. Annoyance scratched with her pen.

Enough was enough. She wanted to know about John, not Alben. Everyone already knew about Alben.

"We all know he became vice president," Minerva said to the air of the room. "Yes, that's quite an achievement for a boy from Paducah. A farm boy who walked barefoot in the snow to school. I'm not sure I believe that part anyway."

When she looked back up, a man stood at the end of the

table. He wore an expression of hurt surprise. "Where did you come from?" Minerva stared at John Wilson Barkley, who was shorter than she expected, and with a solid paunch protruding over his belt. His skin revealed years of being in the fields, bringing in his crops. He still had a full head of silver hair and a mustache that gave him an old-fashioned air. All in all, though, Minerva saw that strength and vigor still dominated this man. Her annoyance evaporated. For the first time since characters had begun showing themselves to her, she wasn't alarmed. Mr. Barkley had a soothing presence, in fact. She thought she smelled cloves, which reminded her of the holidays and her uncle James who always chewed clove gum. She had loved Uncle James.

"Mrs. Place, you are the author," John Barkley interrupted her reminiscing. "I am simply recounting the facts."

"Yes, I understand, but I'm trying to tell *your* story. What about you, John Wilson Barkley? Didn't *you* do anything?"

"In many ways Alben's story was my story."

"I understand," she said, using her patient piano-teacher voice. "But tell me a little more about yourself. Just you."

He cleared his throat and shifted on his feet as if he were about to orate with formality.

"I went to Washington soon after Alben was elected to Congress and served as a doorkeeper in the House of Representatives. This job was the adventure of my life."

Minerva hoped her face didn't give her away. Doorkeeper? An adventure? "Go ahead," she urged, but he swerved off-topic.

"I had hoped Alben would enter the ministry. I had always told Electra that boy had something special. I thought the Lord had anointed him to be a preacher because he had a golden tongue. Have you ever heard him speak?"

"No, I can't say that I have."

"If he's ever in Paducah and gives a speech, you should go hear him. I'm not just saying this because I'm his father. Alben is gifted. Anyway, though he didn't become a preacher, I was proud of his service in Congress."

"Tell me why being a doorkeeper was an adventure."

"I got a kick out of tapping complete strangers on the shoulder, pointing to Alben and saying, 'That's my son.'" John chuckled. Minerva still didn't understand the adventure part, but he did and sometimes it was enough—more than enough—for a person to understand himself.

Her new friend had moved to the wall where the Webster family photographs were hung. He pecked on the glass of one. "Is this your mother? You look like her."

Minerva got out of her chair and joined him by the gallery of photos. "Yes, that's my mother." She'd never considered that she looked like her mother. She frowned and studied the old picture. She *did* look like her mother, she realized. Same downturned mouth. Same angled jaw. Same intense expression in her eyes.

"And I guess that's your father." He pecked on another photograph. "Did you have any brothers or sisters? Oh, is this your sister? I see a resemblance."

"Just one sister." Minerva did not see any resemblance to Geneva, but she thought it would be rude to correct Mr. Barkley. She'd already insulted him about his bloviation regarding Alben.

"Electra and I had eight children." He smiled so big Minerva noticed his fine set of teeth under his bushy mustache.

"I know. Could you tell me what happened to Harry?"

John stopped looking at the photographs, dropped his smile and grew still and silent for a moment. Though his back was to her now, she could feel his tension. When he continued he simply said, "Harry sang for the motion pictures."

"What do you mean? He was in the movies?"

"No, not actually in the movies. In those days Hollywood sent musical scores to accompany the silent films. Theater managers then hired musicians to sing with the picture show." He faced her again and smiled, but he didn't flash his teeth and she saw a dullness to his eyes that wasn't there previously. "Harry had quite a voice, that boy."

"I seem to remember something about you having an affinity for the movies."

The sparkle returned to his eyes in an instant. "Is that right?"

"Yes. Something about you…" Minerva looked at her notes. "Developing a taste for the motion pictures when you went to Washington, especially for westerns."

He cleared his throat again and offered a more sincere grin, one with a trace of the boy he must have been. "I remained a faithful churchgoer but I did acquire one worldly vice in Washington."

"A passion for the movies?"

"Yes, I'm afraid it's true. One of my favorite stars was William S. Hart. One time I got a little overzealous. When the bad guys closed in on him, the ushers had to restrain me because I started shouting, 'Shoot 'em! Shoot 'em!'"

John and Minerva both laughed.

"So, the staunch, church-going Presbyterian hollered at the movies? That would be something like this Baptist organist throwing popcorn at the bad guys when they came on the screen."

"People can surprise you," he said.

Minerva started to reply, but she realized he was gone. Just like that.

"Where did you go?" Minerva cried. She was enjoying John Barkley's company and she had more questions, especially about Harry. The room vibrated with his absence, as though air particles were slamming back into each other. "Oh, Mr. Barkley, please return. I have more I'd like to discuss." She expected a response, a clap of thunder, sparks, something.

Mr. Barkley's last words didn't thunder, but as she waited, the four words did rattle.

"People can surprise you."

"That is the truth," Minerva said aloud for no one's benefit but her own. "Look at John Barkley, for example."

She had expected a serious fellow, a bit full of himself, and he had turned out to be humorous, quite enjoyable company.

But some people were never going to surprise you. Take

Brother Larson. He was always going to strut and skitter and be a nervous Nellie. And Miss Boswell. A know-it-all. Who would ever put the two of them together? She supposed Miss Boswell might be able to stabilize Brother Larson, and he could infuse her with a little life. Not that Minerva was so animated, but for heaven's sake, Miss Boswell crept around the library on cat's paws.

Minerva shrugged. Why was she thinking about that pair again? She tapped the notes about John on the table to straighten them and looked at the folder on Harry, John's other son.

"I wish you'd said more about Harry, John."

She leaned back in her chair and flicked her pen. She suspected John had deflected conversation about Harry because the younger son had been the black sheep of the family. She'd found a clipping about Harry's death and she was almost certain something fishy had transpired. She closed her eyes and thought until Harry's voice began.

Harry Smith Barkley, born October 15, 1885; died August 22, 1910; Old Section 36, Lot 525

I might as well get this load off my chest. Alben did everything right, and I did everything wrong. There. That about summed our lives up. Who can compete with a big brother who was a successful lawyer and ends up being elected county judge—a cushy job—all by age thirty-two?

Minerva fingered the laminated article she had found in the library files. This copy of the actual clipping was filed in the special collections section under "Barkley Family." *The News-Democrat* reported Harry's death on the front page of the August 23, 1910 edition.

HARRY BARKLEY FALLING UNDER WHEELS OF CAIRO LOCAL FREIGHT, WAS KILLED

Brother of County Judge Alben Barkley dies Horrible Death. Body Severed And Mutilated—Fell Back Across Rail and Wheels Pass Over His Abdomen

Falling between the cars of an Illinois Central
Freight train, on which he was riding to Cairo, Illinois, Harry Barkley, twenty-six years old, son of
J.W. Barkley, 512 North Fifth Street, and brother
of County Judge Alben Barkley was killed Monday evening about five fifteen o'clock near Barlow,
Kentucky.

About a mile east of Barlow, toward LaCenter,
Mr. Barkley lost his balance and fell between the
caboose and the last car of the train. The wheels
of the caboose passed over his body, cutting him in
two and bruising him about the face so that he was
hardly recognizable.

Mr. Barkley had come home Monday morning
from Cairo, where he had been for the past few
days. Monday afternoon his brother, John Barkley,
saw him pass Ninth and Trimble streets on freight
train No. 844, which leaves Paducah from Cairo,
Ill., at 4 o'clock. When he reached home, he told
his parents that he had seen his brother and a few
hours later the report came that he had been killed.

He was a potter by trade. He was perhaps better
known to Paducah people as one of the best sing-
ers in this city. His voice was one of unusual quality
and he had appeared many times before Paducah
audiences, where his merits were highly appreciated. For the past few weeks, he had been singing at
moving picture shows in Mayfield, Kentucky.

His was a personality that attracted friends and
he was well liked because of his whole-hearted
disposition and his rare good humor.

Minerva chewed her pen, then flicked it between her index
and middle fingers. She tapped it on the table. Frowned. Chewed
the inside of her cheek. Leaned back in her chair. Tapped the
table again. All buying time before she wrote again.

I went drinking with some fellas after I finished singing

that night. I recall the picture shows were *The Violin Maker of Cremona*, *Her First Biscuits*, and *The Adventures of Dollie*. But what do these details matter? I was whacked. The boys were jazzed about going to a new joint in Cairo, so I went along. I didn't want to risk losing my reputation as a live-wire—the one thing at which I excelled.

I don't remember much from our escapades in Cairo, but the next day I woke up around noon with the worst hangover in the history of alcohol abuse. I thought my eyeballs were going to work their way out of my skull. My tongue was twice its normal size and, I'll swear, moss was growing on it. I didn't look any better than I felt. Dark circles under bloodshot eyes. Ashen skin. Pale lips. A scraggly outgrowth of beard. I splashed cold water on my face and left the house before anyone saw me.

The hair of the dog to cure, I figured, so I eased over to Joe's place by the tracks, away from where I might run into anyone I knew.

Minerva stuck the pen back in her mouth. My goodness, every family has skeletons in the closet, she thought, again forgetting that her truth might not always have been *the* truth.

"You know, Harry, your father should have appreciated your talent and not tried to have squashed you into a mold of Alben. It's ironic your father got in trouble at the movies when he didn't want you to work there."

Minerva wished Harry would appear, but no one came. She had run across a photo of Harry and Alben when they were children. Both boys were handsome, but she could see a rakish air about Harry. He seemed to vibrate with mischief.

"No one should ever have to fit into someone else's mold. Each of us should get to follow our own heart, develop our own talents, pursue our own dreams. Why, I was nothing like Geneva, and yet I wore myself out trying to be a carbon copy of her."

Minerva, startled by this jerk in her thoughts, sat up like a dog on point. How had she veered from Harry Barkley's relationship with Alben to her relationship with Geneva? She was nothing like Harry, and Geneva was no Alben. Still, in the eyes of her parents Geneva had managed to succeed while Minerva had come up short. Even now Geneva was practically living in a foreign country, caught up in a glamorous life. Her parents were probably watching from Heaven, still thrilled with Geneva and disappointed in her.

"Your sister's quite a looker," Manny had said the first time he met her sister. Geneva; her husband, Stanley; and their children, Drake Ross, Rebecca—Becky—and baby Ollie Jane, were in Paducah for a reception after Manny and Minerva were married in a quiet ceremony at the church. Minerva didn't want a big wedding, didn't want the fuss, didn't want her father to have to shoulder the expense. Didn't want the attention. But she did let her mother's friends give a reception for them a few weeks later when Geneva could come home.

"Yes, everyone's always said so."

"You two don't look a thing alike." Manny patted her on the back and, while Minerva knew he wasn't being mean—he had just married her, after all—she couldn't help but arch away from him.

"I think I'll get some more punch."

"Me too," Manny said.

Stanley, who was wearing shiny black cowboy boots that sported silver toe caps and intricate stitching, was talking business with Howard Sherman over the punch bowl.

"So, you got in on the early years of the oil boom?" Howard was saying. Geneva and Stanley lived in Humble, Texas, home of Humble Oil and Refining. Stanley had become a multi-millionaire through his association with Humble, an ironic name, Minerva thought, considering her sister and brother-in-law were anything but. They had the audacity to be smug about surviving the Depression with barely a scratch.

Minerva's line of thinking carried significant guilt with it since she recognized that her dismay over her sister's family skating through the Depression was uncharitable, petty, jealousy-laden, and, yes, mean. But still. Life always had been out of balance for the two sisters. Unfair.

Geneva was golden. That's why she'd monopolized Mother and Father's adoration. The angels had visited her with an outgoing personality. A rich husband had arrived to whisk her away to the mythical land of Texas, where the skies were bigger than anywhere else and where black gold sprang from dirt. Perfect wide-eyed children appeared on cue. Forevermore, Geneva even had small feet.

After Geneva married and moved away, Minerva thought she would finally have her parents' attention. But not much changed. Earl and Lucille Webster talked about Geneva and her husband daily. "Remember how Geneva loved corn pudding?" "Geneva always looked so good in green." "Geneva was so thoughtful."

Geneva is gone! Minerva wanted to say. *I'm still here. I'm here. Why can't you see me?*

Minerva was there right to the end, in fact. A piece of Minerva thought they had died because of her. Why had she relied on a simple country doctor?

If she had only gotten them to a doctor in the city, they might have lived. If only she'd realized how serious their condition was. If only she had done better. If only. If only. If only.

"Oh, Harry," she said to the piece of paper in front of her. "Why did you have to remind me of what it was like?"

Between John's obvious favoritism of Alben and Minerva imagining Harry's tragic end, she had stirred up a viper's nest in her emotions. She shuffled the papers into a neat stack and left the table. If only she had someone.

18

Minerva figured Robert got the idea to ask her to Thanksgiving dinner from the Ann Landers column. When she read the advice column, which hit awfully close to home, embarrassment flooded her.

Dear Ann Landers,
I dread the holidays every year. I cannot tell you how lonely these times are for me. I know I should be happy to see families together at church and in stores, but it makes me sad. I end up crying at home, alone, every holiday. To the world I look fine. I put on a big smile and tell everyone I am A-Okay. If someone invites me to join their family for dinner, I don't go because I do not want to intrude on their family time. I have no living family anymore.

Signed,
Lonely in New Albany

Dear Lonely in New Albany,
You are not the only one who is alone on the holidays. Many people do not have family and make alternative plans to enjoy Thanksgiving, Hanukkah, and Christmas. Find a way to give to others. Locate a church, synagogue, or group that sponsors a meal for needy in your community and volunteer to help serve. This will do more for your spirits than sitting at home alone feeling sorry for yourself. Also, if a friend asks you to come over, do not assume you would be intruding. She would not ask if she did not want you to be a part of her plans. In addition to being lonely, I think you have issues with how you view yourself. I predict if you address your insecurities, you'll see your view of the world change.

Ann Landers

Minerva usually found something to chuckle about in the Ann Landers column. That lady was a straight shooter. Her advice like "stop feeling sorry for yourself and go help someone who is hungry" was practical. Minerva approved of such advice. But the idea of her being the one in need of help both embarrassed and irritated her. Did Mr. McAlpin think she "absolutely dreads the holidays every year?"

"Terrific," she said aloud to the fruit bowl containing a bruised apple and an almost too ripe banana. "He feels sorry for me." Because, she figured, that was the sort of person Robert McAlpin was. He's just that type. She could tell he was soft-hearted. "Well, I don't need his sympathy. I'll go because I've said I'll go and I'm a woman of my word. But once he knows me, he'll see I don't need anyone's sympathy."

Besides, she couldn't think of a reason not to go, and she couldn't bring herself to outright lie—this time.

❧

Early Thanksgiving morning Minerva woke up shivering despite the sheet, blanket, and quilt covering her. She could see her breath, which couldn't be good. She slid the covers down as if she were removing a Band-Aid from a sore, slipped into her house shoes and robe as fast as a fireman, and put her hand on the radiator. Ice cold. Wonderful. Just wonderful. Happy Thanksgiving.

She couldn't do one thing about the problem, either. Nobody worked on the holiday. She knew nothing about radiators except they were powered by the boiler and the boiler was in the basement. The basement, a place she preferred to avoid. Dark. Cobwebby. Musty.

Buck up, Minerva.

The wooden slat stairs to the basement yawned before her, narrow and steep, so she stepped gingerly, holding the railing with one hand and her robe with the other. My goodness, it was cold. The chain from a single light bulb swung behind her, casting a hypnotic shadow on the steps.

For pity's sake. The basement's not haunted. Besides, if it is, you're plenty used to people who aren't real being around. She attempted to tease herself, but she didn't think she was funny.

The boiler, original to the house, which was built in 1932, sat like a lump of dumbness. Silent and bored. Uninterested in fulfilling its purpose.

She considered kicking it, but the metal hulk looked substantial and insolent, so she rapped on the drum as if a keeper might open a secret door and greet her. She stopped knocking and shoved her curled-up fist into the pocket of her robe. The boiler was clearly mocking her. She squinted and frowned. The boiler is not mocking you, she told herself. Don't be ridiculous. Minerva positioned herself so she could see behind the equipment, but this angle supplied no further clues. She didn't know what she was looking for anyway.

"I'll have to get along until tomorrow." She spoke with as much confidence as she could muster into the dimness. "Pioneer women faced rougher conditions."

Minerva relied on pioneers to get her through many difficulties. When she was ill, she reminded herself she owned medicine the pioneers did not have. When she was tired, she chastised herself with the knowledge that a pioneer worked ten times as hard. When she slept poorly, she imagined a pioneer woman sleeping outside with a stone for a pillow. And so on.

Today she took a stab at optimism—a trait that grated on her nerves if it showed up too frequently in others—and addressed the refrigerator, stove, and percolator waiting to be plugged in: "At least I won't get hot baking today." And after eating her usual breakfast of egg, toast, and coffee, this morning with gloves on, she dressed in layers, including a pair of slacks, which she rarely wore, not because she disapproved but because she couldn't find good fits for her large hips.

It never crossed Minerva's mind to ask Buster or Mr. Johnston, who probably knew a thing or two about radiators since he was the church janitor, or Robert McAlpin, an engineer, for help. But she did think, with a semblance of grief, that if Manny were still alive, he could fix it. He was good at fixing things.

Sometimes it got old being on your own, handling every single problem by yourself, making every decision with no one's input. On the other hand, she could do exactly as she pleased.

So she shut herself in the kitchen for the day to trap the heat, thanking God she had a gas stove. By lunchtime, not only had she baked a pie, she had cleaned out all the drawers (including the junk drawer containing stray batteries, ink pens, dull pencils, paper clips, safety pins, a screwdriver, a pair of dice—what was she doing with dice?—a handful of rubber bands, a bottle opener, and the phone book). Plus, she had replaced the aluminum foil lining under each burner and in the bottom of the oven.

Minerva considered making a list of all she'd accomplished so she could have the joy of checking things off but decided that was unnecessary. No, by golly, she would. And that was as satisfying as anything she had done all day.

❧

At four on the dot, Mrs. Place arrived at the McAlpins'.

"Oh, my stars." Minerva could not help herself. The kitchen. Was there one pot, one dish, one utensil not on the countertop? Was there one single spot on the table or the stove or the sink or the floor not covered with food? And yet Robert and George were smiling and accepted Mrs. Minerva Place's pumpkin pie without batting an eye.

"We are so happy you came today, Mrs. Place," Mr. McAlpin said. A stunned Minerva was grateful he chose to overlook the rude exclamation that leaped out of her mouth upon entering the kitchen.

"Yes. So kind of you to invite me." She moved with caution, afraid of causing an avalanche.

"George, show Mrs. Place what you made for her."

Oh, dear Lord, don't let it be food, Minerva thought. I can't imagine that child washing his hands before he does anything.

George bolted for the dining room and stood by a chair. A crooked grin played on his face, and he seemed to have gone shy.

"It's a place mat he made at school," Mr. McAlpin supplied. An oversized rectangle of orange construction paper was decorated with the outline of George's hand, which had been made to look like a turkey, complete with a red beard and yellow beak. A variety of feathers had been glued on the fingers for the fan of the turkey's tail. He had used a black crayon to draw Pilgrim hats in each of the four corners of the paper.

"It's almost too fancy to put a plate on, George. Thank you."

George smiled. "I got the best feathers. Everybody else mostly used the brown ones, but I took the colored ones."

"It's lovely."

"George, why don't you play the songs you've been practicing for Mrs. Place while I finish getting the food on the table? That is, if his playing wouldn't seem like work to you, Mrs. Place…" Robert raised his eyebrows up in question. Minerva was struck by how much George resembled him.

"I'd be delighted. Are you sure I can't help you though?"

"No, no. I've got everything under control."

Minerva doubted this.

Somehow dinner did find its way to the table. Though the turkey was dry, the dressing rubbery, the rolls on the verge of being burned, and the gravy nonexistent (imagine a Thanksgiving dinner with no gravy), Minerva judged she had eaten enough to convey gratitude. The pie was fine, Minerva analyzed, conceding that pumpkin was not her favorite. She detested the occasional grit you run into, so she really couldn't fairly evaluate.

"Mrs. Place, have you always lived in Paducah?"

Time for chitchat, Minerva realized. And, yes, a bit of chitchat did ensue. But the conversation dangerously careened when George interrupted.

"Mrs. Place talks to dead people, Dad."

Minerva sat straighter and became still, but Robert seemed unperturbed.

"What do you mean, son?"

"I mean she talks to dead people. I've seen her in the cemetery talking to the people who are buried under the tombstones.

Don't you, Mrs. Place? Do you have a lot of friends over there?"

Mr. McAlpin and George looked at her with pleasant, quizzical expressions. Minerva wanted to get up and leave. She settled for the tried-and-true tactic of asking a question in return.

"When in the world did you see me in the cemetery, George?"

"Oh, lots of times."

"George," Mr. McAlpin intervened, "you've only been to the cemetery once. When I took you to see what the place where your mother is buried looked like. We saw Mrs. Place then. Is that what you're talking about?"

"No I've seen Mrs. Place lots of times. She doesn't see me 'cause I'm practicing being a spy." Minerva's throat had produced a wad so thick she thought she might choke.

"Now, George, we've talked about you spying on people."

"I know, Dad, but this was important." George recently adopted the word *important* as one of his favorites, pronouncing each syllable distinctly. It was "im-por-tant" for his dad to get him more milk. It was "im-por-tant" for George to watch one more television show. It was "im-por-tant" to have his stuffed animals lined up correctly at night.

"Mrs. Place was probably visiting her parents in the cemetery," Mr. McAlpin suggested, nodding toward Minerva.

"Yes, you're right," Minerva agreed a half second too quickly. "My parents are buried in Oak Grove."

"But she goes to a bunch of different graves and she talks all the time and sometimes she writes on the gravestone and sometimes she brushes them with a toothbrush. Why do you do that, Mrs. Place?"

"George, you should listen to your father and not spy on people." Minerva's neck was starting to splotch now. She itched under her bra.

"I'm sorry, Mrs. Place." Robert reached for George as if a hug would end the conversation. "George, no more spying. Do you understand?" George looked at Mrs. Place with suspicion. Or was Minerva's imagination at work? "George?"

"Yes, sir."

Minerva and Robert smiled at each other. Minerva with a tight, closed-lipped smile. Her heart sped up. She felt damp under her arms.

"George, why don't you play the song you've been practicing for Mrs. Place?"

George's shoulders sagged. "Do I have to?"

Minerva, feeling generous, relieved that the conversation about her talking to dead people seemed to be over, said, "Mr. McAlpin, don't you think we should take Thanksgiving off?"

George jumped on this out and, just to be safe, ran to find something to do in his bedroom.

"Mr. McAlpin," she began, intent on ensuring the conversation remained far away from Oak Grove.

"Please call me Robert."

She paused but didn't reciprocate. He should continue to call her Mrs. Place. She was his elder, after all. "Robert, may I be frank with you?"

"Oh, please do."

"Why is George taking piano lessons? I'm not sure he wants to."

"Well, Mrs. Place, I guess it's because of me. The one thing I always wanted as a child that I wasn't able to have was training on a musical instrument." Robert pushed back from the table and crossed his foot over his leg. "I imagined that playing a horn or a saxophone or a guitar or the piano would bring such satisfaction and joy. Once I came to the States, I began collecting records featuring instrumentals—big band, classical, jazz, hymns—didn't matter. I loved all music."

"You weren't born in the States?"

"I was born here, but I spent my childhood in South America—Brazil."

Minerva thought, *Brazil, I declare*, but said nothing. She didn't want to be rude and ask a barrage of questions.

"Anyway, I was eager for George to become old enough to play the piano. I researched the subject and found that many experts consider the piano the perfect training ground for all musical study. So, I bought that piano." He gestured toward the upright on the opposite wall. "I just knew George would love it."

"Perhaps he will," Minerva said. "Later."

"Yes," Robert continued, "I hope hearing your skills on the organ at church and getting to work with a teacher like you, who is so knowledgeable, will encourage him. I'm just so grateful to you for taking him on."

Minerva smiled. This man so openly shared himself. She was surprised at how comfortable she felt.

"Let me pour you a fresh cup of coffee." He took her cup and went into the kitchen, so she had a chance to look around the room. No doubt about who lived here. The touch of a woman was conspicuously absent. No cross-stitched sayings framed and hanging on the walls. No floral pillows plumping the edges of the brown, nubby couch. Instead of crystal candlesticks on the end tables, there were a couple of books—*Mr. President* by William Hillman and *Kon Tiki* by Thor Heyerdahl—and an open box of crayons, missing a couple of colors. A *Life* magazine served as the coaster on the coffee table, which was free from any decorations except for a bowl of whole pecans that had a silver nutcracker poking out of it at a jaunty angle.

"Here you go, Mrs. Place." Robert handed Minerva the cup of coffee. "You drink it black, right?" She nodded. "Tell me about yourself. Have you always lived in Paducah? I find so many people I meet are native Paducahans."

"No. My family came here because of my father's job with the railroad. I was thirteen. Now I feel as though it's my hometown, though." She blew on her coffee and took a sip. "How do you like Paducah?" Minerva was proud at how she quickly turned the conversation back to him. But Robert was having none of it.

"The railroad? That's interesting. What did he do?"

"He was a vice president with the Burlington."

"I don't know anything about the railroad business," Robert said as George reentered, singing loudly.

"I've been working on the railroad," he sang with the musical acumen of a parakeet. Minerva flinched. "Was your daddy an engineer on a train? Did you ever ride on a train? Did you get to blow the whistle? I got to ride on a train once."

"George, use some manners." Robert laughed and turned to Minerva. "You're probably used to this since you teach piano, but George does seem to have more energy than most kids. Some days—"

George interrupted his father. "Mrs. Place, will you tell me a story about one of those people in the graveyard?"

That again? And now Robert joined in. Forevermore.

"George said you sometimes take a toothbrush and clean the stones. Are you involved in some sort of preservation work?"

They would not let this go.

"I suppose you could say that. I'm interested in who is buried there since it's an older cemetery. I enjoy researching their histories."

"Oh, that's fascinating, I'll bet."

"It is." Minerva stunned herself by talking about this. She had never talked to anyone but Nella and Harriett Boswell about this. But Mr. McAlpin—Robert—was so easy to talk to and seemed so genuinely interested. And she was full of turkey and dressing and pumpkin pie and was inexplicably relaxed.

"Tell us something you've learned." Robert leaned down and scratched George's back as he sat cross-legged on the floor and lined up plastic army men.

"Do you like stories about the Wild West?"

George sat up. "You mean like cowboys and Indians?"

"I don't know if the person I'm thinking about had encounters with Indians, but he did round up a gang of bad guys."

"Did he shoot 'em with guns?"

"I believe he did."

"Tell me!"

And Minerva thought back to the evening she had spent with Colonel Evitte Dumas Nix.

Col. Evitte Dumas Nix, born September 19, 1861; died

1946; Old Section 48, Lot 11, Myrtle Ave., behind Elk's Rest

I sat atop Lone, a sorrel skewbald that stood about fifteen and a half hands, had a remarkably calm temperament, and steady concentration, all of which were key characteristics to have in a horse that day. Those alongside us were snorting and stomping, some throwing their heads back with anticipation. The horses did likewise.

She looked at George's eyes, glowing with anticipation, and warmed to telling the story just the way it had been told to her.

"This is what Colonel Nix told me, George. These are his very words."

My instructions were simple. After the cannon fired, I was to pull my trigger. We lined up across the flat, dusty prairie, more than one hundred thousand eager citizens on foot, on horses, in wagons, on trains, on bicycles any way a man could travel. I don't suppose I'd ever seen that many people gathered in one place in my life.

The air crackled sharp and staccato with the sound of men's nerves keyed up and itching to explode. The noon sun managed to blister my leathery skin and streams of sweat rolled down my back in my body's futile attempt to cool itself. Lone skittered in a tight circle, her only nod to the excitement, the cannon blasted, and I fired my shotgun into the sky.

The Cherokee Strip Land Run commenced with deafening thunder. The vibration of hooves, of feet and wheels, shook the earth until I thought it would split open and swallow us all. The instant thrill of that moment was like nothing I had experienced before or since. I can liken it to what I imagine the Lord's return might be like.

It was the official opening of the Cherokee Outlet and it meant six and a half million acres of land was up for grabs, the largest land run in the history of the United States. September 16, 1893, saw me in as the first United

States marshal over a lawless Oklahoma Territory. I was thirty-two and the youngest man to ever be appointed to such a post.

George interrupted Minerva's story. "So, you knew this cowboy?" His face was as animated as a Saturday morning cartoon character. "Did you meet him sometime and he told you this story?"

"Yes. I…" Minerva frowned and thought what she could say. "It's hard to explain. In a way I met him. You see, George, sometimes when I write I think about the person I'm writing about so hard that he seems to appear to me in real life."

That seemed to satisfy him.

"Tell me more about Colonel Nix."

"Let's see," Minerva said. "I'll skip over the parts I don't think would interest you, about his grocery store business, and being a traveling salesman, and organizing an electric franchise."

"Did he shoot any bad guys?"

"He told me he hired Bill Tilghman, Heck Thomas, and Chris Madsen, who came to be known as the Three Guardsmen, and he supervised over one hundred fifty lawmen. During his three years as marshal, he arrested over fifty thousand and killed some forty-seven criminals."

"Any bad guys I would know?"

"I'm not sure," Minerva said, tickled that she had enraptured him. "Ever hear of Red Buck Waightman, 'Little' Dick West, or Bill Doolin?"

"No."

"Well, you would have known them in the 1890s. You know, I think Colonel Nix told me he grew up carrying a gun."

"Dad! I carry a gun!" Robert and Minerva smiled at each other. George ran to get his holster and set of shiny pistols.

"You have learned so many interesting things in your research, Mrs. Place."

"That I have."

"What do you do with your research?"

Oh dear, Minerva immediately thought. How did she not

see that coming? She sputtered a few "I's" and "um's" between deep swallows before she finally decided she'd just tell him. Why not? It wasn't as if she was ashamed. Nella knew, after all. It wasn't a secret—exactly.

"I write, I guess you could call them, reports."

"You mean like short biographies?"

"Yes, exactly like that. I will admit that since there is so little actual information I can find on each person—in obituaries or old newspaper articles, for example—I flesh things out with my own ideas."

"Your imagination! That's wonderful." Robert looked as though he'd just won a prize at the carnival. "Oh, Mrs. Place, you have to let me read these."

Minerva instantly went from feeling free to feeling trapped in the corner by a large bear. When she didn't reply, Robert rushed in with "Of course, I'd understand if these are personal."

Minerva, not knowing what else to say, reverted to her mother's standard rejoinder from when Minerva was young. "We'll see."

This was exactly why Minerva hadn't told anyone. She didn't want to risk it. With readership came the opportunity for rejection. What if someone read about one of her "friends" and thought her writing was bad? Or, worse, what if they caught a glimpse into who she was? She'd just admitted to Robert that she laced the stories with her own ideas. Oh, she'd gotten herself into a tight spot, all right. Nella never asked to read her work. She simply wanted Minerva to tell her the person's story. It hadn't occurred to Minerva that Robert might ask this. Forevermore, this was the very reason she didn't talk about what she did. It *was* personal. Robert had gotten that right.

But Robert had already moved on to a new topic. Maybe he'd gotten the hint. Maybe he'd leave it alone. Maybe this would help Minerva remember to keep her mouth shut.

Or, maybe she'd think about it some more. Maybe she would wait and see.

19

On her way home from the McAlpins', Minerva noticed the trash cans at the side of neighbors' houses stuffed with surplus. Extra cars were in driveways and carports. Bundled-up children played tag, squealing and running, no doubt banished outside by exhausted mothers. Lights were on in every house, and curtains remained open. She saw families—at a table playing cards, on the couch watching television, working a puzzle, in the kitchen. Abundance everywhere. Everyone and everything full, overflowing. Excess. Minerva fingered the roll of Tums in her pocket.

That evening she fell asleep on the couch still wearing her coat. At some point the boiler revived, and the sputtering radiators snapped and ticked her awake. Static hissed on the television. Such noise and commotion in a house with no one. She picked up *East of Eden* and read until she dozed off again.

❧

The morning after Thanksgiving Minerva woke up when a bird flew into the living-room picture window. She sat up, surprised by the thump on the glass, but more surprised to be in her coat, still wearing her gloves, shoes, and hat topping an unfortunate crick that had set up in her neck. The phone blared before she registered her other aches.

She glanced at the clock on the mantel. Nine o'clock? She hadn't slept that late since she was... Well, she didn't remember ever having slept that late.

She made her way to the phone. "Hello?"

"Minerva! The library is on fire!"

"What? Who is this? Is this a prank call? I do not think this is funny."

"No. Minerva, it's me. Nella. The library is on fire. Buster has his ham radio on, and he picked up the police call. He says they've called for the fire department to go over to the library because it's all ablaze."

"Oh, that can't be right."

"Well, you can believe me or not."

Minerva was saying what she wanted to believe, but her pulse had accelerated. Not her beloved library. She hung up on Nella without a goodbye, gathered her purse and keys, and headed out the back door without a thought to brushing her teeth. She threw Spencer into reverse and floored the gas pedal until a sickening thud brought her back to herself.

A scream. Dogs barking. A neighbor running toward her. Blood drained from her head and she experienced cold weightlessness.

20

Minerva knew the fluorescent lights didn't carry the scent of antiseptic, but she got the idea that if someone would turn off the humming blue glare, the odor would go away. The smell of rubbing alcohol, the high-pitched squealing ballasts, the click of the nurses' heels, the cloying mint green tiles on the walls, the sticky Naugahyde of the waiting-room chairs, the worn July issue of *Life* by *The Holy Bible*. All of it. All of it. It all nauseated her.

Robert McAlpin's leg vibrated. She saw the fidgeting, though he was sitting three seats to her left. Stop. Stop. Stop. Stop. She was close to screaming, close to crying, close to coming undone.

And what would be so awful about falling apart? She didn't deserve a cathartic release. That's what. She reeked of guilt. She deserved to experience the full weight of what she'd done. The relief of tears or cries, the welcome respite of hysteria, belonged to Robert, not her.

George's body had looked smaller than normal when she got out of her car and saw him lying in her driveway. That blasted red wagon. And red blood. Oh, what had she done? Someone had called for an ambulance. The bulky white truck consumed the block with wails and seizure-inducing flashes. How long had she stood there? When did she stoop and touch George's still face, eyelashes asleep on his pale cheeks? When did she reach beyond those curls and put her hand in the spreading pool of blood? When did someone pull her up and away?

She watched the black needle second hand stick at each second on the flat white clock above the exit sign. The heated air threatened to suffocate her. Each blink felt weighted with effort. Her fingernails dug into the backs of her arms as she held herself together. If she let go, pieces of her body might drift away. There goes a finger. There a forearm. There an ear. She gripped tighter.

A doctor with icy eyes peering over a green surgical mask appeared from somewhere. Which door? Where did he come from? He pulled his mask down, and Robert sprang up. Minerva heard "internal bleeding" and "liver," "pancreas," "unknown," "repaired," and "wait." She searched for sense in the words, but Robert's incessant nodding distracted her. She heard him thank the doctor and realized she still didn't know anything. But she didn't want to ask any questions. She didn't want to know the answers.

"Did you hear what he said, Mrs. Place?"

"No, not everything." She tried to swallow, but her tongue was thick. Was she having a stroke?

"Dr. Murray said George…" Minerva watched Robert's mouth move but she couldn't comprehend the words. If he would slow down. She knew his words held meaning but they dissolved when they hit air, a second before she caught them. Something was wrong with her.

"Mrs. Place?"

Had he said her name more than once?

"Mrs. Place, are you all right?" Robert's features pinched together. *Of course, he looks concerned, you fool. His son may die.* "Do you need to sit down? Here, sit down."

Shame strangled her. This young father was comforting her. She moaned and leaned her head back to look at the ceiling when she realized she'd made a noise.

"Would you mind getting a nurse?" she heard Robert ask Brother Larson. Brother Larson was here. Did someone say Brother Brown is on his way too? Oh, dear God.

"No. No. No. I'm fine. I'm sorry."

"Are you sure?" Robert's warm hand was on her arm. She gripped it. Robert drew back almost imperceptibly, but Minerva noticed. Had he winced at her touch?

"You will never know how sorry I am." He didn't look away. And thank the Lord he didn't take his hand out of hers either. A rush of gratitude for this kindness flooded her. "I am so sorry. So sorry." She looked down, no longer able to dam the tears.

"Mrs. Place," his voice scratched with hoarseness and she could smell coffee in his whisper.

∽

Brother Larson insisted on driving her home sometime after midnight.

"There isn't anything you can do here, Mrs. Place," he said, standing above her, his hand on her shoulder. Had he ever touched her before? Had she ever thought of this man as gentle?

He's right. I've done all the damage I can do, Minerva thought, defeated. And I'm so tired. I want to go to bed. I want to sleep. Dear Lord, how can I be thinking about myself? If that child dies… She had arrived at the end of this phrase hundreds of times. She couldn't complete it.

Brother Larson—either from exhaustion or from sensitivity she had never credited him with before—said nothing as he drove Minerva home. She whispered a prayer of thanks for the darkness cloaking the bloodstained driveway.

"You sit tight," he said and patted her shoulder. He came around and opened the car door for her like a boy taking her to the prom. Tears pricked her nose, and she bit the inside of her cheek. She didn't deserve this sweetness. He ushered her inside—she had left the door unlocked when she'd followed the ambulance to the hospital—turned on her living-room light and helped her with her coat. She let him.

"Thank you, Brother Larson. I'll be fine now."

"Could I make you hot tea or warm milk? I know a cup of something warm always brings a little comfort."

"Oh no." Minerva surprised herself with this vehemence. "No. No. But thank you. Thank you. You are kind." How odd, she thought. He is so kind. Am I dead? Is George dead? Is someone dead? Oh. Oh!

"All right then. Of course, we do not expect you to play on Sunday, not with such a shock."

Minerva doubted she would ever play again. She didn't deserve that either.

"I understand."

"Goodnight, Minerva. I'll check in on you tomorrow."

❧

The next morning, Saturday, didn't feel like Saturday, and days do have certain qualities. Minerva had said so all along. Saturdays are imbued with casual crispness. If they were fruits, they'd be apples, Winesap apples. Today was devoid of crispness.

Minerva, you are losing your mind. Only an insane person would be thinking about Saturday being an apple the morning after running over a child. She reached for the small wastebasket she kept by her bed and vomited. Her stomach tightened again, and her chest constricted in a hiccup. She looked at the wastebasket. At least she had put in a paper sack liner. Less mess to clean up.

She hung her head. How could she have a thought of practicality? How could ordinary thoughts ever cross her mind again?

Minerva Webster Place had run over a child.

George! Sweet, ornery, creative, exuberant George. A child who'd been deprived of a mother was now lying in a hospital bed, fighting for his own life. Robert would never forgive her. She would never forgive herself.

Her parents had been right to favor Geneva. Manny had been right to be angry with her. She was a horrible person. Her single-minded focus on her library—it wasn't even *her* library, she thought with disgust—had consumed her. That carelessness had caused devastation.

She glanced out the kitchen window and saw Nella. Before she could whip the curtains closed, they made eye contact and Minerva groaned, "Oh, dear Lord, please don't let her come over."

But not a minute later, here was Nella at her back door.

"Minerva, how are you?"

Nella, her hair in rollers, free of makeup, was still in her housecoat. A gust of November air had entered with her.

"The question should be how is George," Minerva snapped, immediately wishing she hadn't.

"Minerva." Nella moved toward Minerva, but Minerva pulled her robe tighter around her waist and gripped it together at her neck. Nella stepped back.

"Minerva, it was an accident." Nella spoke gently, as if she were trying to calm a hurt animal. "It could just as easily have been me or Maxine or anyone else on this street."

"But it was me." Minerva covered her face as she felt the tears well.

"You sit down right here." Nella pulled out a kitchen chair. "I'm going to make you some coffee."

Minerva was too weak to protest.

For once, Nella didn't talk. It seemed as though she poured Minerva a cup of coffee only seconds after saying she was going to make it. Time was bending and shifting. Minerva looked at her hands and saw the blood. She heard the thud. The disinfectant of the hospital invaded her nostrils again. She picked up the phone and heard Nella's voice say, "The library is on fire." It was all happening again. Out of order. But so real.

"Take a sip, Minerva. Go ahead, honey."

Nella's face was tight with concern. Nobody ever called Minerva *honey*.

Minerva drank the hot coffee and felt the heat trail down to her stomach. She wondered if she was going to be sick again. The two women sat in silence while Minerva sipped the coffee.

"What if he dies?"

"Don't let yourself think that. Those doctors know what they're doing. He'll be okay."

"But what if he's not?"

"Minerva. We're going to pray that he is. We're going to ask God to heal that little boy."

Minerva wondered if God would ever hear her again.

21

At the hospital she located George's room in intensive care. Only relatives allowed. She paced outside the room for who knows how long, trying to glimpse inside when nurses bustled about. Eventually she tired and waited down the hall. She tried to position herself where she could see the activity outside George's room and also watch the elevators. She didn't want someone to take her by surprise. She didn't know who. Anyone.

Robert will have to come out sometime. Won't he? And then she can apologize again. Beg his forgiveness. Tell him what happened. She hadn't seen George or his wagon. She hadn't seen anything at all. She had told George not to leave his wagon in her driveway. She had told him. She had told all the children. More than once. She was so sorry. So sorry. Can he forgive her? Is George going to be all right? Can he forgive her? Can he ever forgive her?

But when she did see Robert, words fled.

They met in the hospital cafeteria. Robert was putting his tray through the window where gloved hands waited to scrub off the Salisbury steak and peas he hadn't eaten. Minerva was behind him but didn't realize it. When Robert turned around, Minerva gripped the brown tray in her hands tighter and pulled it close, right up under her bosom so the gravy from her mashed potatoes got on her cardigan.

"Mrs. Place." He took a step back.

"Oh." Minerva felt as if a chasm had opened with his one step back. He obviously did not want to see her. "Mr. McAlpin."

"Excuse me."

Minerva stepped aside and he walked past her. She blinked, then came to and set her tray down. "Mr. McAlpin. Robert."

"Yes?" Robert stopped and turned back. "I'm in a hurry. I'm

sorry. I don't mean to be rude at all. I…I get nervous when I'm away from George, but the nurses insisted I come down here. I haven't eaten since yesterday."

"Oh yes, yes. I understand. Could I walk back with you?" She could see—what was his expression? Dread?—well up in his eyes. She recognized the look, but she couldn't stop herself.

"Sure."

"I need to tell you… First, how is George?"

"The surgeon said to expect a long road." They came to the elevator and both watched the arrow drop toward the basement.

Minerva was relieved not to be facing him now. "I am so, so sorry, Robert. I never saw him. I never saw anything."

"I know it was an accident, Mrs. Place. I know."

"I'm sick over what happened. Sick." Why was she repeating herself? Her words sounded trite. She was coming off as insincere. "I've been waiting all day, hoping to see you. Hoping to tell you again how sorry I am. I can never apologize enough." Minerva gasped. What was that noise she made? Why was she fighting for a breath?

"I know it was an accident, Mrs. Place." Now he was repeating himself. This was not going well. Not going well at all. How long could it take to get to the third floor?

The elevator opened and Robert held his arm on the door so Minerva could exit first. After he got off, the two of them stood there looking at each other. The elevator doors closed, and the cables stretched over the pulleys.

"Mrs. Place, thank you for coming by."

❧

Minerva drove from the hospital to Oak Grove like an automaton. Unsure how she'd gotten there, she got out of her car and braced her shoulders against the cold. The chimneys of the neighboring houses belched smoke into an ash sky. Brown pin-oak leaves persevered on their branch homes but shivered in the wind. Winter had returned with the intention of winning this time. This would be the year spring refused its right to bloom. Nineteen fifty-three would be the year winter held the world in its grip. The sky would remain colorless, the earth fallow, and the trees bare.

The cemetery welcomed her with nothing new. No changes. Not a squirrel had bothered to move an acorn. This slice of time comforted Minerva, its loneliness a poem. Serenity flowed from the familiar, well-ordered rows. The soothing street names. The unchanging graves. The gray, black, and taupe of granite and marble. Her shoulders settled. Her stomach slackened. Her eyebrows unknit. Her jaw unclenched.

She wanted to visit Emma. Who else could understand? Emma, the murderess. Emma, the guilty. She found the marker, and there, spliced between sky and stone, she tried to talk. Eventually, though, the guilt came tumbling out in drunken waves. Minerva began sobbing so hard she couldn't stand up anymore. She sat on the ground by Emma's headstone and hugged her knees, her head resting on them.

She wasn't even startled when she felt a hand on her back.

Minerva looked up from her tears and said, "Do you understand?"

Emma, just as frail and worn as she was when she first appeared to Minerva, nodded her head and sat down too.

"Let me tell you a little about me," the pale woman said. "The story you won't find in the newspaper clippings."

Minerva didn't care if Emma was real or a ghost. She didn't care whether she was going crazy or not. She only wanted the comfort of someone who knew shame.

Emma's voice was trembling at first, but she became stronger as she went along. She began:

Emma Skillian, born 1878; died January 24, 1937; New Section 13, Lot 298

My life's story hinges on a tale that I believed would destroy me when it began. When it didn't, I began to pray it would. One day I was an ordinary woman who walked unnoticed in the market and the next, mobs of people despised me.

Let me start at the beginning, with my friend, Mrs. Henrietta Wagner. She was an iron-willed woman with strong opinions about most everything. I'll admit, she could run right over me with little trouble. I'm not proud of that.

Henrietta had one great love in her life—Alfred Warren. She had raised little Alf from the time he was ten years old and felt like she was more than a mother to him. She thought she was his rescuer. His savior.

Alf was a timid boy, a lot like me, I suppose. Quiet, shy, not given to cross Henrietta. He was one of those children who blended into the background. I didn't expect he would ever leave home. He grew up making no trouble as far as I could see. He came of the age most boys leave home except he didn't go anywhere. He stayed put with Henrietta. By this time he was well into his thirties, and the two of them had their routines. They seemed to get on well enough.

That is why it was no surprise when Henrietta came completely undone. A woman named Rosetta Simmons entered Alf's life one day and right from the start I could see she was going to be trouble. She was a widow and had two young daughters and a teenaged son. She didn't look to be much older than a teenager herself. When she and Alf made their acquaintance, Henrietta ignored it. She'd say, "What would Alf want with a homely little mouse like that?" But it became obvious that Alf wanted plenty to do with that mouse. He was licking his paws like a hungry Cheshire cat.

Henrietta could not or would not talk about it at first. I think she thought if she ignored the relationship, it would go away. Then, when it didn't, she became consumed with discussing it. That was all I heard from her, in fact.

"Rosetta was the reason her first husband was killed," she told me one day.

"Is that right?"

"It was no accident. That little lady is trouble, and I won't have her ruining my Alf."

"What do you intend to do, Henrietta?"

"I'm thinking on it."

However, despite Henrietta's attempts to derail the relationship—at one point she became so heated she dropped to her knees and put her arms around his legs, all the while sobbing loudly. Despite this dramatic behavior, Alf married Rosetta in December of 1921.

Now Henrietta became so agitated she took to attacking Rosetta whenever she saw her. Why, she even attacked Alfred, who, as I mentioned, was a small, timid man. (Henrietta, who was a big-boned woman, could take either one of those two down to the ground.) What's more, she questioned Rosetta's children whenever she ran into them around town. I might be inclined to call it harassment.

When she found out that Rosetta was pregnant with Alfred's child, she became still more infuriated. She went so far as to tell Rosetta that she would never see her child born. Of course, later when she took the stand, she denied all of this. She said she never had any trouble with Rose except for a few words when Rosetta called her a liar at the market. She also testified that Alf had told her several times that he was dissatisfied since he married. But I'm getting ahead of myself.

It all came to a head before dawn on Monday morning, April 30, 1923. You could hear the explosion for blocks away. I lived three blocks away at the time, on Bernheim Avenue. Houses within a two-mile radius shuddered when the blast went off. Later, when everyone compared notes, they realized most of the folks in the neighborhood woke up in alarm, thinking the town was being attacked.

I didn't hear it myself. I can sleep through anything. But my sister, Lizzie, called me and told me that it sounded like the fire department was over on Trimble Street. Something in me—an intuition? an awful suspicion—wondered about Alfred and Rosetta. They lived one block over from Trimble on Clay Street. I can't tell you why I thought about them, about Henrietta—I mean, Henrietta was my friend.

Of course, when all the information came out, we

learned that dynamite had been ignited directly under Rosetta's bed. I was troubled in my soul, but I said nothing, not
even to Lizzie. Surely Henrietta wasn't crazy mad enough
to do something like blow up a house. I berated myself for
having such an evil thought. Still.

At this point I didn't dream I'd be pulled into the whole
mess.

But to my horror, I was.

It turned out that being her close friend was enough to
implicate me as being involved with the sordid plan. Before
I knew what hit me, I was arrested and hauled to jail.

Minerva interrupted Emma. "Arrested?" Minerva cried.
"You? You hadn't done anything, had you? What evidence did
they have?"

Emma stared at her with those inscrutable, flat eyes.

Minerva felt a stone heavy in her stomach. "Oh, dear God.
Could I be arrested for what I've done?"

22

When Minerva pulled up to her house late that afternoon after her encounter with Emma, she spotted Tiny Johnson loading a bucket and a scrub brush into the back of his beat-up Ford pickup.

"Mr. Johnson," she said, rolling down her window, repeating his name through the crack as it widened.

"Hello, Mrs. Place." Tiny wiped his nose on the sleeve of his forearm and then stuffed a bandanna into the top pocket of his overalls.

Minerva wanted to tell him to use his bandanna, not his sleeve, but instead she said, "Why are you here?"

"Brother Larson asked me to come over and get all this blood up." He turned and spat.

The now familiar nausea swirled back over Minerva. She rolled up her window. She had forgotten to check the fender for blood.

She pulled into her carport and turned off the ignition. Could she bear to look? Did she have a choice?

Yes, there was blood. George's blood. Smeared across the fender. Minerva pulled a tissue out of her pocket and rubbed the dark red streak. It didn't budge. She'd have to get some cleaner and a rag and scrub it off.

But right now, she couldn't face it. Her mind was swirling with what Emma had said. She needed to write to clear her thoughts. A distraction. Oh Lord, please let me have a distraction, she pleaded.

The house seemed emptier than usual. A silence full of despair hovered over her as she sat at the table. Emma's voice came back to her. She could see the wounded bird of a woman in her mind's eye and hear the defeated voice:

Oh, I was done in. My mind turned to jelly, and my stomach and bowels lost their grip when those police came and got me. I didn't know what to do, what to say. If I'd known what was to come—the throngs of people gawking at me, the twisted words of lying witnesses, the stench of jail—I might have committed suicide rather than endure it.

First they jailed Henrietta and me together in Paducah, but eventually they had to move us out of the county because mobs were collecting like angry wasps. It was a trial like Paducah had never seen before. Thousands of people came to the courthouse every day to listen to the testimony. The judge had to call the room to order several times when people just couldn't hold their thoughts on a matter and the talk spilled out like water from a busted hose. I felt like the color had drained from my life and I was living in a picture show. Everything moved fast and slow at the same time.

The worst day for me was when Christine Daughtery, Rosetta's little nine-year-old girl, testified. She said these exact words. I'll never forget them:

"I know Mrs. Skillian and I saw her standing in the yard when I got back. She was in the crowd that stood over her after they had taken Mamma out from the house. I saw her there and she made a face at my mamma."

Then the attorney asked Christine what kind of face and that child screwed her little face into a grimace like an evil imp. I was so ashamed. I don't remember doing that, but if I did, I shouldn't have. I surely shouldn't have.

Eileen Daughtery, Rosetta's twelve-year-old girl, testified that after the explosion she crawled out of the window, which was shattered, and that before the smoke of the bomb had died away, she saw a woman wearing glasses and a pink dress. She said it was me. I would have sworn on the Bible that I'd put on a black-and-white gingham dress that day. She also said that after the workmen had removed the body and laid it out in the yard, she saw me standing by the body laughing "sneeringly." I knew that wasn't true.

Why would that girl testify to such a thing unless someone had told her what to say? How does a twelve-year-old come up with a word like sneeringly? She also said I made a face and walked away. Now, I ask you, why would I make a face? What does that mean, anyway? She said that she and her sister had met me and a tall woman (I'm not sure who that would be…a tall woman? Henrietta was big-boned, but not of a height I would call tall.) on North Tenth Street about a block from their home on Sunday afternoon. That little scrap of a girl said I had scared her by saying that Mrs. Wagner was going to kill her mother and that her mother and Alf weren't married. I don't believe I said that. I do not.

On our way to the train after we left court the day that those two girls testified, a lady in the crowd stuck Henrietta in the side with her hat pin. Jabbed it right into her waist. That hole bled all over Henrietta's dress. The crowd churned like the swarm of angry wasps they were. Though it was hot, I found myself trembling, my teeth chattering like it was twenty below. People from all walks of life came—from high-society women to wives and daughter of laborers, women of the rural districts, all sorts, all vying to get a front-row seat.

The newspapers were full of every detail—some correct, some so wrong you wondered how they could make up such nonsense. I'll be completely forthcoming: I was fearful of soiling my linens. That kind of sick hangs in your gut like a bagful of infection.

In the end, we were both found guilty. Guilty. The word kicked me as hard in the gut as any mule could. The crowd erupted in applause. Just think, they were applauding the fact that I was going to prison. The hatred in that room bounced off each clap; it thundered and swelled until I couldn't hear anything anymore. I couldn't hear myself think. I stood there as the life drained right out of me.

Minerva put her pen down and leaned back in the wooden chair. Before she knew what she was doing, she had fallen to her knees. "Oh dear God, don't let the life drain out of that child. I couldn't bear it. I couldn't bear it. Take my life! Drain the life out of me! I have no one who would care if I were gone. He's an innocent child with a father who has already lost his wife. Oh God! Spare him! Take me!"

She lay prostrate now, her forehead on the rug under the dining table.

"Dear God, take me."

Minerva lay on the floor crying until she was spent. Then she felt foolish. Her hope in God, her faith in his divine help, was in shreds. She pulled herself back up and into her chair; the words on the page before her seemed like an autobiography of her desperation.

Emma's voice continued:

> After I went away, my sister hired another lawyer for me. She said, "We're going to let the dust settle and then get you a new trial, sister." I was not hopeful, but I was grateful that somebody cared. She was the only person in the world who thought I was innocent. Even I had begun to question whether I was guilty. The truth had melted into a dirty puddle.

23

The library had not burned. Turned out to be a false alarm. The city would investigate who had called in the phony emergency, and officials promised to press charges against the culprit.

Minerva stopped reading the newspaper article reporting the false crime. She would gladly throttle whoever had done the unconscionable act with her own hands. They were already guilty hands. What would one more life be?

She tossed the paper to the side of her chair and picked up the roll of antacids she now kept on the table. Maybe she'd write. The manila folders fanned across the dining table like a deck of cards waiting for a magic trick.

> Judge William S. Bishop 1839-1902, Old Section 10, Lot 155, Silent Ave.
> William T. DeBoe, Jr. 1912-1936, New Section 14, Lot 4, Vanmeter St.
> Dollie the Mule 1897, Old Section 1, Lot 12, Faith Ave.

"Ha," Minerva barked. She picked up the thin file on Dollie, adjusted the pillow for her back, and rolled a piece of paper into her new Underwood typewriter (which was a whole other story).

> Dollie the Mule February 25, 1897, Old Section 1, Lot 12, Faith Ave.
> *I am an ass.*

Imagine burying a mule in the cemetery, right alongside people of importance, she thought with disdain. Wasn't right.

Minerva yanked the piece of paper out of the carriage. The words "I am an ass" weren't accurate. Donkeys are asses. Mules are donkeys bred with horses. Mules are partial asses. She couldn't even curse correctly.

She rolled in a fresh piece of paper. Her recent conversation with Emma Skillian was going to interfere with anything else she might write. She might as well get it over with. She had left Emma receiving the guilty verdict. Now she finished:

A conversation I'd had with Henrietta kept troubling me.

"I'm taking care of the situation," she had said to me one afternoon as we visited over the phone, a habit we'd gotten into.

"By 'situation,' do you mean you're taking care of Rosetta or Alf or what?" I was scribbling on a notepad, only half listening to her. She had gone on so many times about what she called "the situation" that I just let her rant. I knew she'd eventually have to get over it. What was done was done. Those two were married and had a baby on the way.

"You know exactly what I mean," Henrietta spat back at me. "I've got a plan."

Now, right then and there, I should have pressed her more. What plan? What did she mean exactly? I could have dissuaded her from such a preposterous idea. I could have saved that poor Rosetta's life. And her baby's. But what did I do? I kept right on scribbling and changed the subject.

"What are you fixing for dinner?" I said. Even though Henrietta's voice sounded different this time. Even though I could feel a steely glint to her words. Even though that simple phrase cut through me for a reason I couldn't have known at the time, an intuition, a gut feeling. Even though. I asked her what she was fixing for dinner.

I could have reported my suspicions to the police, but I didn't have any real proof that Henrietta was going to kill Rosetta. She hadn't come right out and said it. Still.

When we were in jail, I asked her how she'd done it.

"It was simple," she said. "I bought some dynamite, took a taxi over there at night, and hid it under the house."

"You mean to tell me you crawled under their house on your own and lit the fuse yourself?"

"It was a long fuse. I wasn't in danger. And who else

was going to do it? It had to be done to save Alf from that despicable woman."

I stared at her with disbelief. I couldn't reconcile her actions with the woman sitting beside me in a prison eating a tough piece of meat smothered in some sort of gravy. It was all surreal.

Minerva paused. Surreal. Yes, that was the word.

She had gone to the hospital to check on George, to see Robert, but the nurses wouldn't let her in. He was in intensive care and no visitors except family were allowed. Robert must be staying at the hospital around the clock because no one ever answered their home phone. She had no way of knowing how the little boy was doing.

She thought about asking Brother Larson if he knew anything, but she was too ashamed to call him.

Shame. Guilt. They were back to taunt her, to strangle her, to keep her awake at night. Just like when Manny beat her, the shame covered her in its heavy mantle, swallowed her like a python. She had brought about this terrible situation. She had been impulsive and careless. Manny and her mother had always accused her of not paying attention, of letting her imagination get away from her, of being no earthly good.

It was true.

"It's your fault, Minerva. It's all your fault."

24

The next morning was Sunday, but Minerva had taken a "leave of absence" from playing the organ. Surely someone who mowed a child down with a car should not be leading people in worship, she reasoned. To Brother Larson she said, "I'd like to take a break." He had readily—eagerly?—agreed.

She set a cup of coffee down without a saucer straight on the dining-room table. Leaving one finger looped through the handle of the coffee cup, she used her other hand to pull her robe together. This would be the perfect time to smoke a cigarette, although she had never smoked (barring her experiment smoking cigars with Cat Gray).

The word UNDERWOOD hypnotized her for a moment. She wished she could take the machine back, but she had used it and doubted she could. The episode that had led to the purchase was so trivial, yet she remembered it vividly. She was writing about Emma when her hand cramped. She put her pen down and considered the pain. Three prominent callouses—one on the inside of the first knuckle of the middle finger where the pen rested, and the other two on her thumb. Why the thumb? she wondered. She picked the pen back up and held it as if she were going to write, but instead she studied her thumb. She sat there several minutes trying to figure out the callouses. She sat there long enough for her neck to start aching. That's when she retrieved the newspaper out of the kitchen trash can and rustled through the pages until she got to the next to last, the lower left three columns, where Wilson's Office Supply advertised the Underwood SX-100 Rhythm Touch.

Oh, the weighty box was a fine piece of equipment. Sturdy. All business. She mastered typing in no time. Her fingers were limber from the piano and organ, and she had learned how to type years ago anyway, back in high school. A million years ago. Lucky for her the keyboard hadn't changed. F-F-F-J-J-J and so on. She sipped her coffee and tucked the edge of her robe between her crossed legs.

She didn't deserve a typewriter. She couldn't believe she had allowed herself such a luxury in the middle of such tragedy. The purchase had been purely self-indulgent, an act attempting to absolve her.

One of Minerva's rules was to eat breakfast in the kitchen while she read her thought for the day from a pocket-sized pamphlet she picked up at church each quarter. But she hadn't been to church to pick up a new booklet, and she had tossed last quarter's. She wouldn't have re-read those anyway—too much about Thanksgiving and Christmas. Without her devotion, which ranked as Number One in the Rules of the Day, all subsequent rules relaxed.

She cocked her eyebrow at her own rebellious behavior as she eyed vestiges of last night's dinner on the counter. A loaf of bread sat out rather than owning its proper place in the bread box. A plate sat unrinsed, sporting a used fork with a wadded napkin crumpled in surrender beside it. She glanced at this morning's coffee cup on the dining-room table—not in the kitchen. The prodigal cup lacked even a saucer to suggest respectability.

She sighed and yanked the paper out of the typewriter. A coffee cup with no saucer. Wayward bread and napkins. Sitting in the dining-room in the morning. She'd given herself over to a complete disdain for decorum. She fretted with a loose thread in the seam of her robe until it pulled two inches of sewing out. The clock on the wall judged her with every tick. She'd frittered time until mid-morning, for Pete's sake. Lounging about all day undressed. A total lack of discipline.

A little boy is in the hospital close to death because you ran over him, Minerva Place. What do you have to say for yourself?

She put her head on the table in cradled arms, but she didn't cry. The comfort of tears had dried up and left her.

෯

The sun rose and reminded Minerva where she was. She reached for a stretch and rolled her head in a slow circle. Her back ached. Her foot was asleep. She bounced her leg to urge the blood to circulate. Her hands and wrists hurt from pounding the typewriter keys; they were more stubborn than piano or organ keys. She made fists, then spread her fingers wide. She'd been writing about Emma Skillian all night. The piece differed from anything she'd written before, but Emma wasn't like the rest of them.

Minerva stood and her back caught, so she slowed, letting the muscles uncramp. For a while she didn't move at all. The yellow morning air held her steady, allowing her to breathe, to swallow, to blink.

"Emma, what happens to women like us? Women no one wants, no one trusts, no one loves."

The refrigerator hummed a bored solo and the house stuttered and creaked getting ready for another day of sheltering life. A new layer of fine dust gathered. Minerva had read somewhere that most of house dust was dead skin that sloughed off. She was leaving evidence of her own death every day. She breathed in deeply through her nose and shut her eyes for a moment longer than a blink. Emma's words from the cemetery swirled in her head.

Emma Skillian continued...

Sleet alternated with rain for days in January of 1937. A man wrapped in a raincoat and muffler knocked on our door two days ago and told Lizzie and me we needed to leave the house. He looked familiar, and I puzzled over who he was.

"The river's rising, and everybody needs to get out," he said, his voice pitched above the wind. "You need to find family or friends who live on higher ground."

"Well, my word, he doesn't have to yell at me," Lizzie said, throwing her shoulder and hip against the front door to persuade the swollen wood to shut.

"Where will we go, sister?" I asked because Lizzie always kept a plan in her pocket.

"I don't know. I suppose we'll think on it for a day or two."

But we both knew there was nothing to think about, nothing to plan. No place to go. We'd outlived all our kin. Friends had walked away long ago. We knew positively we didn't want to go to the shelter at the elementary school and endure other homeless folks, people we might or might not know. One was as bad as the other and besides, imagine the smells. So we waited and watched the rain from our little house. Liz said we were too far from the river to be in real danger.

A week after that official came by, the rain still held us hostage. Vertical sheets like brushstrokes of crystals coated the air. Frigid water seeped into the two-room, shotgun house, leaking through the soaked towels and rugs we had stuffed into the doorways.

"Somebody will get us out of here." Lizzie peered out the front window at the encroaching river as she rambled. Sometimes her words felt like they would drown me before the water could.

But I let Lizzie talk. She was the oldest and was used to being in charge. I knew her nerves had triggered the endless chatter.

I shook my head and rearranged the pins in my bun. My hair had gone white within a month after I was convicted of murder. Seemed like it had happened overnight. I didn't look like myself anymore. I was an old woman.

"Hush, Emma," Lizzie scolded. "Somebody'll come."

"I didn't say anything." I wondered if she was starting to lose her mind. I turned away and stepped over a puddle forming in front of the pie safe.

"Get the mop and get that water up," she ordered.

I ignored her. My shoes left wet outlines on the bottomless floor.

Two days later, at least two more inches of rain. Now I stared out the front window and tried to remember when the water had covered the neighbor's fence. I didn't see anybody moving through the scrim of curtains across the street. The Taylors must have left. We hadn't seen them go, but the house appeared lifeless.

We didn't talk much to our neighbors. We didn't talk much to anyone. Though I'd been exonerated in the second trial, the people in town never considered me innocent. They remained leery of me. "Where there's smoke there's fire," I'd overhear people say, while their eyes shot in my direction, and their heads were tipped down as if confiding a secret.

I may not have killed Rose, but I was guilty.

I rubbed the window with the heel of my palm. The wavy glass was frosted with ice and grime and the gesture did nothing more than smear a little of my breath's steam. The yard was now a swirling mixture of water and sludge, a flat reflection of the gray-soaked sky.

I moved from the front room, through the bedroom, into the kitchen, an L-shaped room with a black stove, a pie safe, and a large white porcelain sink. Liz had made a skirt from leftover pillow ticking to fit around the base of the sink, and we kept Clorox, soap flakes, rat poison, and rags there. A dark rim teased the hem of the fabric now. Water, our new enemy, advanced.

My hands and feet were numb from the cold, so it was like watching someone else when I tried to slice a piece of bread. I moved like I'd had a stroke. Finally I dropped the knife and stared at the solid brown loaf. Then I dug into it with my numb fingers, leaving a jagged, uneven break that would upset Lizzie. The stale bread tore apart like tough meat.

In the front room, Lizzie sat on the horsehair stuffed love seat, wrapped in an orange and tan afghan, the only color in the world. The blanket reminded me of the sun that hadn't shown itself in months. I hadn't seen the moon or the stars, for that matter. Clouds had settled over the town like a shroud. No movement but the slice of rain and gusts of wind. No noise but staccato drops. No warmth. No dryness. Only cold, filthy water. Icy and determined. Brutally, efficiently swallowing us.

I eased into the rocking chair across the room from Lizzie and gnawed at the hard bread. While I chewed, I watched Sister nod until her gray head came to rest at an uncomfortable, odd angle. She'd complain later, but I was too tired to do anything about it. Spittle formed at the corner of her mouth and ran down her chin. Her face hung slack as she sat there, unaware, her skin loose in fleshy folds.

I had this idea that Lizzie's arthritis was seeping across the floor like a mass of congealed gravy. It would work its way to me and seep up my body like the water stain on the sink skirt, rising from my feet and knees to my hips and shoulders and neck. I couldn't do anything about it, so I rocked and rocked the pain away until I fell asleep too.

I found the piece of bread later. It had fallen from my lap and absorbed the water, swelling to twice its size.

Every day brought more precipitation, as if God had decided to empty heaven of all its crystal seas. But heaven is supposed to be beautiful, and I saw nothing but raw sewage and flotsam, remnants of furniture, bottles, and an occasional boot bobbing along. The Ohio River had spilled over the mound that was supposed to protect the town and had covered block after block with the diligence of a troop invasion. The National Guard and other volunteers were cruising in johnboats between houses like slow-moving fishermen trolling for bass. We kept the curtains drawn so nobody would try to persuade us to leave again.

How were we to know what craziness was happening outside our house? That the Hustons, over on Sixth Street, had somehow finagled a cow up to the second floor, and you could hear the poor beast lowing all over the neighborhood from its unfamiliar perch on the porch. That hundreds had been dragged from their homes, some of them on the verge of dying from exposure, some fighting fevers and ragged coughs. That hysteria was kept at bay only because people were too cold to work up a panic.

At our house, baskets, potatoes, books, and a waste can all floated in the murky mess. We gave up trying to salvage belongings. The water had reached a foot high inside. We curled together on my bed. Lizzie was in the front with her back to me, and I wrapped my arms around her. A sour mix of fear and staleness drenched the familiar peppery, cinnamon scent of my sister.

We had piled all the blankets we owned on top of ourselves, but when the fabric absorbed the water, comfort dissolved. So we lay huddled, shivering and silent, and drifted in and out of consciousness.

When I was awake, my thoughts smacked together, out of order and peevish. Angry imps jerked me back to the trial. I remembered how the *Sun-Democrat* had followed the whole ordeal. A hound dog on a scent. Huge headlines dominated the pages and column after column written— so many untrue, unkind words right there for all to read. Crowds formed outside the courtroom during the procedures.

I still can't reconcile that I, who was guilty of nothing but being Henrietta Wagner's close friend, was arrested as being a co-conspirator in the murder of Rosetta Warren. I was innocent. Henrietta was the guilty one. She had planted the dynamite under Rosetta's bed herself. That crazy woman had planned and executed the whole affair. Henrietta was the murderer. I was innocent. Innocent.

I can still picture Rosetta's two scrawny girls sitting in the witness box, one right after the other, lying about me. My throat tightens up like I'm going to choke when I remember how they both said I was laughing at their mama dying.

"I did not laugh like some lunatic," I whispered to myself. "I did not. Those girls got everything wrong. All I was guilty of was being friends with Henrietta. That was all in the world I'd done wrong. Those people had to realize I wasn't guilty. They wanted to lock me up with Henrietta."

"What are you going on about?" Lizzie mumbled, her voice coated with blurriness.

"Nothing. Nothing." I squeezed Sister closer, in case a hug could discover a hint of warmth.

Then the imps jerked me to the second trial, the one where they acquitted me. After it was over, I had stood and thought, *There now. All's been made right.*

Yet nothing was ever right again. One by one my friends no longer stood with me at the market to chat. The butcher gave me the worst cuts of meat. People crossed to the opposite side of the street or looked at the ground when I passed. I caught children throwing rocks at my windows at night or knocking on the door and running. Gradually everyone stopped looking me in the eye. I became invisible.

I tried to put these things out of my mind, but they itched at my thoughts. Through the years I questioned the verdict myself. I became uncertain. Henrietta blamed me on the train that day. She said I was responsible, that I came up with the idea. Was that the truth? Had I?

"Emma," Lizzie breathed.

"Hmmm?"

"Nobody came."

"No."

"We're going to die."

I said nothing.

"Are you scared?" Her voice sounded like it had when we were girls. I'm ashamed to admit this, but the briefest surge of vindication coursed through me right then. Usually Lizzie was the one to comfort me, but today, in this last hour, our roles were reversed.

"Be quiet, now," I told her. "Close your eyes and sleep."

Her lips were pale purple and her eyes, sunk deep into their sockets, were ringed in dark olive shadows.

I saw a mist, I believe it was Sister's spirit, hover above the bed.

I waited to see what the mist would do.

"It's time for this to be over, Lizzie," I whispered, more to myself than to her. Then I closed my eyes and prayed, "Lord, forgive me. Forgive me. Forgive me."

Nobody found our bodies for weeks. Then one day, Ferris Collins passed our house and noticed a gut-wrenching odor. He gagged reflexively before he pulled out his bandanna and held the rag over his nose.

Junk, remnants from the Ohio, lay strewn across the patch of mud that was once a yard. Maybe people thought nobody lived in this house. Nobody who cared much anyway. Or maybe they thought it had been abandoned during the flood. Many had moved away for good.

Ferris looked around and, seeing no one, walked to the door and knocked with his free hand. He squeezed his nose tighter with the other.

"Anybody home?" he hollered. "Anybody there?" The stench of rotting horse conjured an uneasy dread.

After knocking, stomping noisily around the house, and trying to get a glimpse through the curtains, Ferris scratched his head. I could see he was deciding. I figured he was thinking whether to report this to officials. They might arrest him for trespassing. A Negro didn't knock on a white woman's front door without consequences.

Sometime after noon, the sheriff drove over to check out Ferris's claim that something was dead. He pounded his clenched fist on the door. Nothing. He knew I lived there with my sister. In fact, he was the official who had come by and told us to leave. I knew he looked familiar. I suppose I didn't recognize him because he had been bundled in a heavy coat, muffler, and hat. The poor man was about to find out we hadn't followed his advice. He knocked again.

This time when there was no answer, he threw his shoulder into it, trying to bust through. The door wasn't locked but was jammed. He grunted as he slammed against the warped wood again, making less than an inch of progress. I wanted to tell him that he'd hurt his shoulder if he kept this up. Finally he wrapped his coat around his fist and broke the window.

I could see he knew right off something was wrong. Something more than the destruction of the flood. It must have smelled like the inside of a slaughterhouse because he took out his handkerchief and covered his nose as he negotiated his way through the grime-coated remains.

Then, there we were. Two ravaged bodies huddled together in one bed. The scene, draped in stench and sorrow, triggered disgust, and the sheriff vomited.

"Damn," he said to the dead bodies, wiping his mouth on his sleeve. "Damn it all to hell."

He probably was like everyone else and thought, *That Skillian woman was no doubt guilty of something.* He'd heard stories about the trial, about how they loaded the two suspects into a train and whisked us away from Paducah's outrage. Oh yes, Emma Skillian was guilty of something.

But did anyone deserve this kind of death?

A few folks gathered outside the house and the sheriff pointed to a gangly boy. "Go get the coroner and Charles Lindsey." Of course, not much could be done. After the coroner announced the cause of death, the Lindseys, with professional pride, packed each of our remaining pitifully decomposed bodies into pine caskets reserved for paupers.

The winter sky attended us at Oak Grove. No one was there besides the gravedigger, one of the Lindsey brothers, and an assistant in training. Charles Lindsey walked over to the edge of my grave and opened a book containing appropriate prayers.

Then Charles turned to the gravedigger, a hairy man with beefy hands and forearms, and gave him the go-ahead.

The sound of the mud hitting those caskets reminded me of the bitter, icy rain that had stolen our lives. Shovels full of mud fell in a rhythm, like enormous fingers drumming on a wooden table.

I wondered if Charles remembered that he had attended my trial with his mother when he was eight. When she spoke to me of that years later, she said the police's explanation of the dynamite explosion had fascinated little Charles. Strange what people said to me. Why would Mrs. Lindsey tell me this?

And did he still remember the cab driver, a scrawny ferret-faced man? Or how the little girl mimicked my laugh? Mrs. Lindsey said her boy attended school with the girl. What was her name? Catherine? Christine?

After the girl testified, he became terrified of me. The kids told stories about me breaking out of jail and killing them. Then, when I was freed, the stories continued, becoming more fantastic and gruesome. Sometimes, on a dare, a boy would sneak up to try and peek in one of our windows.

I wondered if Charles remembered any of my story. He certainly had a solemn expression on his face. Then, who knows why, he blurted out, "Nah."

The gravedigger looked up, a shovel loaded with mud in midair. "What?"

"Nothing."

I watched as my grave was filled in with mud. It was over.

Minerva stared at the words. *I'm going to end up dead and forgotten. A guilty woman. This is what I deserve.* Were those Emma's words or her own?

࿇

On the fourteenth day of George's stay in the hospital, a little after seven in the evening, Minerva's telephone rang. When she placed the receiver back in its cradle, her heart palpitated a Morse code signal to her brain, but she couldn't translate it.

25

Ah, the romance of childhood. Carefree summers filled with daisy chains and games of tag. Piles of leaves waiting to be jumped into and ghost stories around a campfire. Christmases with Santa eating cookies that had been left on a plate. Winters full of snow for sledding and making snow angels.

But what about this? The wasp hovering over the clover of the daisy chain. The person not chosen to play tag. The skinned knee. The Christmas tree with no presents. The flu. Mumps. Chicken pox. Childhood.

Minerva Place's childhood and Robert McAlpin's childhoods could not have been more different. And in those long evenings at the hospital after the accident, they discovered this.

How had they gotten here? From the awkward elevator conversation to a personal, intimate exchange of conversation every evening. Minerva wondered. She certainly did.

The only people she knew this much about were dead.

Her friend Cat had told her intimate thoughts, but they were just girls. They'd only accumulated thirteen years of life. And could you count the first two if you retained no memories of them? Minerva thought not. Which left you with eleven, and of those eleven she and Cat focused on only the one year they were living. Thirteen-year-old girls tend to dream of what might be, not long for what has been.

She and Nella were friends, sure. But they mostly talked about recipes, the weather, other people. She didn't know what Nella feared or dreamed about in the depths of her soul. Nella complained about her husband in a good-natured way. She rolled her eyes about her children's faults like any proud mother. But who was she outside of her plum cake at Christmas and her tried-and-true tips for getting greasy stains out of sweaters? Had she ever been betrayed by someone in whom she had sunk her heart? Did she ever long to escape Paducah and see the Eiffel Tower or an aborigine in a jungle? Did Nella ever worry that God didn't exist—or if he did, whether he could ever forgive her for the hideous thoughts she'd had, the evil she'd committed?

Robert revealed more to her than Cat ever had, more than Nella, more than her friends in Oak Grove did. This transparency scared Minerva. He had called her on that fourteenth day to tell her that George was being moved out of intensive care. He thought she would want to know.

"Oh, thank you so much for calling, Robert," she had said before hesitating. "Would it be all right if I came up to see him? I would be grateful."

To her tremendous relief he had agreed. And she had started going every evening, right after dinner, to help him wait through the last hours of his day. He didn't really have anyone either, after all.

Nausea accompanied her every time she entered the hospital—even before then, when she got in her car to go to the hospital. In fact, Minerva remained bilious most of the time despite the antacid tablets. But she considered this penance, to use a Catholic term. The Baptists missed out in that respect, she thought. Penance was a necessary concept. She owed a debt. She owed her sorrow. She owed her comfort. She should be unwell.

Some evenings she marveled that Robert trusted her with so much about such personal details. He was a kaleidoscope of information. She never imagined anyone had ever lived such a foreign life. She never imagined Robert had. That was certain.

❧

When Robert was six, his parents packed him a bag of all his worldly goods and sent him to the Sao Paulo International School. Until then, he'd enjoyed life in a one-room house on the edge of the jungle (The jungle! Minerva's mind tilted), sleeping in a bed tented with mosquito netting. At night, that filmy net and a bright embroidered piece of cloth hanging from a ceiling beam were all that separated him from his parents.

Robert's father, who boasted a PhD in linguistics, and his mother, a trained teacher and no slouch in the intellectual department, never considered teaching their only son at home. The privileged went to school, and they considered themselves privileged—not financially privileged, no, but in other ways. The McAlpins considered experiences and education to be perks of their life's work. What an opportunity for Robert to learn alongside the children of diplomats and other officials. He would be exposed to wealthy, sophisticated leaders, have excellent instructors (Brazil was famous for its educational opportunities), and then develop his spiritual and moral fiber with their guidance in the months he was not in school.

But as a boarding student in Sao Paulo, an unfettered, curious Robbie had been forced to exchange the chatter of monkeys and the pulse of unseen creatures for the artificial noises of the city and incessant whir of humanity. He traded a jungle canopy for classroom lights, calluses on the bottom of his feet for blisters from shoes, and monkey squeals for recess teasing—none by choice.

"I wondered why I was being punished," he told Minerva. The two of them sat in George's hospital room and Minerva fancied it was a jungle of sorts. Strange sounds and beeps. Doctors and nurses speaking foreign languages. Otherworldly colors. "Why were my parents making me give up everything I loved? I couldn't understand it. I ended up one furious little boy—although at the time I would not have been able to tell you why I was angry."

Robert told Minerva all this the first night he had called her from the hospital and allowed her to come. Once in the room, she sat screwed to the seat, ready to take her punishment, certain banishment was coming. Listening to him talk about his temper. Waiting for it.

He said his temper became a serious issue. Teachers attempted to control him with thrashings. They placed him alone in the corner. He couldn't eat meals with the other children. In time, his behavior improved. But the anger never went away.

"I was surprised when George asked me one day if I'd ever hit anybody," Robert said. He sat in a chair beside the bed, across the room from where Minerva sat. The white sheets on the hospital bed were crisp and tucked, never disturbed by George, who looked so different when he was still. "I stalled by saying, 'Why do you ask, son?' George simply went…" Robert shrugged and hummed the words "I don't know" to indicate George's response. "So, I changed the subject. I didn't think I should tell him about my frequent fights."

"Why did you fight?" Minerva asked before she checked her words. She wasn't as in charge of herself as she normally was, and after she spoke bile rose in her throat. The question reeked of intimacy.

But Robert didn't seem to mind. He cocked his head and looked toward the far corner of the room as if seeing a movie reel. And like a movie, a story unfolded. "I only remember the reason for one of those fights," he said, "the fight with Eduardo Saboia.

"Eduardo's father, was prefeito of Sao Paulo from October 3, 1932, to December 28, 1932, and again from April 2, 1933, to May 22, 1933." Robert stopped and grinned at Minerva. "I know those dates are peculiar, but Brazilian politics were peculiar. We had to memorize all sorts of dates for school and for some reason they stuck with me. Anyway, I was completely uninterested in politics, but more than a little interested in girls. So, typically, this information—the dates and the unrest surrounding his father's terms—would have been a piece of information I collected for the weekly civics quiz. But when Eduardo Saboia and I became rivals for Aimee de Hereen, every piece of knowledge became a weapon.

"One day on a break between classes Eduardo and I got into an argument. I have no idea what started it or why we were arguing; we were just mad at each other all the time. I guess we were in competition over Aimee, who seemed so glamorous to us. I remember she dared to wear her hair parted on the side and swept up into a barrette, not in braids like all the other girls." Robert smiled. "I said the ugliest thing I could think of—Você é da família não é nada, mas merda de cachorro.

"I can laugh about it now, but I was dead serious then. I cursed at him in Portuguese because I didn't curse in English, only in Portuguese. I gave myself that parameter for some strange reason.

"He—the Brazilian—replied in English: 'My family is dog shit?" Robert interrupted his story to apologize to Mrs. Place, and she closed her eyes and nodded her head as if absolving him. "'You don't even have a family. Your parents are a couple of holy rollers who think the savages are more important than their own son.'"

Robert, unable to tolerate another moment of inaction, threw a right rounder to Eduardo's jaw, producing a bloody tooth, which flew out of the poor kid's mouth to both boys' surprise. After a stunned instant, the two flew at each other in all-out warfare. Filthy, bloody, hair amiss, and sweaty, the boys eventually were pulled apart by Senor Rodriguez, the science teacher, and Senor de Carrollo, the custodian.

"I am a little ashamed to admit this, Mrs. Place, but that fight thrilled me." Robert looked at his hands, now curled into fists. "A part of me came alive. The pain was worth it." He laughed self-consciously. Minerva shifted on her chair.

"What happened with the girl?"

"Well, neither one of us ended up winning Aimee de Her-een's affections." He chuckled and shrugged. "But," Robert continued, "I was still bothered by the fight for other reasons."

He remained upset over the insult the Portuguese boy had hurled at him. The accusation that his parents wanted to get rid of him had stung. Were they more interested in their work than in him?

Through the years he had told himself to shake off the words, but the memory still felt like a ragged hangnail. An urge to hit someone when that voice sounded in his head never settled. "I think that's why I called you," he concluded.

Minerva scooted sideways, re-crossed her legs, blinked rapidly, sniffed, and blinked more. She was uncertain she wanted to hear what Robert might divulge next.

He wasn't looking at her anymore, though. He stared at George. Perspiration beaded on her upper lip and under her arms. She surreptitiously scratched her scalp, then readjusted a bra strap.

"As I sat in this room watching George, so little, not moving, and I wondered hour by hour if he would live, the familiar rage returned. The rage I'd felt as a kid. My anger felt like a beast trapped in a corral with a herd of incompatible wild animals all vying for dominance."

Minerva swallowed and waited. She debated whether she should call for a nurse. Maybe Robert was getting worked up. Would he harm her? Here in the hospital?

"I felt things I hadn't felt in years. Emotions I thought I had dealt with, I realized still had a foothold in me. I was angry with my parents. Why did they abandon me to fend for myself when I was only six? I was angry with Marilynne. How could she have died, leaving me with a child to raise on my own? And I was angry with you."

Minerva's throat tightened. She stopped fidgeting, stopped blinking, stopped breathing.

"When I saw you in the cafeteria I thought, 'She looks like one of the dead people she talks to.' I'm sorry. I know this isn't nice to hear, but I think I must tell you.

"I questioned myself. I wondered what I had been thinking, having you over for Thanksgiving, sending George to you for piano. Standing there in the cafeteria, in just those few minutes, I convinced myself you were odd. Too odd. I thought, 'Just because you feel sorry for someone doesn't mean you should invite them into your life—especially when they're crazy and possibly harmful.' I'm sorry, Mrs. Place. I know these aren't kind words."

His eyes brimmed with tears. A numbing cold had settled on her. If she could have collapsed into a neat folder that could be filed with the ones at home on her dining-room table, she would have.

"Then I came back from lunch and I opened the door to George's room. My boy looked so helpless. I sat next to the bed and dropped my head. The pattern of the tiles, the hum of the machines, the ticking of the clock—the world crumpled in on me. Just buckled like a house of cards." Robert rubbed his neck. "I thought, 'I can blame Mrs. Place, but George's accident was my fault. Like Marilynne's death was.'"

It took Minerva a beat to register what he'd said. What? His fault?

"No, Robert." Minerva's voice was raspy. She cleared her throat and shook her head. "No."

He pressed the heels of his hands into his eyes while the machines beeped and shushed. He spoke without looking at her. "I thought, 'An eighteen-year-old girl died because of me and now a six-year-old child might too. How could I have taken a nap that day? What kind of parent falls asleep and leaves his child free to roam the neighborhood?'"

He rubbed his neck and looked at the ceiling.

"But then I asked myself, 'Who doesn't check the rearview mirror when backing out of the driveway? With the number of children in the neighborhood, surely everyone checks and double-checks their mirrors and turns around. I always turn around. I don't trust the mirrors. Why didn't she turn around?'

"Then I switched to 'it could have been any one of those children. But it was George. Why'd it have to be George?'"

He pounded his knees with a quick whack. Minerva startled.

"I knew to call it an accident. Of course it was an accident. Of course you didn't run over George on purpose. But you did run over him. My child. I was angry. So angry I couldn't feel anything else. Why was my child unconscious, lying in a hospital bed, in a sterile room full of machines making noises and nurses swishing in and out? Why George? He was innocent. He is only six years old. What kind of God did my parents give me up to serve? What kind of God was I worshipping? What kind of God let this happen?

"And then, the strangest thing."

Minerva held her breath again, fearing his anger yet hoping he would vent the fullness of his wrath on her. She deserved his fury and more.

Robert looked at her and the distance in the room closed, sounds disappeared, George melted into the sheets. Robert and Minerva stared at each other.

"I remembered Dub."

26

Reginald "Dub" Dublin had been in Robert's army unit, Second Brigade of the Seventh Infantry Division, stationed in the Aleutian Islands. The Ohio State football player, an all-state high school quarterback, had been known as much for his quick tongue as his quick feet. The reason his humor was always so well-received—though no one analyzed it at the time—was that Dub made sure the jokes were ultimately on himself. This often involved his less than beautiful singing voice and lack of dancing skills. He also encouraged the guys who were the most discouraged or homesick.

That's why the tragedy seemed more than simply unfair.

Robert sat beside Dub's hospital bed and looked at the bandaged stump ending at Dub's knee. Dub's ticket to athletic fame had been amputated, and Robert was embarrassed by his reaction to the sight. He was morbidly fascinated with the ghostly lightness with which Dub moved the abbreviated appendage.

"So much for 'Light, Silent, and Deadly,'" Dub finally said to break the awkwardness. He was referring to the division's motto. "But we got a lot of those Japs, didn't we? And I guess you could say I'm a little lighter now."

His voice broke the spell. Robert laughed uneasily.

"Yeah. Yeah. Dub, I'm just so—"

"No, no." Dub held up his hand for Robert to stop. "The Lord giveth and the Lord taketh away. Blessed be the name of the Lord."

"What?" Robert wasn't sure he heard him correctly.

"I said, The Lord giveth and the Lord—"

"I heard you, but what are you talking about? Your leg?" Robert felt sure Dub was still in shock, though three weeks had passed since the amputation. Robert was ashamed that he had delayed visiting his friend for so long. He had waited on courage that wasn't coming. Finally, he'd forced himself to go.

"Yeah," Dub said. "I'm talking about my leg. Look, God gave me life. He didn't promise to give me a perfect life or an easy life. He has every right to take it away from me at any time he chooses. Or he can take away parts of it—like my leg. He has his reasons. I trust him."

"How can you say that?" Confusion mixed with anger—indignation?—scratched at Robert's emotions. "You can't blame God for this."

"I don't blame God."

"You just said he took your leg."

"I guess it's like this. I believe God is the ultimate authority. He oversees everything, including me. I am his child and because he loves me so much nothing happens to me that isn't okayed by him first. The Bible tells me everything happening to me will somehow work out for good in the end because I am his. So this"—Dub gestured toward his stump—"is going to work together for good somehow. Doesn't mean I like the fact that my leg's gone. Doesn't mean I don't get upset about it. I'm not dancing a jig." He smiled, but his joke fell flat. "Oh, man, I wish it were different. I can't figure out how something not there hurts so bad, by the way. Somehow I can still feel the leg." Dub shook his head. "Still."

At the time, Robert told Minerva, he thought Dub was nuts.

"*Nuts* is the precise word I used when I talked about him with the guys later. But I remember thumbing through my Bible trying to find the verse he quoted. I really thought he had turned into a religious fanatic. You heard about people having come-to-Jesus moments all the time, especially when a guy had a traumatic experience like Dub."

Minerva watched Robert. "But you don't think that anymore?"

"No," he said. "Now I think I understand what he meant."

"Well, I don't." A vague pulse of annoyance beat in her temple. Had Robert called her over to the hospital to tell her about some strange religious experience? Was he trying to convince her God had ordained her running over George? What a repugnant thought.

Robert looked pained when he smiled. "I'm not explaining it clearly."

"No," she agreed.

"What I'm trying to say is…" He stopped and swallowed. "Mrs. Place, I'm not angry with you. I don't want you to worry about what happened."

What? An unexpected bath of irritation blanched her emotions. Instead of receiving the angry lashing she deserved, she was receiving forgiveness? Mercy? No, it wasn't right.

Minerva understood guilt. She had carried it as she might have carried a suitcase full of items for a trip. At various stops along the way in her life, she'd opened the case and added to the load. Her mother and father had given her pieces to put in. Manny had contributed many items. Her sister had donated. People at church had given. Now the hard-sided luggage bulged so she could barely drag it along. But she did. She dragged it with ferocity. She had to. It was hers to carry.

ॐ

That night Minerva knew she'd never go to sleep. She watched *The Arthur Murray Party* for a while, read a while, but nothing helped. She pictured Robert at the hospital. He probably couldn't sleep either, or if he did it was in snatches.

"I'm so grateful for this cot," he would probably be saying about now to Nurse Turner, who started her shift at eleven. Minerva was impressed with the young nurse's uniform, which was starched stiff and white, and her cap, which was pinned to her jet-black hair with black bobby pins. That stark white against such black. It was a pleasing contrast, Minerva thought. Plus, she noticed, the cap was different from the other nurses' caps, a little wider, with more striping. But she doubted Robert noticed all that. Men rarely noticed the details. They simply knew if a woman was pretty or not.

"You are welcome," Nurse Turner would have said in response to Robert, "and if there is anything else you need, please ask." She would smile and shake the thermometer. "Everything looks fine here." She would make a note on the clipboard hanging at the end of the bed. "Try to get some sleep, Mr. McAlpin."

He would be grateful for more than the cot.

Minerva tried to put her mind to rest, to stop thinking about Robert and George. But though her body ached with tiredness, she couldn't find sleep. She mulled over what all Robert had told her.

One thing was certain, Robert had never experienced normal grief over Marilynne's death. For starters, they were just kids when they married, and they were married for no time. *You're one to judge, Minerva. It's not like you and Manny were so experienced or married for decades.*

࿇

"Is this going to be a dozen?" The young woman behind the counter tapped her fingernail on the glass case.

"No. Um, yes." Minerva was picking up doughnuts to take to Robert at the hospital. He said he'd never had Munal's before. She had told him that was a crime she would rectify. Standing here before the variety of Long Johns, fritters, jelly-filled, cake, and glazed, she felt a little dizzy. She'd never bought more than two at a time. Plain glazed. She asked the uninterested girl for a mix but thought better of it as she watched her skip over the cinnamon bun.

Back in the car the warm cakes instantly filled the air with sugar, but her thoughts ricocheted back to Robert and his lack of grief. She suspected that a vague emotion broke through the murky surface occasionally, nibbling at him, causing him anxiety. But she doubted that he named the feeling grief. She wondered if he ever felt as she did about Manny—relieved. Highly unlikely since that was an abnormal response. Who feels relieved when their spouse dies? Minerva had never told anyone that she had, and never would.

No, Robert had not felt relief, but he had felt confusion. Since Robert was in the Aleutian Islands and at the mercy of bureaucratic red tape, he missed Marilynne's funeral. So all he had to go on, the only proof of her death, was her marker and a gravesite already assimilated into the surrounding grassy area.

"I don't know what I expected—a mounded bulge of freshly turned dirt, complete with wreaths of gladiolas and carnations?" He had laughed mirthlessly when he told her this during one of their talks in the hospital. And then there was the fact of being handed a baby boy as he disembarked from the plane that had returned him to Virginia.

"I went from being a newlywed to widower to father in an instant," he said, snapping his fingers. Minerva understood—there was no time to process a loss. A death. Finality. Complete absence. The kind of gone that was forever. "Sometimes I still think she is just away, like I might get a letter from her."

The hospital room had become a sacred place for Minerva and Robert. What an unlikely pair they made, Minerva sometimes thought. A young, unmarried father who had grown up in Brazil and an old widow who knew little past Paducah. But grief was a binder, and they shared the tenuous uncertainty of having floated untethered in their pasts.

She thought it was shocking that Robert had revealed what he had, and like a child afraid of being caught listening to a private adult conversation, she'd developed a habit of holding herself still when he spoke. Though he really seemed to have forgiven her, she continued to doubt. He is going to look at me and remember what I've done, she told herself, and who knows what he'll say then. I wouldn't blame him if he threw me out.

But her imagined scenario wouldn't occur today.

"Thank you for these," he said, studying the box to decide which one to eat next. Minerva nodded. He picked the cream-filled one first. She'd never tasted a cream-filled one, had never considered eating one. Now he was licking his fingers as seriously as if he were studying his next move in a chess game. Funny, his licking his fingers would have annoyed her in the past, but something between them had altered. No, something in her had changed.

Today's conversation didn't seem congruent with doughnuts.

Robert wanted to talk about the day he received the news that Marilynne had died in childbirth.

"I heard the words, but I wasn't able to process the information," he said. He leaned back in the hard chair looking at the ceiling. He'd eaten four doughnuts. Four.

"The words were nothing more than air, eiderdown. You hear the phrase 'it hit me like a ton of bricks,' but it wasn't forceful or dramatic. It was more dreamlike. I took out the photograph I carried of her and studied it. There she was smiling, one hand waving at me, the other perched on her cocked hip, her head tilted to the left." Robert lifted one hand and tilted his head. "I could smell the almond-scented lotion she wore. I could feel the silky smoothness of her hair. All those feelings lifted right out of that snapshot. She looked so alive."

A trace of confusion passed over his face for a moment and Minerva waited, trying to become more still than still.

"Anyway." He looked at her and shrugged. "The army discharged me to go home to care for George. No one else was available. Marilynne's father was dead, and her mother suffered crippling rheumatoid arthritis and required care herself. My parents had returned to Brazil. I'm not sure they knew she was pregnant yet."

After swimming through the red tape, Robert was ill-prepared for what awaited him in Virginia. He tried to anticipate the situation, but "as every first-time parent knows," he said with a grin, "thinking you know what it's going to be like having a child is totally ridiculous and completely unachievable."

Still, he said, he imagined himself holding a baby, burping a baby, changing the diaper of a baby. Nurses at the clinic on base gave him tips. Army buddies who were fathers warned him he wouldn't get much sleep. They cautioned him to enlist the help of a woman. Various well-meaning friends hinted that raising a baby on his own might be impossible—though they never used that word.

But the true shock was the wash of emotions that poured over him when he saw his velvet boy wrapped in a pale blue blanket, contentedly sucking on a pacifier bobbing gently in a pink kiss of a mouth. George shone with beauty. He was amazing. Miraculous. Breathtaking. When Robert held his baby for the first time and those dimpled fingers curled around his thumb, words lost meaning. George's skin was warm satin, translucent, glowing with light from within—his soul? His mouth a bow turning up so, so slightly on the corners, giving him a constant pleasant expression. Marilynne's dark eyes. Fine pale curls scented of caramel. A stork bite where his skull met his neck shaped like a lopsided heart. Paper-thin fingernails. Perfection.

Sadness and longing almost strangled Minerva, who still grieved when she considered that she'd never know such joy. And yet she didn't believe she deserved it.

Robert found an apartment close to the university and paid other students—always fresh-faced home-ec majors—to care for George when he was in class. His GI Bill covered the rest of his education, and he worked as the maintenance man for the apartment units where they lived. When George was awake at night, Robert would hold him on one side of his lap and prop a book on his other knee. This was how he studied and finished his senior year.

After he graduated, Union Carbide offered him a job. He and George stayed in Virginia for the next six years. When they received the opportunity to move to Kentucky, Robert thought an adventure, a fresh start, was what they both needed.

"I told George that Kentucky was known for its bluegrass, and he won't let me forget that. We've got a running joke now. I tell him to be on the lookout for it and he reports back, 'I didn't see anything but green grass today, Dad.'"

Minerva smiled, barely. Robert rubbed his knees with the palms of his hands.

❧

The next evening Minerva returned with a loaf of banana bread. As she and Robert settled in for their evening visit, Robert commented that his mother had never baked anything when he was a boy. "She said Brazil was too hot, but I suspect she didn't like to cook. I didn't know then, but I do now—I did not have a conventional childhood. What about you? What was your childhood like? What did you enjoy doing when you were a little girl?"

Minerva acclimated to Robert's unusual questions—at least to her mind they were unusual—and was reluctant to admit it but enjoyed the routine the two of them established. She sat in the Naugahyde chair and Robert in the wooden one. Minerva had given up protesting this early on. The monitors beeped and hummed with a gentle rhythm. George slept. A stuffed bear missing one eye and a wad of fur on its forehead was tucked in beside him.

"What was your favorite activity as a child, Mrs. Place?"

"Oh, I don't remember. Marbles. I guess marbles."

"Is that right? I would have pegged you for a reader."

"Yes, books too. I did love to read."

"What were your favorite books?"

"Anything I could get my hands on."

"Surely you preferred some. One or two that stood out."

"I don't suppose I've ever been asked. Let me think." Minerva felt compelled to tell Robert the truth, so she sifted her memory. "Oh yes. *Five Children and It* and *The Enchanted Castle*. Both by Edith Nesbit. I loved her books, all of them. And I loved Francis Hodgson Burnett's books. *The Secret Garden.* I lost myself in that book." Minerva was flush with the success of coming up with an answer.

"I haven't read any of those."

"No? Everyone should read Edith Nesbit. Everyone. You would appreciate her books as an adult. George too."

The quiet room held them a long while between sentences.

"What did you read?" she finally asked.

"Only what they made me. I didn't like reading. I would have rather solved a math problem or done a science experiment."

Minerva was slightly disappointed, since one of her top ten rules was *people who are smart love to read.*

She sniffed and took a tissue out of her purse to dab her nose (why was this room so cold?). The machines shushed like a train perpetually preparing to leave the station. Robert pulled his ankle up onto his knee and pushed down to stretch his hip. Minerva shifted.

"If you don't like to read, you don't like to read. None of my business." She sniffed and dabbed the tip of her nose again. "Seems they could afford to turn the heat on in this place. You go down to the cafeteria and you'll be blazing hot. Up here in the patients' rooms you are ice cold. Now that doesn't make sense."

Minerva smoothed her hair (which was already smooth) and ironed a wrinkle from her lap. Robert vibrated his grounded leg until Minerva abruptly stood.

"How about a coffee?"

"No, thank you, Mrs. Place. I'd better not have any more coffee tonight."

"Water?"

"No, thank you."

Minerva hesitated at the end of George's bed, then reached out and patted the mattress. "I believe I need a cup of coffee."

Nurse Turner smiled at Mrs. Place as they passed in the hall. Minerva's eyes narrowed and her lips thinned. She was not at all sure about that one. Too pretty.

27

Sleep eluded Minerva. She struggled to go to sleep and couldn't stay asleep if she did. Just when she began to drift, a hot flash overtook her, and she'd get ringing wet. Ringing wet. Wetter than a— Oh, she couldn't remember how the phrase went. That was another thing. She couldn't remember squat. She needed sleep—she would remember if she could just sleep. This insomnia was becoming a serious problem.

A couple of advertisements in the back of one of her *Good Housekeeping* magazines promised relief from the blasted night sweats and hot flashes.

Feel Peppy Tonic—Over 40 Doesn't Have
to be the end…
Men, Women Over 40 Don't Be Weak & Old.
Feel Peppy, Years Younger. Take Ostrex.
Contains tonic often needed after 40—by bodies
weak & old solely because lacking iron. Get regular $1
size now only 89 cents! Try Ostrex Tonic Tablets to
feel peppy & younger today. Also contains vitamin B1
& calcium. For sale at drug stores everywhere.

Then there was Lydia E. Pinkham's Vegetable Compound:

You Women Who Suffer From Hot Flashes
If you suffer from hot flashes, dizziness, distress
of "Irregularities," are weak, nervous—due to the
functional "middle-age" period in a woman's life—try
Lydia E. Pinkham's Vegetable Compound. It's helped
thousands upon thousands of women to relieve
such annoying symptoms. Follow label directions.
Pinkham's Compound is worth trying!

Neither product helped, and she concluded she should save

her money when future products promised dazzling results. Nobody talked about being overcome by heat, so maybe it was a rare disorder. But then why would there be a tonic? Minerva shrugged her shoulders.

She tried to take her mind off the awful thoughts that crowded in at night by making lists. Lists of names beginning with the letter A, then B, then C, and right on down the alphabet. It used to work by the time she got to M. Unfortunately, she'd been getting to X, Y, and Z. The only names she could come up with starting with Z were Zelda, Zachariah, Zertha, and Zebediah. Zaccheus, sure, but nobody named their child Zaccheus these days.

She'd heard of counting sheep, but she didn't quite comprehend what this exercise involved. Was she supposed to imagine what a sheep looked like, then label the animal with a number as it passed through a gate in her mind? Sheep were dirty and dumb animals anyway.

She tried naming the members in different sections of the choir. The sopranos: Ida Fae Marble, Judith Beiderman, Maggie Dunn, etc. The second sopranos. The altos. The tenors. The baritones. The basses. She could put everyone in the correct chair. Sometimes this exercise put her out, but not always. Sometimes she just got agitated, especially when she named the sopranos, which she usually did first. So the whole time she was annoyed, thus defeating the purpose, which, of course, was to relax.

She ran through the books of the Bible. She tried listing herbs and spices, the aisles of the grocery store, the forty-eight states, the states and their capitals, her aunts, uncles, and cousins, every bird she could recall. She was exhausted but still couldn't sleep.

She couldn't sleep because she was hot, yes. But she couldn't sleep for other reasons. Despite her lists and tricks and tonics and warm milks, Minerva could not clear her head. At night, the silence that was once her friend now taunted her. Despite Robert's forgiveness, she still heard the noise the car made when she hit George. She heard the awful thud, the scraping. The sound of the scream. Whose scream? She never knew, but it was a sound she'd never forget. She heard the dog bark. Strident voices. The ambulance siren. And the sounds were always followed by sickness. She had stopped vomiting, thank goodness, but nausea hovered nearby. She smelled the hospital. She heard the machines. She saw George lying there. Blood on the driveway.

She was too afraid to talk to Robert about why he'd forgiven her. Maybe he would change his mind. Maybe he would say, "Forgiven you? I haven't forgiven you. I am just being nice to you because you are a pathetic old woman." Maybe he would say, "What you did was unforgivable. I will never forgive you for what you have put my child through, for what you have put me through. I forgave God, but not you."

So she took what he offered and didn't ask questions. Just in case.

ॐ

Minerva's first Sunday back at church teetered somewhere between hell and purgatory, a place Minerva most certainly did not believe in, as that was a Catholic belief and she was a Baptist, a Southern Baptist. But she did know what purgatory represented. At least, she was almost certain it represented a place of limbo. And limbo was torturous. Why, oh, why did she allow Brother Larson to persuade her to return?

She did her best to draw out the benediction so she could keep her stiff back turned to those passing out of the sanctuary. Eventually she outlasted everyone but Tiny Johnson, who was gathering stray copies of orders of worship and candy wrappers. Mrs. Place saw parents giving their children candy in church and did not understand why. First off, a child should be able to endure one hour without a piece of candy. Secondly, any reasonable person would clean up after himself. But, no, week after week Mr. Johnson did this. She wondered if he ever found the occasional nickel or dime that had sneaked out of a gentleman's pocket. She guessed he did. She wondered if he kept these coins.

"Mrs. Place?"

Oh no. Mr. Johnson stood between the fourth and third pews, holding a bag of trash. He didn't look smart. Why did she think he looked dumb? Minerva. Get a grip on your thoughts! He is God's child. You are in God's house. Stop making judgments. Still. His face was slack. He looked as if he might start to drool.

"Mrs. Place, I was wondering how that little boy is doing."

She had managed to pass through the morning without discussing George one time. She knew it was too good to be true.

"He's in God's hands, Mr. Johnson." (She had practiced that sentence just in case.)

"Boy, when I went over to your house to clean up his blood, I figured he would die right off. I can't believe the little fella is still holding on. I guess you never know. God might have something big planned for him, don't you suppose? I guess he would have died by now if he were going to die. Don't you?"

Minerva blinked rapidly. "Mr. Johnson, thank you for your work. Have a pleasant Sunday afternoon." She hit her thigh on the corner of the organ as she exited.

❧

God's plan, Minerva thought that afternoon as she walked along Peace Avenue. Did God plan for her to run over George? What a thorny question. If God is who he says he is—all-knowing— then he knew Minerva would run over George. But if he is who he says he is—good—then why would he allow this tragedy to happen? The thoughts slid around like mercury from a broken thermometer. She thought about the Ohio football player who had convinced Robert that everything works together for good. Did she believe this?

A mockingbird called from the branches of a Norfolk pine. It sang, "Dirty bird! Dirty bird!" Minerva pulled her coat tighter, but the cold penetrated anyway. The forecast predicted an early snow. She hoped not.

She felt the folded paper in her pocket and stopped walking. She forced herself to take it out and read it. The words on the page seemed to choke her. It was a list of children buried at Oak Grove.

Why had she felt compelled to make this list? Why was she torturing herself this way? She had never recorded children's gravesites. Of course, she had known there were markers for children, but her interest was in telling stories. She didn't consider children as having lived long enough to have acquired significant stories. Guilt swelled in her when she recognized her lack of regard for children. She really was a terrible woman.

As she went from lot to lot, locating these gravesites, she noticed the children's headstones usually did not have a birth date, only the day they died and their ages.

Mervel Wallace, died May 6, 1925, ten years old (New 14, Lot 24)

Lillard Abbott, died February 1, 1917, one year old (New 12, Lot 22)

Pearl Mathis, died October 4, 1915, five years old (New 11, Lot 162)

Frank Tapp Jr., died July 15, 1928, four years old (New 10, Lot 220.5)

Nelson Irvin, died January 22, 1917, four years old (New 8, Lot 102)

Maynard Alexander, died March 9, 1931, five years old (New 5, Lot 58)

Which was worse? Having a child who died at birth before you knew what color his eyes would be? Or having time to know his personality, his fears, his preferences, and then lose all of that?

Minerva turned toward the Old Section and walked along Oak until she got to Charity. A flock of blackbirds startled, and she paused to watch the graceful swirl pepper the sky. She wished she could join them. Fly away from this place, this world.

Her body knew the way without her having to think. A

numbness carried her until she stood before the simple rectangle where more than one life had ended.

Manfred Earl Place, born October 30, 1923; died October 30, 1923; Old 15, Lot 35

They'd named him for Manny and for Minerva's father. She'd never seen him, this being she'd carried in her body for eight months. She'd felt his hiccups, knew when he was awake by his squirming, recognized an elbow bulging through her skin. He was real. A real person. Someone she loved. And then he was gone without a goodbye.

She woke up in her hospital room to the ashen face of Manny.

The funeral had occurred on a bright blue, outrageously lovely day. The sun shouldn't shine on such grief, but it had. Minerva felt as if she were a shell that had been scraped hollow. Her body hadn't been able to sustain life. She was death itself.

The weight of fresh grief held Minerva like an anchor at her baby's gravesite, a place she never visited. She longed to weep, to be rid of all the tears, the pain, the loss. But no such solace came. Only the frigid air. She took off her glove and wiped her nose with the back of her hand. She didn't bother wiping her eyes. The cold caused them to water. That would have to do.

If George died, she couldn't imagine how she would continue.

28

Mrs. Place!" Robert's voice boomed so loudly out of the telephone that Minerva jerked her head back. He didn't wait for her to answer. "You've got to come to the hospital right now."

Oh no! What had happened? Had George taken a turn for the worse? The doctor said his brain could be affected. Maybe his heart stopped. Maybe he quit breathing. Maybe he'd died.

"What's wrong? What is it?"

"He's awake! He's awake! My boy's awake!" The line went dead. Minerva stood holding the receiver for a moment before the words sank in, then she shook her head and dropped the phone.

God had answered her prayers. The prayers she had not formed into words. The prayers she had only dared to breathe with every murmur of her heart in the sacred stillness of solitude, deep in the hours of night when the feeblest shred of faith clung to the hope that God was awake too.

She didn't remember how she got to the hospital, or to his room, but there he was. Sitting up.

"Oh, George."

George's eyes were open, and he looked good to her despite the gashed cheek and bandaged head. Minerva's heart broke all over again to think of what she'd almost done, to think what she'd been spared.

"Has he said anything?" She kept staring at the little boy who looked as though he could barely keep his eyes open.

"He hasn't," Robert said. "He's drifting in and out. But the doctor said that was normal. He said this was a very, very good sign. The turnaround we've been praying for."

Robert smiled at George and encouraged Mrs. Place to have a seat.

"I shouldn't. I don't want to tire him out."

"It's fine."

"I won't stay long."

A nurse came in and flicked a thermometer, popping it into George's mouth with a gentle admonition to keep it under his tongue. She held his wrist and watched the second hand on her Timex.

"You're looking good, young man." She patted George and made a note on his chart. She turned to Robert. "Can I get you anything?"

"No, thank you. I've got what I needed."

Minerva quizzed him on what the doctor had said.

"He said expect it to take some time. Expect it to be slow. He'll likely wake up completely over the course of the next few days. He'll start talking soon. We think he'll be able to eat on his own soon."

"When will we know if there's permanent damage?" Oh, Minerva, she thought, why did you ask that?

Robert didn't hesitate. "We'll know more when he starts talking."

29

The news was good, wonderful, so why was Minerva irritated? She pursed her mouth and blinked rapidly.

"I see."

"Yes, isn't it great?"

"I suppose."

Robert was folding George's pajamas and George was transferring the Jell-O he'd been eating from one cheek to the other.

"Betty says it's no trouble. No trouble at all. We shouldn't need her more than a couple of weeks, Dr. Malvern says. Isn't that some news? A couple of weeks."

Minerva thought *she* would be staying with George when he was dismissed from the hospital—wasn't that logical? Betty, of the Nurse Turner variety, requires no sleep? How was this girl—Minerva doesn't care how young she is, she needed sleep—how was she supposed to care for George during the day and then work at night? Had Robert thought this through, or was he enamored with her pink cheeks and raven hair? My goodness, the girl could be the heroine of one of those dime-store romances with such looks.

"When will Nurse Turner sleep?" There. She was compelled to ask.

"Oh. I guess I didn't tell you."

Robert was awfully bright, too bright. Yes, George was going home, which was wonderful, just wonderful, but Robert needed to be cautious. So much could still go wrong.

"Betty's being moved to the day shift, and she's going to take her unused vacation days before she starts."

Of course she was. She knew a good thing when she saw it. She figured if she could take care of George, Robert would be forever grateful. She was out to snag a husband.

George blew bubbles through a straw in his chocolate milk.

"The arrangement's a gift. I cannot tell you how grateful I am." Robert vibrated with joy. Nurse Downaliese, a seasoned, stocky woman who, though under five feet, two inches, filled up a room, marched in to dispense dismissal instructions.

Minerva sat on the wooden chair by George's bed. While Robert was occupied, she leaned closer to George.

"George, what do you say about Nurse Turner?"

"She's pretty. And funny."

Funny.

"Will you like her being at your house?"

"Sure." George was pretending the milk carton was a car.

"Good." Minerva didn't know what she was trying to accomplish with this line of questioning. She checked her urge to touch George's curls, which were longer than usual.

An orderly appeared with a wheelchair.

"Oh, boy." George threw back the covers and knocked a fork to the floor.

"Hold on there, chief." Robert moved quickly to George's side. "You're not dressed yet. You're going to wear yourself out before you get out of bed."

The wheelchair, like the bed, was too big for George. They shouldn't have to make wheelchairs for children; her thoughts were as painful as sharp pinches to tender skin.

The nurses and orderlies and any doctors who happened to be on the floor all clapped for George as the candy striper pushed his wheelchair down the hall. Red hearts and doilies with nurses' names written on them were pinned to the bulletin board. Someone had draped streamers from one red cardboard cutout of Cupid to another. Valentine's Day arrived in two days.

"Don't come back." Laughter. "Never want to see you again, George." Clapping. "Later alligator." "After 'while crocodile."

Minerva had offered to drive the McAlpin men home. No, that was not accurate. Robert had asked Minerva if she would take them home. How could she refuse?

Minerva pulled the car (she had stopped calling it Spencer after the accident) to the area where patients were dismissed, and Minerva went ahead of Robert to open the door for him and George.

"Slow down." She frowned at the candy striper, who whipped the wheelchair through the door so quickly the darned thing practically tilted on two wheels. Teenage girls.

"Right here. Right here." She opened the passenger door and backed out of Robert's way. George scooted out of the wheelchair and climbed into the front seat of Minerva's car while Robert put the small suitcase in the back seat. The candy striper blew a bubble from the gum she'd been popping and waved at George. "Bye-bye, Georgie Porgie Puddin' and Pie."

Minerva put her hands on her hips. They ought to teach these girls to be more professional.

By the time they got George put to bed at home, he was exhausted. Robert didn't look so well himself. Minerva said, "All right, then, I'll be on my way. Let me know if you need anything."

"Don't go yet."

She paused, her arm extended in mid-attempt to collect her coat from the back of the kitchen chair.

"Do you have to leave?"

Minerva blinked, confused. She was all set to go. She didn't want to be in their way.

"I don't suppose so. No." There was his smile, the one recently returned. Minerva wanted to touch him, to pat his arm. She didn't. Of course not.

"I went to the market and picked up George's favorite foods." He cut his eyes over and when he did, he looked so much like his son. "Can I offer you a Twinkie and chocolate milk?"

Oh my. Minerva internally groaned. That sounded revolting. "Thank you."

Robert handed Minerva the cellophane treat and a glass filled with milk, and Minerva did her best to look pleasant. She reminded herself why she was here—surely she could manage to ingest a Twinkie and milk—and nodded as Robert talked.

He looked pale and wrung out, but he was talkative. Why was he chattering on about Popsicles and pudding? This Twinkie wasn't so bad. Might have been better with coffee.

"When you go through a situation like we have, you learn what a person's really like in a short amount of time."

What was that? What had she missed?

"She was the first person since Marilynne who I've wanted to spend any time with. Do you know what I mean, Mrs. Place?"

She said yes, but her brows were furrowed in puzzlement.

"Robert, you are at a vulnerable place right now. I wouldn't be making any decisions when you've just been through what you and George have been through." Dear Lord, what was she saying? He wouldn't have been through anything if she hadn't put him there. She had some nerve offering advice.

Minerva took the last bite of her Twinkie and watched Robert chug his entire glass of milk. He looked as if she'd just kicked his puppy. She hesitated, then spoke.

"Goodness. What am I saying? Don't listen to an old woman. That's wonderful. Wonderful. Nurse Turner seems quite pleasant."

"Nurse Turner?"

"Isn't that who you are talking about? Nurse Turner?"

"No."

Minerva frowned. Of course he was talking about her. That black-headed nurse. Nurse Turner. Turner was her name, wasn't it?

"You thought I was talking about Betty all this time?" Robert laughed. "No, no, no. I'm talking about Carole. Carole Brennan."

"Who in the world is Carole Brennan?" Embarrassment agitated her confusion. Who was this person? Why did she not know her? Betrayal sidled up to her confusion, although, she reminded herself, she had no right to that emotion.

"George's teacher. I know you met her. She came to the hospital all the time."

"Oh."

Minerva tried to recall having met Carole Brennan. Nothing.

"Very pretty."

"'Very pretty' doesn't tell me a thing." Minerva didn't mean to sound so sharp. "I mean, there were so many pretty girls who visited you, Robert. (This wasn't entirely true, but Minerva was groping for a way out of her edginess.) Can you describe her a little more specifically?"

"Okay. She has brown hair and hazel eyes. Comes about here." He put his flat hand above his eyebrow like a salute.

Robert's gesture elicited a memory. One evening, early, right after dinner, Minerva recalled seeing a woman walk toward her down the hospital hallway. The woman reminded Minerva of the nurse who was in charge during the evacuation station during The Flood. Not in looks, but in authority. Minerva had itched to salute her. She also looked at the woman's shoes to see how high her heels were. Not very. She was a tall woman. Minerva had liked that. Could she be who Robert was talking about?

"...and was from South Carolina, so she has a Southern accent, not a Southern accent like people around here, but real Southern. Do you know what I mean?"

Minerva tried to smile.

"She certainly sounds lovely."

30

The debut of Paducah's spring surprised the community every year. Locals had seen everything from frozen landscapes to sultry storms. This year crocuses and daffodils popped up like excited guests who couldn't wait for the party to start. Fuchsia and white azaleas blended with pink and milky-white dogwood blooms. Forsythia and pale green wraps of leaves danced with memory and grace. Tender fescue resurrected the yards. Cherry blossoms flowed and dripped like waterfalls. Tulips stood at attention in a flagrant color riot. All of nature intersected and harmonized to the delight of the proud residents on the newly formed Civic Beautification Board, who tended to take credit for Mother Nature's display.

Minerva supposed taking pride in your community was fine, but how could you take credit for what God had done?

Oh, well.

Life had stubbornly returned to normal.

Minerva looked at her list for the week. Monday through Saturday lacked imagination. So did Sunday, for that matter. Visits to the cemetery. Piano lessons. Errands. Tending graves. Research. Writing. Organ practice.

Neat. Orderly. Normal.

Except nothing felt normal. Her world tilted about an eighth of an inch off-kilter. She felt the same dissatisfaction as when the bottom of her calloused foot itched and she couldn't fully scratch it. If forced to put words to this vague sensation lurking in her subconscious, she might say she was out of sorts.

Minerva tied a scarf around her ears and locked the door behind her.

This Monday morning, she walked to Oak Grove to enjoy the exceptional weather. Even Minerva had grown tired of this year's gray and rainy winter. Fresh air and sunshine would do her body good today. Plus, a walk meant she didn't have to complete that awful exercise routine she'd put herself on.

Minerva had run across an article suggesting that older people fall because of balance issues. This made sense. She had determined to work on her balance by exercising. She wouldn't mind trimming down a bit either. That remark Mr. Johnson had made about her being a big gal had stung—even if the man wasn't quite right in the head.

The *Good Housekeeping* she'd marked gave detailed instructions for what she should do.

The column read:

> One cannot expect to whittle down inches in a week or two—it requires diligent, daily exercising and a stern will regarding one's food. While heavy thighs can often be disguised with clothes chosen to minimize them, a bathing suit inevitably reveals their true measurements! So, begin now to work off that "thigh-bulge" which is so unlovely.

Minerva never intended to wear a bathing suit again; she did desire stronger thighs with which to squat and rise in the cemetery. If said hips happened to slim in the process, maybe every single dress wouldn't need altering and wouldn't that be nice.

> The following three exercises are presented through the courtesy of the American Women's Association Contour Corner—this was the fourth group of the refashioning routine. These exercises will, if practiced daily without fail, reduce your thighs and will give your body greater flexibility!

The article's heavy use of exclamation points jarred Minerva; it was like a coach yelling at her. She conceded she needed forceful urging, however, so she read on.

On the Mat You Get!

She double-checked the drapes to make sure no passersby could sneak a peek, and then eased to the floor.

Minerva rolled onto her side and grabbed hold of the legs

of the sofa, her head lying on her left arm, just as the instructions directed. Then she hoisted her legs and attempted to kick. A sturdy grunt was the only result. She tried again. Thwump. This was going nowhere.

The article pointed out that you could expect difficulty if you were not limber. So, she sat with her back against the couch and reached for her toes. Her fingertips made it to her kneecaps.

She wiped the perspiration beading on her forehead and lip. That was round one, day one. The routine had improved in ease, but not in enjoyment.

And physical effort couldn't salvage her mind, which was slipping. If it could have fallen as she had in the cemetery, it would have. It would be sprawled out for everyone to see its awkward, clumsy, sad, sorry state. She could exercise all she wanted, but it wasn't going to help her mind, which was definitely in decline.

For instance, take last week when she couldn't remember her own cousin's name. So what if she has several cousins. Thirteen or fourteen on Mother's side. Well, which was it? Thirteen or fourteen? Let's see, there was Dorothy, Margaret, Nathaniel, James Samuel, Thomas, Rufus, Matilda June, Flossie, Suella Lucille, Marvin, Lester, Bill, May Esther. Thirteen. All those double names were throwing her off. No, wait, she had not counted Leta. Fourteen. Leta was who she couldn't remember. Yes, she was losing her mind.

And what about little what's-her-name's piano lesson she'd rescheduled and then forgot? Now she couldn't remember the child's name. Then there was the incident in the car. She'd driven all the way to the river before she remembered she was headed to Boaz's to pick up the shoe she'd had repaired. Losing her ever-loving mind.

Rhew-Hendley Florist had put together a fresh spring urn for her to deliver to her parents' gravesites. She hadn't laid any flowers on their graves since last Memorial Day. Quite unlike her. She "tsk'd" herself.

"Here you go, Mrs. Place."

"Thank you, Estelle. I like the forsythia you used." She was about to leave when Brother Larson appeared.

"Mrs. Place!" He was jolly. Effervescent was the word.

"Brother Larson."

"What a lovely spray."

Before Minerva had a chance to respond, Estelle launched in. "We have you all set, Brother Larson. I think they're just beautiful. Beautiful. A classic bouquet. Aren't they lovely? We would have been glad to have delivered them."

Brother Larson's and Minerva's attention swung toward a magnificent bouquet of red roses tufted with baby's breath.

"Ahhh. They are beautiful. She will love them." Brother Larson was rocking back and forth on his feet. Minerva thought this was a peculiar reaction to flowers. Such a twitchy fellow.

"They are lovely," Minerva agreed, realizing the "she" who would love them was no doubt Harriett Boswell. Evidently that petite librarian still had her hooks in Minerva's Baptist minister.

With nothing left to say, Minerva turned and wrangled the cemetery spray out the door. "Thank you, Mrs. Place." She lifted her free hand in a wilted wave.

Minerva hoped her face hadn't given her feelings away. She didn't know why she didn't like that Harriett woman. She just didn't. Did she have to have a reason for everything?

☙

By the time she got home, evening had pulled the temperature back down to the 40s. That was the trouble with spring. It was all over the place, unable to make up its mind about whether it wanted to be warm or cold.

Minerva pulled a bobby pin out of her bun and scratched at the psoriasis. The scaly red patches were worse lately. A flurry of white scattered across the table. Disgusting. She whisked the dandruff away.

She hadn't seen Robert or George for two weeks. Her throat tightened when she counted how long it had been. She looked out the window at Nella's and speculated.

Buster had been home for about an hour. They were finishing dinner about now. Minerva was having Saltines and apple juice she'd bought for George for her dinner. She wondered if George and Robert had eaten yet. She finished another cracker and stared at the empty wrapper in her hands.

She had eaten all of them. No wonder she couldn't lose weight. Taking another sip of apple juice she muttered, "That's detestable," and dumped it in the sink.

31

Minerva was writing about a deep-sea diver when the phone rang. She thought about letting it continue to ring because she was at a critical spot. Her character was bringing up charred bodies from the bottom of a ship-wrecked vessel. She had the most extraordinary friends.

"Mrs. Place. Hello."

Robert. Her pulse quickened. A mild flush.

"Hello, Robert. How are you? How is George?"

"We are great. Just great. How are you? We've been out of town over the Easter break. I believe I mentioned we were going back East for George to see some of his relatives, Marilynne's family? Anyway, George and I have missed you, and we are calling to see if you might come over and visit."

Minerva didn't know where to begin. He had said so much. Her mind scrambled to catch up. She figured she should have been accustomed to this rapid pace of the younger man's conversation by now, but she floundered. Should she answer his inquiry about how she was, or should she ignore it and ask about their trip? Should she say she missed them too?

Oh dear Lord, no, she could not say that. What did he say last?

"I suppose—"

"Great. That's just great. We've got to tell you all about our adventure. What about tomorrow afternoon? Between two and two thirty?"

❧

After church the next day, Minerva could not shed her girdle fast enough. Why was she so excited? she chastised herself. You are utterly ridiculous about those two. Just settle down.

She could not settle down, though. She had bought a new

girdle for Easter and the contraption was not broken in yet. The girdle waistband rolled below the bulge around her middle. Why, the whole point of a girdle was to corral such unwelcome features. She had half a mind to return the elastic torture-wear even though she'd worn it. She wouldn't, but she had half a mind to. Now she wrestled the blasted thing off with tugging efforts that caused the bedsprings to squeak like a flock of geese. Goodness gracious.

That morning she'd spotted Robert and George sitting in their regular pew (funny how quickly people established personal real estate in a church), and that odd sensation of warmth blossomed in her. Not an attraction. Oh my goodness, no. She could have been Robert's mother. Could she have? She was almost old enough to be. Anyway, that feeling. What was it? Tender. Yes, and vulnerable. She hadn't felt this vulnerable or exposed since she fell in love with Manny. And look how that turned out. Minerva was so distracted with this analysis she missed a pedal switch during the choir's cantata. Really, Minerva, she reprimanded herself.

George opened the door that afternoon and grinned at Mrs. Place, who returned his smile but said nothing. No one would ever have imagined that two months ago he had been in a hospital bed. Children were resilient. They were.

"Come in, come in." Robert stood right behind his son and popped his hand on top of George's head while motioning Minerva in with the other. "It's so good to see you."

Since George had been discharged from the hospital, Robert and Minerva hadn't spent as much time with each other. Of course they wouldn't. Minerva knew life must return to normal. Sitting in a hospital room every night, visiting with a young man while the boy you ran over with your car recovered. Well now, that wasn't going to last forever. Minerva felt shame that a part of her had hoped it would.

"I saw you just this morning at church." Why did she say that? Minerva knew she sounded snippy.

"Oh, sure, but we haven't gotten to visit. You know. Like

we did in the hospital." Minerva fought an impulse to respond with gratitude. She managed to keep her smile to her usual controlled, closed-lip offering. Inside she was dancing.

"Come on into the kitchen. George and I tried making peanut butter cookies. Do you like peanut butter?"

"Oh my." Minerva couldn't help herself. Not one square inch of the counters was free of evidence of their endeavor.

Robert picked up a cookie sheet and put it right back down. He grinned. "We aren't what you'd call tidy."

"I do like peanut butter." She spied an open peanut butter jar with a spoon handle sticking out.

"Here. Please try one." Robert handed her a cookie from a plate. Others were still lying on waxed paper, cooling on the counter.

Minerva accepted it but stood there holding it.

"Robert?"

He lifted his eyebrows.

"Robert…" She stopped. He was so young. She swallowed and blurted out the rest. "I want to thank you."

"Oh, sure. We've got plenty."

"No. Not for the cookie." His smile was goofy, she thought. Goofy's the word. His nose veered to the left and his bottom teeth were crooked. He didn't look old enough to shave, and he had a son. He held a job. He was an engineer. He was looking at her as though she should be strapped into a straitjacket, as if she was a crazy old bat. She *was* a crazy old bat. She wanted to reach out and hug this young man and tell him how he had transformed her life.

She chickened out. "For having me over."

Robert laughed. Minerva could not imagine laughing so easily in front of another person. Before she met Robert, she mistrusted people who laughed like that.

Rosamond Greenley came to mind. Rosamond laughed at anything. Minerva hadn't thought about that girl in years. They'd gone to high school together.

Rosamond was not pretty—her eyes were too close together

and her nose was a notch too big—but no matter, everyone thought she was lovely. Boys walked her down the hall, carried her books to class, asked her to dances. And girls liked her too. Except for Minerva. Minerva doubted this Rosamond was genuine. She laughed all the time, for one thing. How could everything be worth a laugh? What's more, her laugh seemed contagious. In class, a teacher, for crying out loud, could make a comment that tickled Rosamond, and she would let loose with that laugh of hers (Minerva conceded it was quite musical). Soon the entire classroom, teacher included, would be laughing.

Rosamond was an extreme example, but Minerva had observed others through the years. She noticed people who laughed readily. She doubted, though, the sincerity of all that laughter. Come now, she often thought, it isn't that funny.

She labeled easy laughers frauds.

But she didn't consider Robert a fraud.

"Of course. You know we think of you as family." Robert munched on a cookie without using a dish or a napkin. Crumbs fell to the floor. Minerva wanted to tell him to get a napkin. She wondered where he kept his broom. Then the word he'd just used registered with her. Family. He thought of her as family? The woman who ran over his son?

"These cookies are delicious," she said.

32

Minerva was tinkering with the idea of taking a trip. "You should go visit your sister," he'd first said to her last month when they sat on her porch after his piano lesson. Robert had slipped into George's former slot on Tuesdays. He'd taken eight lessons, and he seemed to have a natural talent. Minerva hoped she had found a student who would develop into a pianist.

When he first asked her if she would take him on, Minerva balked. She didn't teach adults, never had.

"Is there a reason?" Robert asked. "I've always wanted to play an instrument, and we have this perfectly good piano just sitting unused in our house. I sort of forced lessons on George before he was ready. But why can't *I* learn? He might want to take lessons someday, but I can right now."

Minerva couldn't think of a solid reason to refuse, so she said they could try. She had a hard time saying no to him.

And now the evening held out hope for summer. Ivy crept around the violets, forsythia gold had yielded to green, and Robert talked of travel.

"So, you think I should?" She swayed in the glider, and he rocked in the gentle porch swing. They moved in time with each other.

"I do." Robert watched George catch fireflies in a Ball jar Minerva had supplied. "Traveling expands your mind. I hope to take George to all forty-eight states."

"I've been to Illinois, Missouri, and Kentucky."

"If you go to Texas, you'll get to go through Tennessee and Arkansas, and if you come back a different way, you can take in Louisiana, maybe Mississippi too."

Minerva nodded. She was enjoying her new car. She had traded the Buick for a Chevrolet with a mint-green-and-white exterior and a dark green, almost black-green, interior. Sharp. This vehicle's brakes were more sensitive than Spencer's were, and it boasted more pickup. She'd decided not to name this car. Getting so attached to a material possession was unhealthy, perhaps sinful.

"I'm not sure a woman should make such a long trip on her own. What if something were to happen?"

"You have a point. Can you change a flat?"

Minerva laughed out loud.

"No, I can't change a flat tire."

He laughed too.

"You know, Minerva (He called her Minerva now, when they were alone, and she didn't mind. In fact, she was the one who'd suggested it.) I could always go with you."

She looked at him as though he'd sprouted a horn from his forehead.

He laughed again. "What's your expression mean? You're giving me a funny look."

"Why would you go with me?"

"Well, I've never been to Texas either. I'd be able to check off three or four states from our list. Texas sounds like fun. I'll bet there are cowboys there and horses, and they say the sky goes on forever."

"So I've heard." Minerva had wanted to go to New Mexico and Arizona since they became states when she was twenty-two. She wondered if she could work the two youngish states into a trip to Texas.

"What do you think?" He stopped swinging and leaned forward, his elbows on his knees, hands dangling, neck jutting forward. "I think you've got a great idea. I've got two weeks of vacation time since I've worked at the plant for over a year. We can go right after George gets out of school in May."

"What about Carole?"

"What about her?"

"Wouldn't she mind me taking her men off for two weeks?"

"I don't suppose so. She has plenty to do at the end of the

school year, and I know she wants to visit her parents in South Carolina sometime. I imagine then would be as good a time as any." Carole and Robert were dating, but they weren't engaged. He said he went fast the first go-round with Marilynne. This time he wanted to move slowly. Minerva wondered how his timetable sat with Carole. But Robert and Carole's relationship was none of her business. She wasn't one of those nosy women who asked all sorts of questions.

They rocked together awhile longer until—for the likes of her, Minerva couldn't figure why, but it had been true since she first heard Robert McAlpin's voice—the answer welled up in her. Yes. Yes.

"Okay," she said. "Let's do it. Let's go to Texas." For some reason she couldn't fathom, her heart opened, and her voice rose in response to this man who had forgiven her. It wasn't really a question.

33

When Minerva's rubber boots squished in the mud she remembered when she and Cat had snuck out the back door of the Websters' house during a rainstorm. The girls put on galoshes, slickers, and rain hats and played in the summer shower as if they were four years old instead of fourteen. Her mother opened the screen door about five minutes into their shrieking good fun and called out, "Minerva. Catherine. What are you two doing out there? You get inside this instant."

Today Minerva stomped in a puddle as if she were still replying to her mother. The resulting splash coaxed a laugh out of her.

She was on the corner of Myrtle and Charity in Oak Grove. A storm system had passed through yesterday, leaving sticks and leaves littered around cockeyed wreaths and tousled memorial flowers. Minerva bent to right a plastic vase of red, white, and blue silk carnations marking a veteran's grave. At least she assumed it was a veteran's grave. Why else would somebody choose red, white, and blue flowers? And forevermore, why would they have left them until they faded to pink, gray, and purple? If you want to honor someone... Minerva stopped herself mid-thought. She was not going to make judgments. The person who had placed that bouquet might have had a perfectly reasonable explanation. She might live in California for all she knew.

She sniffed and nodded as if she needed a physical gesture to realign her thinking. There now. That was better. She was back on track.

She took the familiar route to Emma Skillian's marker, the summer sun casting shadows that glimmered. Minerva breathed deeply and walked with purpose, taking care on the gravel. She didn't want a ridiculous tumble to detour her. She carried a burden of words that needed to be born here at Oak Grove. The story she'd written about Emma was in its file folder tucked away in her cemetery supply bag. She slipped it out now and scanned it, stopping to focus on the last two sentences.

I watched as my grave was filled in with mud. It was over.

Minerva had been reconsidering that ending. She'd been thinking about Emma and her other friends, friends she'd made in the chair at the dining-room table. Friends she'd met at Oak Grove, gotten to know better at the library, then invited into her own home. Friends she had imagined into life.

Margaretha, who stirred up feelings of being unloved and unappreciated. Della, who—like Minerva—hadn't understood what real love was. Harry Barkley, who had been the black sheep of his family, which was how she'd always felt. John Barkley, Harry's father, who had taught her that parents are wrong to have favorites.

And dear Emma. She had imagined Emma all wrong the first time. She realized from Emma that you really could judge people wrongly. Minerva had related to Emma most of all, her loneliness, her being misunderstood, her sadness.

Now Minerva placed the story about Emma alongside four pens, a hard notebook, and the urn Mr. Petty had sold her for half price (not too many people in Paducah chose cremation). She laid out a worn towel next to Emma's marker and squatted, noting as she did that the exercises had helped her. Her new strength was gratifying, and she smiled.

Now she would finish Emma's story in the way she began writing the first story about Della Barnes, with paper and pen.

As she wrote, her measured handwriting felt like a familiar meditation. Place and time folded into that dimension only writing could expose. The present collided with a place in the past, a diamond glint on the spectrum of time. Thoughts became reality, and words swam together, laboring into real people. And these people were like all people—enigmas, surprising mixes of lights and darks with stories that refused to relinquish their shades of grays. Minerva could hear Emma's voice.

Today, on this side of eternity, I am a woman at peace. Words cannot explain how this transformation happened. You'll unfold the sacred secret at your time. I can only offer assurance.

If you have placed your trust in what the Bible says, God himself will meet you at that silvery point where your spirit slips from the clutches of your weighted world into uncharted waters. He will welcome you with kind eyes and firm embrace. He will say, "All is forgiven. All is forgotten."

When you hear those words, if you're harboring a grudge or clinging to ill will toward anyone—including yourself, you will realize this: you've been trying to be something—someone—you are not. You see, we humans, we don't have the right to withhold forgiveness from others. And we don't have the right to withhold it from ourselves. That right is God's alone. If we don't forgive ourselves, we are saying God's forgiveness is not enough. That's the real crime.

I lost sight of truth in my life. The law declared me guilty. The law declared me not guilty. I knew I was both. I knew I was neither. I spent my entire life blaming others or myself. I chose unforgiveness, and so I chose misery. God intended better for me.

Minerva rolled up the pages, slid them into the urn, and reached to place the package in front of Emma's simple marker. Like her other words, nobody would read them. But that had never been the point anyway. She patted the pale, thin blades of grass starting up out of the grave, then stood back up.

What do you know? She got herself up out of a squat. That exercise regimen really was paying off. She didn't notice her joints hurting at all.

Well, not as much. Okay, she hurt, but she was not going to complain.

Right now.

ACKNOWLEDGMENTS

So many kind and generous people helped me on the way to publishing this novel.

First, a huge thank-you to my husband, Kent Buchanan, who supports me in whatever I want to do. You don't say a word about me traipsing off to writing workshops or holing up in my office with imaginary friends. And thank you for the privilege of being one of the few authors you've read who wasn't writing about theology or physics. I'm honored.

And thank you to my parents, Karen and Maury Dodson. Everyone should have such cheerleaders rooting them on in life. You both have encouraged me about my writing forever—or at least since I was six and started writing stories. That's a lot of encouragement.

Speaking of cheerleaders, thanks to my sons and their wives, Ben and Amy Buchanan and Brent and Keighlee Buchanan. All four of you have encouraged me many times, and—as if I deserved more—I see those seeds of encouragement sprouting in our grandkids too. (Special thanks to our first grandchild, George, for letting me use your name!) What a blessing and privilege it is to experience life alongside you all.

And, in the vein of vividly imagining the deceased, I want to thank my grandmother, Glenda Wilson. Like Minerva, I felt "Gabby" hovering in the room as I wrote. She was definitely an inspiration. Not a scary ghost at all.

All my early readers—thanks from the bottom of my heart. You read some of my first drafts and managed to find something positive to say about them. Cathy Hancock, Darlene Mazzone, Brenda McElroy, Paulette Petty, and Jill Wagner, you are generous friends.

Many thanks to Laura Yorke. I don't think the book would have been published without your insight and suggestions.

Susan Reinhardt, Gwynne Jackson, and all who participated with me in the Collegeville Institute's Writing Spirit, Writing Faith workshop—each of you had a part in birthing this novel, whether it was laughing at the right time or offering practical advice.

Colossal thanks to Jaynie Royal and Pam Van Dyk for loving Minerva as much as I do, for guiding me through my first publication experience with professionalism and kindness, and for making the manuscript sparkle. A special shout-out to Elizabeth Lowenstein for buffing it further.

A big salute to Bobby Wrinkle and Vonnie Shelton, outstanding librarians in the Special Collections department at the Paducah-McCracken County Public Library. You were always happy to point me in the right direction when I was researching. And to Pam Souder, whose mother was sexton of Oak Grove Cemetery for many years, thank you for helping me navigate old records. Most of the ghosts Minerva encounters were real people who now reside in the cemetery.

Thank you to Gayle Frye for asking me to write scripts for several of the City of Paducah's Oak Grove Cemetery tours and the Paducah's Flood Wall Murals celebration. And thank you City of Paducah for featuring my work.

Which leads me to this acknowledgment…I am grateful to the community where I live—Paducah, Ky., a creative haven with endless inspiration. Thank you for allowing me to dig into our rich, rich history and for sharing amazing stories. This book is, of course, fiction but its characters and places are true bits and pieces of history that I've mined and cobbled together to create the population of *Toward the Corner of Mercy and Peace*.

Finally, thank you reader. Without you my words would sit imprisoned upon unturned pages. I'm so grateful that you have set them free.

Soli Deo Gloria.